365 Days

"One of the most real books I've ever read. It frequently made me giggle out loud to myself while muttering, 'OMG, RIGHT?'"—*AfterEllen.com*

"Payne captures Clemmie's voice—an engaging blend of teenage angst and saucy self-assurance—with full-throated style."—Richard Labonté, *Book Marks*

me@you.com

"A fast-paced read [that] I found hard to put down."—*C-Spot Reviews*

"A wonderful, thought-provoking novel of a teenager discovering who she truly is."—*Fresh Fiction*

Another 365 Days

"Funny, engaging, and accessible."—*Kirkus Reviews*

The Road to Her

"A wonderful, heart-warming story of love, unrequited love, betrayal, self-discovery and coming out."—*Terry's Lesfic Reviews.*

By the Author

365 Days

me@you.com

Another 365 Days

The Road to Her

Because of Her

Visit us at www.boldstrokesbooks.com

BECAUSE OF HER

by
KE Payne

A Division of Bold Strokes Books

2014

BECAUSE OF HER

ISBN 13: 978-1-62639-049-2

THIS TRADE PAPERBACK ORIGINAL IS PUBLISHED BY
BOLD STROKES BOOKS, INC.
P.O. BOX 249
VALLEY FALLS, NY 12185

FIRST EDITION: MARCH 2014

CREDITS
EDITORS: LYNDA SANDOVAL AND RUTH STERNGLANTZ
PRODUCTION DESIGN: STACIA SEAMAN
COVER DESIGN BY SHERI (GRAPHICARTIST2020@HOTMAIL.COM)

Acknowledgments

Thank you to each and every one of the folks at Bold Strokes Books who make publishing my books such a pain-free journey. To my editors, Lynda Sandoval and Ruth Sternglantz, for guiding me through the editing maze, to Sheri for another amazing cover, and to Cindy Cresap for making sure everything moves along so smoothly. Thank you all.

Thank you, as ever, to Sarah Martin for being such a fantastic beta reader and supporter (not to mention chief advisor on busted knees). A massive thanks also to Mrs. D for your constant encouragement, words of wisdom, and support. It's truly appreciated.

To BJ: I don't know what I would have done without you. Thank you for your hours of dedication—even though at times you were so knackered your eyes were crossing—and for frequently saying all the right things to me when I was stressing.

Finally, a huge shout out to all the readers who continue to buy my books and who take the time to contact me. I truly appreciate every e-mail, Facebook comment, and Tweet that you send me. Your continued support is immensely important to me—thank you all so much.

Chapter One

It was 10:32 a.m. yesterday when I first saw her.

The Girl.

I was a week into my first term as the new girl at Queen Victoria's Independent School for Girls, sitting in my biology class with Libby, both of us earlyish for a change, and in walked The Girl, looking hot as hell, all long hair, beautiful eyes, and sexy walk. She was with a group of other girls, but she stood out so much I didn't even notice them. As she sauntered past my desk, she flicked a casual look my way, her stunning eyes holding mine in the brief moment when she saw me, and then away again. The quickest of glances, but long enough for me to see she had the most amazing eyes I'd ever seen: grey blue, but piercing, as if they were looking right into me.

And that was it. I was hooked.

I had no idea who she was, and I hadn't noticed her in my classes the previous week, but all I knew as she wandered past me and sat down was that I had to have another look at her. So I did. I glanced back over my shoulder and saw her towards the back of the room, staring straight back at me. I jerked my glance away and opened my books in a fluster.

"Got a pen? Mine's finished."

I turned and looked blankly at Libby.

Libby Coulson. My new friend. I'd met her the first day I started at Queen Victoria's, along with a lanky, bespectacled guy called Greg Slater, one of only a handful of year-twelve boys who attended the mainly all girls' school.

Anyway, Libby and Greg had ripped the piss out of me about my strong Durham accent, asked me out for a drink that night, and a friendship had been cemented. They were my lifesavers. If I'm honest, without them, my first week at my up-its-own-arse new school would have been hell.

"What?" My voice sounded strange, I don't know why.

"A pen?" Libby asked, waggling hers at me. "For writing with? Mine's empty."

I handed Libby a pen, wanting to ask her who The Girl was, but not knowing how to bring up the subject. I couldn't concentrate all through the whole damn lesson after that either. I was aware of her presence in the room and the temptation to turn around and study her, to get another look at those amazing eyes, was all I could think of. Our teacher droned on about photosynthesis or something like that, oblivious to my plight. To be honest, my mind was so puddled, he could have been telling us about photo booths for all I noticed.

After the lesson had finished, I deliberately stayed at my desk, knowing that The Girl would have to walk past me to get to the door. I wondered if she'd make as much of an impact on me as my first glimpse of her had. She did. Big time. As I made a show of packing my stuff away, she slid past me again, still with the same group of girls. I looked up from my books just as she crossed parallel to my desk, secretly hoping she'd catch my eye like she had on her way in, but she was mucking around with one of the girls, laughing and joking, pushing her as they both tumbled from the room.

I watched her for as long as I could before she disappeared from view.

"Gotta let everyone know they're around, haven't they?" Libby scraped her chair back and frowned.

I looked up at her.

"Who?" I asked innocently.

"That lot." She tossed her head towards the door they'd all just gone through. "Love the sounds of their own voices, they do."

"Who are they?" I rose from my chair and hitched my bag over my shoulder.

"Bunch of prima donnas, that's who," Libby muttered. "Think they own the school, you know?"

"Right." I nodded.

But who was The Girl?

"They're a proper little clique, very tight-knit," Libby said as we left. "And, my God, they really think they're something special. It's just been the three of them since year nine, and they show no sign of ever falling out with each other or growing up."

They walked together down the corridor, a little way ahead of us. My eyes were still drawn to her. "Mm-hmm," I said. "Names?"

I don't care about the others' names—just give me *her* name.

"Hmm, okay. You've got Beth on the left there." Libby waved a hand to the left. "She really thinks she's it. She's in a band and seems to think she's going to break into the big time, like, tomorrow."

"Beth, okay," I repeated.

"Then next to her there's Gabby—man mad and she's the gobbiest of the lot. Total loudmouth. To be avoided at all times," Libby said. "For Gabby, read Gobby."

"Gabby, gobby. Okay."

The Girl was walking next to Beth.

"And her?" I lifted my chin towards her.

"That's Eden," Libby said. "She's okay, actually. Probably the best out of all of them."

Eden.

I said it to myself slowly. I liked the way it sounded, and as I repeated it to myself, the letters of her name appeared clearly in my mind. Eden lodged herself in my brain as if she was meant to be there.

"Eden what?" I found myself asking.

Libby shrugged. "Palmer, I think."

Eden Palmer. Nice.

"She's the same age as us, I take it?" I asked.

"Yuh-huh. Seventeen."

"Do you know what other subjects she does?" I blurted, before I'd realized what I'd said.

Libby looked at me strangely. "No idea, no. I only do biology with her."

"Right. Sorry."

"Anyway, what are you doing for lunch?"

Libby's question stirred me from my thoughts of Eden and her lovely name.

"Shall I see you at the canteen?" I asked. "Same time as yesterday?"

"Fab." Libby hooked her bag up higher onto her shoulder. "See y'later."

❖

He'd finally done it. My father, that is. And I was in London, hating every second of it, purely because of him and his burning desire to make something of himself. Screw everyone else, that was his attitude. He'd been headhunted, so he'd proudly told us a few weeks before over dinner, by a company in the City, 280 miles south from our modest but happy existence in the northeast of England. It meant a six-figure salary, two company cars, and all the corporate parties a high-flying financier like him could handle.

It didn't matter to him that moving down south would upend not only my life—tearing me away from my girlfriend Amy—but my mother's and my brother Ed's as well. He didn't seem to care. He knew I'd always hated change, but he just went ahead and did it anyway. I was shit-scared at having to start over at a new school, but my tears fell on deaf ears. I tried to appeal to his better nature. He didn't have one. As long as my father was okay and could now scramble up his greasy ladder to success, then the rest of us could just fall in with his plans, and there wasn't a thing we could do about it.

That's how I came to be at Queen Victoria's. Because of my father and his aspirations. He thought the new fancy school would make a lady of me, whatever that was supposed to mean. Why? Because I was different from other girls. I knew I was different. I just didn't need every idiot on the planet—including my father—

telling me that, and I sure didn't need some posh private school trying to mould me into something I absolutely wasn't.

Okay, so I wore my hair short and floppy. I liked having my hair short and floppy! I liked that I could feel the air on my neck, that it hung untidily over my eyes, but most importantly I liked that I didn't have to fiddle with it for hours before leaving the house. People told me that I was cool but messy, just because I liked wearing scruffy clothes—hoodies with sleeves that hung over the ends of my fingers, that sort of thing. To me, they were just clothes. I felt comfy in them, so what? Why would I wear something that makes me feel uncomfortable, something that I know doesn't suit me, that makes me walk differently, act differently? Why would I want to look the same as every other kid in this damn school?

Queen Vic's was considered to be one of the best schools in London. Of course it was. Would my father have put me anywhere else? Founded by Queen Victoria herself in 1886, it sat on a leafy avenue just a five-minute walk from Sloane Square Underground station.

Rumour had it the annual fees were knocking on £7000 a term, but as my father refused to discuss any money matters with me, I didn't ever get that verified. However much he was paying, I guess he thought it was worth it. It was an impeccable school, but I figured if you were paying that amount, you'd kinda want that standard of perfection, wouldn't you? As far as I was concerned, the only good thing about the wretched place had been spotting Eden that first time. At least she would give me something to look at while I was biding my time. But if the school—and my father—wanted excellence from me, they were fooling themselves. It was never going to happen. Instead, I knew I was going to do my damn hardest to get the hell away from the school and from London, and on the first train back to Amy just as soon as I could.

CHAPTER TWO

Libby was sitting in the canteen in the spot she favoured most days when I finally found her: central, so she could see everyone coming and going, but slightly towards the window, so she could watch students scurrying back and forth outside. She always told me it was because she liked to keep herself clued-up on what was going on in and around the school. I preferred to think it was just because she was nosy. Not that I'd ever tell her that, of course.

As I walked in, my head still full of the sonnet that Mr. Roberts, my English teacher, had drummed into us for the entire previous hour, my eyes were drawn, as if by magnets, to the far corner of the canteen. Before I'd even seen her, I just knew Eden was there. She was sitting with Gabby, in Gabby's preferred spot, perfectly positioned for her to admire the view out across the football pitch where the year-twelve boys' team practised. If a visiting team also happened to be using the pitch, so much the better: twenty-two boys to eye up, rather than the usual eleven.

I bought myself a sandwich from the hatch, then weaved my way through the maze of chairs and tables towards Libby. I plonked myself down just as she was pulling a textbook from her bag.

"You've saved me from the misery that is the binomial theorem," she said, gratefully snapping her book shut again. "I was just about to start reading."

"The bionic what?" I asked, unwrapping my sandwich.

"Exactly." Libby grinned. "How was English?"

"From fairest creatures we desire increase," I said, throwing my hand up dramatically, *"that thereby beauty's rose might never die."*

"You what?" Libby opened her can of Coke with a satisfying fizz.

"Shakespeare," I said. "We did Shakespeare for an hour."

"Kill me now." Libby groaned.

I stole a glance over to Eden. "Where's Greg today?" I asked absently. "I kinda thought he might be here, too."

"No idea." Libby narrowed her gaze. "You know he likes you, don't you?"

"What?" I stared at Libby.

"Greg," she repeated, "likes you."

"Has he told you that?" I asked, my brow furrowing.

"Nah, but it's obvious." Libby unwrapped the cellophane from around her sandwich and screwed it up into a tight ball.

"Obvious how?"

"How he's always hanging around us."

"He's a friend." I laughed. "He doesn't hang around. He's a friend, so we do stuff together. Like friends do."

"But he looks at you, like, all the time."

"He does not!"

"Does so."

I unscrewed the top from my bottle of water and took a long drink from it. "Well, even if he does like me—which he doesn't—I don't like him." I wiped a droplet of water from my mouth with the back of my hand.

"You could do worse," Libby said. "Okay, he's a bit of a geek, but he's a funny geek."

I rolled my eyes. "Don't even go there."

"Why not?" Libby leaned closer, her eyes mischievous. "Tabby and Greg. We could call you Treg. Or Tabreg. Or something."

"Or Gabby?" I grinned.

"Ew. Nasty."

"Trust me, Libby," I said, pulling a sliver of tomato from my sandwich, "nothing in this world would ever make me want to go out with Greg."

"Well, I think he's nice," Libby said, "and I thank the day this place decided to let boys attend a girls' school after year twelve." She bit into her sandwich. "Boy, was there an outpouring of hormones that first day."

"You go out with him if you like him, then," I said. "Or are you already seeing someone?"

Libby shook her head. "No and no. Are you?"

"What?"

"Seeing someone?"

I took a bite from my sandwich, dusting the crumbs that showered from it off my top.

"Your silence tells me you are."

"Well, kinda," I mumbled.

"Ah, you have someone back home?"

"Yeah. Someone back home." I pictured Amy in my head and smiled.

"You must miss him something awful," Libby said, opening a packet of crisps.

"Yeah," I said eventually, glancing over towards Eden. "I do."

I shook my head as Libby offered me a crisp from her packet.

"Actually," I said, my heart beating just a little faster, "he is a she."

"Hmm?" Libby looked up from peering into her packet of crisps.

I cleared my throat. "The person I have back home and who I miss more and more every day is a she, not a he."

"Oh. Right." Libby raised her eyebrows. "I didn't realize you were—"

"Gay?"

"Mm. Gay."

"You never guessed?" I waved my hands up and down myself.

"Well, I suppose now you mention it…"

"Not a problem is it?" I asked. "'Cos if it is, I can go and find someone else to sit with and eat lunch with every day."

"God, no!" Libby's eyes widened, apparently appalled at herself. "'Course it's not a problem. I just didn't realize, thassall. Sorry…I hope you didn't think…?"

I shook my head.

"My cousin thinks she's gay," Libby said, taking a drink from her can. "Well, she says she's dabbled with it, anyway."

"Dabbled?" I asked "You make it sound like it's the occult."

"Oh, no! I didn't mean—" Libby's face flushed with acute embarrassment.

"It's okay," I said. "I was kidding."

Libby offered me another crisp. Again I shook my head.

"So, what's your girlfriend's name?" she asked.

"Amy," I said, turning the ring on my finger at the thought of her. "She's called Amy."

"Who's called Amy?" Greg flopped down next to me and immediately reached over to take a crisp from Libby's open packet.

"No one." Libby snatched her crisps back, holding them against her chest so Greg couldn't reach.

"My girlfriend," I said. I figured if I was coming out to one new friend, I might as well come out to the other at the same time. Two birds, one stone, and all that.

"Nice name," said Greg, without missing a beat. "Does she come to this place?" He looked around, as if he expected to see her sitting behind him.

"No," I said. "She still lives up North."

"That's got to make life tough," Greg said. "It's not like she's even just an hour away, is it?"

"Yeah, it's not good." I looked down at my uneaten sandwich. "But we're managing."

It was in the northeast that I fell in love with the girl next door. Such a cliché. Amy is seventeen, like me, and while it took me a long time to notice her, once I did, it was like a light being switched on inside me. My life was never the same again after that. She was the local wild child—the antithesis of what my father would seek in a friend for his daughter—and she'd reeled me in with her don't-give-a-shit attitude from the moment I'd met her.

"Can I ask you something personal?" Libby asked.

"Shoot."

"When did you know? That you were gay, I mean."

"Right from an early age." I sat back in my chair. "When all my friends at school used to talk about boys and actors they liked, I never got what they were talking about. I never felt it, you know?"

Libby nodded, then reconsidered. "Well, no, actually. But carry on."

"And then when we all got to the boyfriend age," I said, "that was when I met Amy. And all the fireworks shit that friends were talking about getting from their boyfriends? Well, I was getting that with Amy. That's when I knew for sure."

A crack of laughter from across the canteen drew my eyes over to where Eden was sitting. My aching thoughts of Amy were temporarily sent scuttling as I saw Eden laughing heartily at something Beth was showing her on her phone.

"That's kinda cute," Libby said.

Cute. Eden? I blinked at Libby. "Cute. What do you mean?"

"Your story."

"Oh. Yeah."

"You want that?" She pointed to my long since forgotten slice of tomato. I shook my head, and she reached over for it. "So, anyway." She rolled her hand for me to continue.

"Yeah, it was cute, but scary at the same time," I said. "I mean, I knew I was different from other girls, but getting together with Amy just confirmed it."

"So why was it scary?" Libby asked, eating my tomato.

"I guess I didn't want to be classified as the lesbian at first," I said. "Being gay is just another part of who I am, and what I like," I continued, looking directly at Libby. "I mean, I like girls, you like boys. I like English, you prefer maths, with its bionic thermometers. I like white bread, you like...I dunno...Granary?"

"Well, I prefer a nice seeded batch if I'm honest." Libby grinned and wiped her hands on her napkin. "And now?" she asked. "Does it get any less scary as you get older?"

"A bit," I said. I couldn't help but look over towards Eden as her laughter continued. "But I guess I'll always be coming out to people throughout my life, every time I meet new people."

"Do your parents know about you and Amy?" Libby asked.

"No," I replied firmly. "My father and I have a strange relationship, and he absolutely loathes Amy." I chuckled. "Probably because she's led me astray on more than one occasion."

"She sounds like trouble."

"She is. We were always skipping school, hanging out together," I said. "I kinda thought I'd be the same down here." I slid my eyes over towards Eden, still deep in conversation with Gabby.

"You miss her?" Greg asked.

"Yeah, but we'll be together again soon," I said. "I made a vow to her"—I picked at the crust on the sandwich—"shortly after my parents coldly told me, when I was in pieces over leaving her, that I'd find other friends in London."

My mind flickered back to the night before I'd left. I remembered the tears, the hugging, the promises. The relentless ticking of the clock bringing me ever nearer to leaving her.

"Don't be sad, Tabs." Amy had pulled me to her, but it had done little to ease the burning fury I felt towards my father and the whole injustice of the situation he'd forced me into.

"I just don't know how he can do it to us," I'd mumbled into her sweater. "Uprooting us like this. Taking me away from you."

"Long-distance relationships suck, I know." Amy was appeasing me. I knew it. "We just need to get through these next two years, then we can think about getting a place at university together."

"I can't wait two years." I'd pulled myself from her. "I won't wait that long."

"We can Skype and stuff in the meantime," Amy had said, but she wasn't convinced. The distraught look on her face had told me that.

I'd shaken my head. "No. I told you, I won't wait that long. I'm going to do everything I can to get back to you as soon as possible."

"But in the meantime"—Amy had lurched over the side of her bed, retrieving a small box from under it—"you can wear this and think of me until we can be together again."

Inside the box had been a plain silver ring.

"It's fab." It was exquisite. "Thank you! It's perfect."

"I know you don't like anything fancy, so…"

I'd leant up and kissed her, her words getting lost in my kiss.

"It's perfect," I'd repeated. "Just like you."

"Sounds like your parents really know how to push your buttons." Greg's voice filtered in to my thoughts.

The conversation had continued without me. I'd been turning Amy's ring over and over, lost in my thoughts of her. "Sorry?"

"Your mum and dad."

Another splinter of laughter from Eden's corner pulled my attention over towards her. She was listening intently to something Beth was telling her, her face a picture of delight.

I stopped turning Amy's ring. "My parents know exactly how to wind me up." I drew my eyes away from Eden and back to Greg. "But, no matter," I said. "One day me and Amy will be together again. I'm going to make sure of that."

CHAPTER THREE

I was in the library, trying to finish off an essay, when I first spoke to Eden Palmer. Well, kind of spoke to her. It was more like a mumbled garble of words, but never mind. It was an interaction of sorts, at least.

I was hunched over my books, alone, when a crew of girls entered the room and sauntered over to my table. One of them spoke. It was Beth.

"This free?" She dumped her bag onto the table before I'd had a chance to answer. I clumsily gathered up my books, which were scattered across it.

"Help yourself." I snapped one of the books shut, cursing that I hadn't thought to look and see what page I was up to.

"I don't think we've met." The girl raised her chin in greeting to me as she sat down. "I mean, I've seen you in biology but we've never spoken. So, hi."

"Yeah, hi." I mirrored her greeting.

"I'm Beth." Beth reached into her bag and pulled a folder out. "This is Gabby and Eden." She rolled a hand in the general direction of the other two girls as they sat down, too.

"Tabby," I said, looking from one girl to the next.

"Like the cat?" Beth asked.

Yeah, like I'd never heard *that* one before.

"Like the cat," I confirmed.

"So, what's it short for?" Gabby asked.

"Tabitha," I said, cringing as I always did when I spoke my full name.

"I'd never have you down as being a Tabitha," Gabby said, looking me up and down. Her disdainful eyes settled briefly on my shirt, half hanging out and with the sleeves rolled up, as always, to reveal my beloved collection of shabby leather bracelets. "No offence."

"None taken," I replied truthfully. It wasn't the first time I'd ever heard that said, either.

Eden hadn't said a word yet. I glanced towards her and, seeing her steadily watching me, looked quickly away again, feeling a quickening of my heart.

"So you're not from around here, then." A statement, not a question.

I looked at Gabby, who'd said it. Libby's quip about her being more Gobby than Gabby swam into my head. I fought the urge to smile.

"No, I'm not," I finally answered. "I'm from the northeast. Place called Cragthorne. Near Durham."

"Wow!" Beth looked as though I just told her I came from Mars. "That's got to be a culture shock moving to London then, hasn't it?"

"You could say that," I said, amused at her expression.

"So what brought you down here?" Beth asked.

"Apart from the train," Gabby interrupted, pulling a dumb face at Beth.

"My father's job," I replied, aware of how much my strong northeast accent was standing out against Gabby and Beth's flat London ones.

I suddenly wanted Eden to speak, to hear what she sounded like, but she stayed silent.

"What does he do?" Gabby asked.

"Head economist at Global," I replied.

"Swiss bank in the City," Beth said, evidently enlightening Gabby.

"Yes, I know." Gabby flashed a look of irritation towards Beth.

They smiled as they quite blatantly looked me up and down in unison, both processing that little nugget of information. I knew just what they were thinking though: How could a scruffy girl like me possibly have a father who was the head economist at a European bank?

"Did you find it a wrench? Moving?" Eden's voice punctured the silence.

Her voice was lovely. Soft, measured, and educated—quite unlike Gabby's and Beth's. It was warm, too, almost velvety, and made her even lovelier than before. Her eyes held mine as she spoke, totally flummoxing me.

"I...yes," I stuttered, feeling like I'd just been enveloped by her voice and her eyes. "Wrench. Yes. I mean, it was, yes." I stared down at my books, my face burning.

We didn't speak again. Gutted that I'd been unable to string even a few words together in reply, I worked on in silence. Every so often I glanced across at Eden, who sat immediately opposite me. I let my brain filter and process little snippets of information about her each time I did.

Her hair was amazing. She occasionally tucked it behind her ear as she worked, and it was much darker than mine, with soft curls. For some crazy reason I wanted to know if they were natural or not. Her eyes, which had captivated me the first time I'd ever seen her, were now hidden from me as she gazed down at the books in front of her in adorable concentration, allowing me precious time to look at her long enough to fully appreciate her. I started playing a game of chance, testing myself to look at her for longer and longer each time, praying that neither she nor Gabby or Beth would glance up and see me looking.

They didn't.

I bowed my head and tilted my eyes slightly towards her. All three girls were still busy working.

Eden was wearing a blue-and-white striped long-sleeved T-shirt, the sort of top I favoured myself—quite unlike the garish, revealing tops that Gabby and Beth were wearing. Each time she moved her left arm, I could see a brightly coloured cloth bracelet, similar to one of mine, dangling from her wrist.

I liked it. It suited her.

On the middle finger of her right hand she wore a simple silver band with an unidentifiable green stone in it, the ring sitting perfectly on her long, slender finger.

The sight of her ring compelled me to look down at the one Amy had given me. I felt a stab of guilt as I touched it and thought about her and everything we'd said to one another the night before I left. My memories were swiftly accompanied by a feeling of loneliness, making me look away from Eden and reach down to take my phone from my bag. Hiding it under the desk, I fired off a text to Amy, telling her I loved her and was thinking about her, assuaging only some of my guilt.

I reluctantly returned to my books, knowing that I needed to concentrate on them rather than on Eden. I hated myself at that moment. My girlfriend was 300 miles away, missing me, and here I was, sitting in the library trying to make eye contact with a girl who'd barely said three words to me. I looked down at the desk, my book open at the same page it had been for the last ten minutes.

Time to concentrate.

If only it was that easy.

How could I focus on my books when Eden was doing this amazingly cute thing of chewing on her bottom lip while she wrote, making my insides flutter?

Finally, after what seemed like just five minutes but was probably more like an hour, Eden leant back in her chair. She linked her fingers and stretched her arms out straight in front of her. Stifling a yawn, she snapped her books shut, then roughly shoved them into her bag, scraping her chair back and standing up.

"I'm done," she said. She looped her bag over her head and diagonally onto her shoulder. "Catch you all later."

And she was gone.

I'm done.

That was all she'd said.

I followed her retreating back as she picked her way around the other tables in the library and made for the exit door. I glanced at Beth and Gabby. Both had their heads bowed over their books, oblivious to the fact their friend had left. I looked back at the space Eden had just vacated, wishing she'd come back again. She didn't.

Any hope of more work was over for me after that. Instead, I sat staring down at my books, thinking about the one sentence she'd said to me, and rueing the fact I hadn't even been able to answer her coherently. She must have thought I was a complete idiot! I stared blankly at the desk, thinking about the sound of her voice, how her eyes had secured mine when she'd asked me the question, and how it had made my head spin. It had been the shortest and simplest of questions, yet I kept replaying it over and over, wishing we'd spoken more than we had, and wondering just how Eden Palmer had managed to get under my skin in so short a space of time.

Chapter Four

I t's hell." I squinted at a book on the shelf in front of me. "Well, it's hell without you, anyway."

"How can London be hell?" Amy's laugh filtered down through my phone. "Isn't it supposed to be the place everyone wants to be?"

"Not me."

I was in the library. It was a week after I'd sat with Eden, Gabby, and Beth, and Eden had asked me that question which I'd been unable to answer lucidly.

And three days after she'd smiled at me in the corridor and I'd walked into the lockers.

"When are you coming to visit?" I nestled my mobile in the crook of my neck and pulled a book from the shelf.

"Soon. I promise," Amy said.

I flicked through the book, uninterested, and placed it back in its slot.

"So tell me more about Libby and Greg," Amy continued.

I shot a look over to the table where I'd left Libby, busy with her biology books.

"They're fun," I said. "They make this place bearable."

"Met anyone else yet?"

"No." My answer was clipped.

"It's not the same up here without you," Amy said. "Everything's changed. I hate it."

"It won't be forever." I lowered my voice. "I promise."

My words died on my lips as I saw Eden in the aisle opposite, scanning the shelf for a particular book.

How long had she been there?

She pulled one out and skimmed through it. While Amy carried on talking, I watched as Eden bent her head slightly to read from it, making her hair fall softly across her eyes. Occasionally she'd run her hand through her hair, lifting it away from her face again.

"...that's what he reckons anyway."

"I'm sorry?" I turned to look out of the window, away from Eden.

"Michael. He reckons...were you actually listening to me?"

"Of course."

I turned back. Eden had gone.

I drew in a deep breath. "I better go," I said. "I'm in the library, getting looks. Fill me in on the rest of the story later?"

"Skype tonight?"

"You bet."

I returned to my table and pulled my notepad out in front of me.

"So, remind me what a disaccharide is again," Libby said, looking up as I sat down next to her.

"Disaccharide?"

Where was Eden?

"Uh, it's a type of carbohydrate, isn't it?" My finger underlined something I'd written in that morning's lesson.

"Like sucrose and lactose and that type of stuff?" Libby frowned at her book.

"Mm."

I bent over my book, cradling my head in the palm of my hand, and surreptitiously glanced around the library.

"So what's an oligosaccharide, then?" Libby's face was creased in confusion. "Too many saccharides. I can't cope."

"Well, according to my notes," I said, flipping the page of my notebook, "an oligosaccharide is some sort of polymer."

"What's a polymer?"

"Lib, remind me why you're taking biology again."

"I ask myself that every day." Libby sighed, rubbing at her face. "Should have done English, then all I'd have to do is read sonnets all day rather than learn about bloody saccharides."

Finally I spotted Eden, by the door. She was leaving. Disappointment burned in my chest as she headed through the exit. Ignoring the voice in my head telling me I was being crazy, I thought if I left the library right at that moment, I might catch her up in the corridor. I imagined the scenario: It could be one of those moments like you see on the TV. A kind of *Fancy seeing you again, isn't that a coincidence?* type of thing.

Telling myself that if I had any sense at all, I'd resist going after Eden, I tried to replace her image in my head with one of Amy. I desperately wanted to kick-start the guilt complex I knew I ought to be feeling at my urge to follow Eden. But reason goes out of the window when all you want to do is get to know someone a little better.

And what better time than when she was without Gabby and Beth?

So despite all the voices urging me to not, under any circumstances, leave the library, I snapped my books shut. If I didn't go now, I'd never catch her. I was Skyping Amy later, wasn't I?

"Gotta go," I suddenly said to Libby, opening my bag and putting my notepad in. "Can't concentrate up here."

Wasn't that the truth?

"Oh." Libby looked up from her book and then glanced at her watch. "I'm gonna stay here for a bit. I've got sandwiches. See you in the lab after lunch?"

"See you there."

Giving a cheery goodbye to Libby despite my thumping heart, I hurried from the library. Just in time, too—Eden was disappearing around the corner and heading towards the canteen.

I kept a steady distance behind, not wanting her to think I was stalking her, but wanting to stay close enough to keep her in sight. If she turned and saw me? Well, I'd figure that one out if and when it happened.

It didn't.

Finally we both reached the canteen and joined the queue, Eden being four places in front of me. I grabbed a tray, occasionally glancing towards her, hoping she'd spot me and ask me to join her for coffee. I tried to make myself look visible, like you do when you're desperate for someone to notice you. I coughed a few times and scuffed my foot on the ground, looking around me, over to Eden and away again. It didn't work, but it evidently pissed off the person in the queue in front of me, who frowned to himself at every cough and scuff.

We shuffled on down the line. I watched as Eden chose a bottle of water, a panini, and an apple for herself, feeling pleased when the person in front of me suddenly left the queue, allowing me to get closer to Eden.

One down, two to go.

I turned my head a little and watched her through the corner of my eye as she asked the person serving to heat up her panini. Her profile was beautiful: lightly tanned skin framed by her fabulous dark hair, a perfectly straight nose dusted with freckles, and full lips, which curved upwards slightly, giving her a natural smile.

I thought I could stare at her all day and never get bored.

Just as I was watching her, she turned and saw me staring straight at her. We locked eyes for a moment, me too mesmerized to pull my attention away from her. She lifted her chin in recognition, then looked away again as the server asked her a question. My cheeks burned because she'd seen me gaping at her. What would she think? That I was like some freaking stalker, standing in a queue and blatantly staring right at her?

We shuffled along the line a bit more, and I allowed myself another quick look at her, dropping my eyes instantly this time as she turned and finally spoke.

"Hey! I didn't see you there."

Chapter Five

My heart hammered. I knew I should reply, but my voice box felt curiously squeezed, and I was worried that if I did try to speak, it would be nothing more than a squeak.

Don't just stare at her. Speak. You'll be fine.

"Hey, Eden. You all right?" A familiar voice sounded behind me, and I jumped slightly as an arm was suddenly flung casually around my shoulder. I swung round and saw Greg grinning over to Eden.

"Not bad. You?"

"Good, yeah." Greg looked down at me. "All right, squirt?"

"I didn't know you knew her," I said, indicating towards Eden.

"Eden? Yeah, I know her."

Eden paid for her food and wandered off into the canteen. My heart sank. Another opportunity to try and talk to her, wasted.

"I've been thinking." Greg reached past me and opened the clear plastic cupboard in front of him. He pulled out a tired-looking egg sandwich, wrapped in cellophane.

"Hit me, Einstein," I said, reaching in as Greg held the door open for me to pick out my own sandwich, too.

We shuffled further down the line.

"We need some new members to join our fencing club or there's a danger it'll be dropped." Greg turned to me. "Fancy it?"

"Fencing?" I gave Greg a withering look. "Isn't that a bit nerdy?"

"What's nerdy about fighting someone to the death with a sword?" Greg picked up his tray and walked over to the till.

He handed the cashier some money then stepped away, waiting for me.

"To the death?" I handed the cashier my money. "Sword?"

"Okay…" Greg fell into step with me as we made our way across the canteen to an empty table. "Maybe not to the death, but you do get to fight hard and dirty sometimes."

"And wear dumb clothes and have a sieve over your face," I said, sitting down. "I don't think so, thanks."

"Fencing is more than wearing dumb clothes, Tabby." Greg huffed. "It's about outwitting your opponent, it's about one-on-one combat, it's about—"

"Fighting to the death?" I mumbled. I took a drink from my can.

"Come on, it'll be fun!" Greg said. "You look like you know how to handle a weapon. You'll fit in straight away."

"Gee, thanks."

"We really do need new members, Tab. You'd be perfect."

"I'll think about it."

"Really? Awesome!"

"I only said I'd think about it."

"So I'll put you down to come next Tuesday, then?"

"Do I have any choice?"

"Nope."

❖

"We've already learned that the cytoplasm contain enzymes for metabolic reactions together with sugars, salts, amino acids…" Mrs. Hamilton's voice droned on in the background, like an irritated bee in a jar.

It was Tuesday, last lesson of the day. Libby was slumped low in her chair next to me, chewing on the end of her pen. "I sometimes think," she whispered, "that Mrs. Hamilton's voice should be bottled and used as a cure for insomnia." She stifled a yawn. "'Cos she's sure as hell sending me off."

"Can't be any worse than my philosophy class this morning,"

I said. "We talked about repressive desublimation. At nine o'clock in the morning." I looked at her, then back to the front of the class, trying to concentrate on what Mrs. Hamilton was saying. "This is a walk in the park in comparison."

"Do you sometimes just feel like giving it all up and going to live in a forest?" Libby pulled herself up straighter in her chair in an attempt to wake herself up. "Foraging for mushrooms all day and keeping chickens? It's got to be better than this, hasn't it?"

"So, homework delivered to my office by four o'clock tomorrow, please." Mrs. Hamilton snapped her laptop shut and stepped down from the desk at the front of the classroom.

"Homework?" Libby looked aghast. "What homework?"

"She just put it up on the whiteboard," I said, closing my books. I glanced at her, seeing panic on her face. "I'll text you the question later, okay?"

"Glad one of us was concentrating." Libby put the lid back on her pen with a loud snap. "I was busy in my forest, collecting mushrooms."

"Right, I've got to go," I said, reaching down and grabbing my bag. "I've been roped into going to fencing class with Greg tonight."

"Fencing? You?"

"Tell me about it," I groaned.

"Isn't fencing supposed to be elegant and sophisticated? Graceful and poised?"

"Yeah, you're funny. You should be a comedian, you know that?" I stood.

"Love you." Libby grinned up at me.

"Up yours."

"You around for coffee tomorrow morning?" Libby stood and walked to the door, stepping to one side to allow the swarm of students leaving the room to pass.

"Should be, yeah." I walked out into the corridor, my bag hitched up on my back.

"Try to be nice to everyone tonight. No stabbing people when you realize you're not cut out to be a swordswoman. Get it? Cut out? Swordswoman?" Libby called after me as I walked away.

"Try being funny for once," I said, sauntering down the corridor, one hand in my trouser pocket, the other lifting a middle finger to Libby as I turned the corner.

"See you," I heard her call to me.

"Seeya."

CHAPTER SIX

I didn't know anyone in the fencing group, of course.
I stood looking around the gym, hoping to see a familiar face, and cursing Greg at the same time. Finally I spotted him over in the corner talking to some girl.

"You came," he called over to me when he saw me.

"You said I didn't have a choice, remember?"

"Right, well let me go get you some protective clothing and a foil before I do anything else," Greg said, beckoning me to follow him.

I slung my bag down in the corner of the gym, along with everyone else's bags, and meekly followed Greg. While I waited for him outside the kit room, I saw a few more people arrive, each of them looking like they knew exactly how to handle a fencing foil.

I wondered for the hundredth time just what on earth I was doing there.

"These should fit you." A pile of white clothes flew out of the kit room and landed by my feet.

"You're a gent," I said, reaching down to pick them up.

"You don't have to wear the whole lot today, just for practice." Greg came out of the kit room, two foils under his arm. "Just wear the top and keep your sweats on for today's lesson."

"So what have I got here?" I said, holding an item of clothing and screwing my face up.

"Padded jacket." Greg prodded the jacket with his foil. "But put this on under it. It's an underarm protector. Stick it on under your jacket 'cos it'll give you double protection on your sword arm side and upper arm."

"You think I'm going to get stabbed?"

"You'll need this, too," Greg said, ignoring me and handing me a thick glove. "It's got a gauntlet on it that'll stop your opponent's foil from going up your sleeve."

"Terrific," I said. "Remind me why I'm doing this again?"

I put the glove onto my hand and waggled it in Greg's face.

"Don't worry, I won't make you wear the breeches today," Greg said, waving to someone as they came into the gym. "We'll save that for another time."

I stopped waggling.

"Breeches? You're fucking kidding me, right?"

"Matthew!" Greg called over to someone by the door. "Hang on, Tabs. I'll be right back."

I stood, jacket, protector, and glove in my arms, and tried to picture myself in white breeches. Shaking the image from my head, I was just heading to the girls' changing rooms when I saw her, standing over to the side of the gym.

Eden.

She was already dressed in her whites and talking with a small group of boys. I stopped in my tracks the moment I spotted her. She was standing with her back to me, but it was definitely her. I immediately recognized her hair, the curve of her waist, the way she was standing. When I finally caught the sound of her voice, drifting across the gym towards me, it was all I could do to try and calm the thudding of my pulse in my neck.

Quit it, Tabs.

I shook my head and, realizing I was still standing in the middle of the gym with a pile of white clothes in my arms, hurried towards the exit before she could see me. I didn't know what to do. Should I stay? How could I let Eden see me in breeches one day, for God's sake? I had legs like pipe cleaners at the best of times. I could only imagine what they'd look like in a pair of dumb, pristine white breeches when the time came to wear the stupid things.

Breeches! For the love of…

Nope, there was no way I was joining any idiotic fencing group now I knew she was in it, too. I would just have to…

"Tabby! Over here."

I stopped dead, my clothes hanging limply in my arms. I turned slowly and saw Eden waving to me from the other side of the gym.

"Hey!" I waved shyly, dropping my foil in the process.

She came over to me. "It is Tabby, isn't it?"

"Mm-hmm." I bent over to pick up my foil.

"How're you?" Eden asked.

"Good. You?"

"Good, yeah."

She stopped a few feet from me, looking hot in her fencing gear, her jacket clinging nicely to her top, a pair of scruffy, loose sweatpants sitting on her hips. I kept my eyes resolutely fixed on hers, probably making me look like a startled rabbit, but I knew if I wasn't vigilant my eyes would start roaming over her body, taking in every bump and curve.

"I didn't know you were into this kind of thing," she said, nodding her head towards my foil now tucked under my arm.

"Greg talked me into it." I laughed and looked around. "No Gabby or Beth?"

"Nah," Eden said tightly. "They think it's nerdy." She thought for a moment. "And they think I'm geeky enough as it is, so I don't really tell them I come here, to be honest."

I remembered how I'd told Greg I'd thought fencing was nerdy and couldn't help smiling.

"What's funny?"

"Ah, nothing." I turned away from her and gazed out across the gym. "When Greg first asked me to join, I think I might have said to him I thought it was nerdy."

"You want me to show you how nerdy I am?" she said, flexing her foil and raising an eyebrow.

"Trust me"—I rolled my eyes—"you'd whup my arse. I've never done anything like this before."

"Really?" She cocked her head to one side. "I'd have thought you'd know how to look after yourself."

"Perhaps. But I also have two left feet, so I don't think the grace and guile needed to fence is going to be my thing."

"We'll see," Eden said, looking at me for so long I was forced to break the gaze first.

❖

"Right, so if you'd all like to gather round." Rob, our instructor—a tall, muscular man drafted in from a fencing club from across the Thames—clapped his hands, immediately silencing the hubbub in the gym.

I wandered over to the edge of the group, feeling embarrassed in my white jacket, my glove tucked into the waistband at the back of my sweatpants.

I'd only put that on when it was absolutely necessary.

"Welcome, everyone," Rob greeted us, "and especially to our new members tonight."

Greg put his arm around me and pulled me closer to him, nearly making me topple over.

"So, I want everyone to get themselves a partner. The more experienced ones here, please nab yourselves a novice." Rob started walking amongst the group. "We're going to practise parries and ripostes. So one of you will attack your opponent, while the other will defend it, then attack back. Clear?"

"As mud," I muttered under my breath. I turned to Greg.

"So I come at you with this thing"—I wobbled my foil—"and you fight me off, right?"

"No offence, Tabs," Greg said, looking behind him, "but I'm fighting with Tim. Sorry."

"Hang on, Greg." I put my hands on my hips. "You dragged me here. The least you can do is practise with me! I've never used one of these things before." I held the foil up, narrowly missing Greg's nose.

"My point exactly," Greg replied, wandering off to join Tim.

I glowered at him, absolutely fuming as he crossed the gym. While my eyes bored into his retreating back, I was aware of Eden watching me. She smiled when she caught my eye and came over.

"I think I've just been dumped." I laughed.

"Want to practise with me?" Eden asked. "I can't say I'm as good as Greg but I'm okay."

"I've never done this before, you did get that bit, didn't you?" I said. "If I take the tip of your ear off or something with this thing, you won't hunt me down, will you?"

"You'll be fine! Quit worrying."

Eden jogged to a mat and stood, waiting for me.

"And I'll be gentle with you, I promise." She winked, making a small part of me crumble inside.

I took up my place opposite her and tried to look like I knew what I was doing.

"Okay, so I'm gonna aim for your torso and it's up to you to stop me, yeah?" Eden said.

"Go for it."

Eden lunged at me, making me say a very loud *shit!* which echoed embarrassingly around the gym. So that's how she was going to play it, huh? Hard? I could play hard, too. I lifted my foil and parried her attack, forcing her backward on the mat.

"Ooh, you're good!" she called. "Again."

I moved closer to her, aiming for her white jacket, but each time she'd move herself a certain way and immediately block my attack, then lunge at me harder than before.

"Again!"

She lunged at me, making me stumble three or four steps back, our foils clashing before I managed to fend her off and take control again. I stepped into her, jabbing my foil closer and closer to the target, getting frustrated when it kept missing by inches. She was fast, her right arm bringing her foil up quicker and more accurately each time.

Finally, after around twenty minutes of constant stabbing, she stepped back and waved her arm at me. Chucking her foil onto the mat and placing her hands on her knees, she bent over, breathing hard. She looked up at me, a light sheen of sweat on her face, her hair a little plastered across her forehead.

"You're awesome!" she breathed. "Are you sure you've never done this before?"

"Never," I said, my sides heaving with the effort. "Good fun, though."

"I said, didn't I?" She grinned, looking up at me for a good few seconds.

We carried on like that for the rest of the two-hour lesson: fighting hard, stopping to rest while Rob tried to instill some basic technique in me, then fighting on again. It was great. I loved it, and despite being pissed off with Greg for initially abandoning me, by the time we'd all finished I could have kissed him for buggering off and leaving me with Eden. She'd surely want to practise with me each week now, wouldn't she?

"So you think you'll come again next week?" Eden asked me after we'd changed out of our gear. She was leaning against the wall of the changing room, watching me stuff my fencing clothes untidily into my kit bag after Greg had told me to keep them for next week, too.

"Sure." I bent over my bag. "It was great fun!"

"Not nerdy?" Eden's lips twitched.

"Definitely not nerdy," I said, straightening up and lifting the strap of my bag over my head.

"So, phone number?" Eden pulled her phone from her pocket.

"Mine?" I asked stupidly.

"Well, not Greg's," Eden replied, tilting her head to one side and making big eyes at me. "I wanna text you later in the week, remind you to get your arse here next Tuesday for another whupping."

"Another whupping, hey?" I said, pulling my phone from my pocket and removing the alert on the screen about my two missed calls from Amy. I gave my number to Eden, who was still leaning against the wall, one hand in her pocket. How stoked was I right now?

"So, see you tomorrow at school, I guess." Eden shoved herself away from the wall and sauntered from the changing rooms, slowing slightly as my phone rang. "That's me, by the way. Now you have my number, too." She looked back over her shoulder and flashed me a smile before pulling the door open and leaving the room.

❖

I'd just returned home from fencing and had gone into the lounge, looking for my iPad, when my father collared me.

"So?" He put down the paper he was reading and studied me.

I'd been riddled with guilt by the time I arrived home. I felt guilty for having had such an awesome evening with Eden, and even guiltier at the casual way I'd dismissed Amy's missed calls to me with barely a thought back at school. By the time I stepped in through the door, I was ready for a fight. My father would do for starters. I sighed, wishing I'd just gone straight up to my room. At least that would have saved me from the third degree which I knew was now coming.

"So…?" I repeated.

"How was your first class?" he asked.

"Are you interested?" I spotted my iPad on the coffee table, just in front of my father. If I timed it just right, I could grab it now and make my escape up to my room where I could Skype Amy without having to answer too many questions.

"Of course I am." He stretched his legs out and crossed them at the ankle. "I'm always interested."

"It was okay, I suppose," I said, reaching over and picking up my iPad.

"What did you learn tonight?" my father persisted.

"Jack-all," I lied. "We were given some lovely white clothes to wear, and then I spent the rest of the evening trying not to go mad and stab everyone in a fit of excitement."

"Why do you have to be so sarcastic all the time?" He glowered.

"Years of practice."

Ed came into the room behind me, cuffing me gently around

the back of the head as he passed me. "So?" he asked. "Stab anyone tonight?"

"Just the boys," I joked, catching Ed's eye and grinning.

"I've got tickets for the theatre, by the way." My father reached onto the windowsill behind him and picked them up. "This Saturday. Are either of you interested?"

"Freebies?" I asked. "Perk of the job?"

"A valued customer kindly gave them to me, yes," he said piously. "If that's what you mean by freebies."

"I've already got plans," Ed said. "Sorry. Football night out."

"Tabitha?" My father held the tickets up again.

"No, thanks." I brooded. "Not really my thing."

Exasperation rose in his voice. "We live a Tube ride away from the West End, with any play or musical you could wish for, and what? It's not your thing?"

"Nope."

"So, what is your thing?"

"Cragthorne's my thing," I said simply. "London sucks."

"Not this again." He chucked the tickets down on the table in front of him. "I don't know how clear I have to make it, Tabitha. London's our home now, and that's all there is to it."

"And my feelings don't count?" I swung around. "You know how much change freaks me out. You know I can't cope with any upheaval but you still just went ahead and moved us all here, didn't you?"

"Tab." Ed's voice was warning.

"No," I said, trying desperately to block thoughts of Eden. "I'm sick of it. I miss home, I miss my old school." I hesitated. "I miss Amy."

"How can you miss your old school when you were never there?" my father asked drolly, completely ignoring my reference to Amy.

"I hate London," I said. "I hate everything about it."

"Perhaps if you broadened your horizons," he said, getting up from his chair, "and met different people, you'd see what both London and your school have to offer."

Eden. I've met Eden.

"I joined the fencing team," I said savagely. "What more do you want?"

"A peaceful life, Tabitha." He sighed and walked to the door. "Just a peaceful life."

CHAPTER SEVEN

A pparently, if you put Mentos into a bottle of Coke, you can make it explode." Libby leant over her chemistry textbook and looked up at me, excited.

"You didn't know that?" I looked at her in disbelief. "We were doing that in, like, year five, Lib!"

We were in the canteen, having just come from a spectacularly boring chemistry lesson, where we'd learned about particles. Or something. While Libby had been enlightening me on Mentos and Coke, I'd been aware of Eden, my eyes magically drawn to her as she arrived in the canteen and made her way through the maze of chairs and other people. I looked around, expecting to see either Gabby or Beth with her, but she was alone.

As I sat down, I saw her settle at a table over in the far corner. She got out a magazine from her bag and opened it, then unscrewed the top of a bottle of water, and took a long drink. I skimmed my eyes over her long slender neck, freckled nose, and lovely jawline, my stomach melting as she gently wiped her lips after she'd finished drinking.

"Greg not coming today?" Libby's voice stirred me, and I drew my eyes away from Eden.

"No," I said, twisting my apple round and round until the stalk came off. I placed it on my plate. "He's gone to the physics lab to speak to Mr. Giles about something, so he said."

"Right. Okay."

Focus, Tab. Look at Libby, not Eden.

"Ew! Radishes!" Libby pulled two radishes from her salad and placed them on the table. "Who would think to put radishes in a salad? Evil."

"And what did they ever do to you?" I asked. "Hmm?"

"God, I am *so* tired," Libby said, ignoring my question. "Do you think I could concentrate in chemistry just now? How am I supposed to learn about fundamental sodding particles when it's all I can do to stay awake?" She yawned loudly, not bothering to cover her mouth.

"Never mind," I said. "It'll soon be half-term and then we can all have a rest."

"That's another thing." Libby forked up a slice of tomato and waved it at me. "How can it be the end of October already? Where did all those weeks go?"

"Sucked up into a swirling eddy created by Dr. Thompson and his fundamental particles, no doubt," I said, grinning.

Libby turned over a piece of lettuce and screwed up her nose when she found yet another radish. "See? They even try and hide them under the lettuce leaves, hoping I won't notice."

"Hmm?" I slid my gaze back over to Eden. She was still alone, eating her lunch and still reading her magazine. I watched her, elbows on the table while she read, face cradled in her hands. I looked back to Libby and, seeing her still fussing about with her radishes, allowed myself the luxury of glancing back over to Eden. She was staring right back at me.

I spun away, heat spreading up my neck. Even though I knew I shouldn't, I slid my eyes back towards her, curious. She was still looking at me but, like I'd just done, immediately pulled her eyes away when our eyes met.

"Radishes."

"What?"

"Radishes in my salad."

"Will you stop going on about your bloody salad?"

"Who's bitten your arse?"

"No one."

Was Eden looking at me again?

Don't look over. Concentrate.

"You're distracted." Libby put a piece of cheese into her mouth and chewed. "I can always tell."

"I'm not."

"So are."

"Not." I took a bite of my apple. While Libby fussed with another piece of cheese, my eyes unthinkingly strayed back to Eden.

So much for concentrating, then.

This time Libby turned around to see what—or rather who—I was looking at.

"Why do you keep looking over there?" she asked as she faced me again.

"I don't."

"You do."

Putting another piece of cheese into her mouth, she twisted around in her chair and gazed out across the canteen. I saw her chewing slow as her searching settled on Eden. She turned slowly to face me again, both eyebrows raised so high they were practically touching the top of her head. She frowned. Turned one more time towards Eden. The little hamster wheel of thought eventually kicked in, a realization-dawning look spreading across her face.

"Her?" She tossed a look over her shoulder and grinned.

"Who?" I played dumb.

"Eden Palmer."

Just the sound of her name said out loud made me swallow involuntarily, like a hungry dog having a sausage waved in front of its face. I coughed, embarrassed.

"I've no idea what you're talking about."

Libby leant towards me. "You've been staring at Eden Palmer since the moment we came in here," she whispered.

"No, I haven't."

"Yes, you have."

I sighed impatiently.

"You can't take your eyes off her." Libby turned in her chair and looked over at Eden.

"Stop staring!" I reached over and flicked her hand.

"Why? That's all you've been doing for the last ten minutes."

"Because I don't want her to see."

Libby straightened herself in her chair again and grinned. "You've got the hots for her, haven't you?"

"No." Then, "Yes."

"Sweet!"

"No, not sweet," I said. "Pointless."

"Now it all makes sense," Libby said. "Why you were asking me questions about her before."

"Go figure."

"Well, I'm sorry to tell you," Libby said, squashing another square of cheese into her mouth, "that you're fighting a losing battle there."

"With Eden?"

"Yuh-huh. Last I heard, she was dating some guy called William."

"Story of my life," I said, sighing.

"So, what is it about Eden that's caught your eye?" Libby asked.

Apart from her gorgeous eyes, her fantastic figure, her lovely hair, and her infectious laugh?

"She's just nice," I said.

"Is that it?" Libby leant back in her chair.

"Well, I dunno," I said. "It goes like that when you like someone, doesn't it? You just see them and think, ooh, nice."

"Well she's nicer than Dumb and Dumber who she hangs out with, anyway," Libby said. She looked at me. "And I really hate to burst your bubble twice in as many minutes," she said. "But you have a girlfriend, remember?"

"I know, I know," I said. "So it's just as well Eden's straight, isn't it?"

"Because you couldn't possibly lust after Eden when you have a girlfriend so far away." Libby made big eyes, making me laugh. "Imagine the guilt!"

"Couldn't I lust just a little bit?" I asked, making big eyes back at Libby. "Nah, I love Amy. Eden's straight. It's a non-starter all around." Well, I thought I sounded pretty convincing.

"Because you have a girlfriend." Libby stressed each word.

"Because I have a...yeah, yeah." I grinned, sliding my eyes back over towards Eden. "Oh, but you should see Eden in her fencing gear," I said dreamily, still looking at her. "Did I tell you she was there?"

"She fences?"

"Yeah." I laughed. "I couldn't believe my luck when I turned up for the first class, and there she was."

"Yeah, like you didn't know!"

"Seriously."

"With Beth and Gobby, too?"

"No, just her."

"Well, thank God for that." Libby shuddered. "I wouldn't trust the pair of them with a pair of scissors, let alone a sword."

"It's a foil, but I see your point." I paused. "She was very keen to tell me that she didn't want the other two knowing anything about her fencing," I said. "She said they thought it was nerdy and they'd take the piss out of her for evermore if they found out."

"Sounds about right."

"So don't mention it to them, yeah?" I said. "Just having her to myself for two hours a week is fab. I'd be gutted if she left."

"My lips are sealed," said Libby with a grin.

Chapter Eight

It was Tuesday again. Strangely, though, since I'd signed up for fencing, each Tuesday now took forever to come around. I felt like a kid waiting for Christmas. That's how it was for me now. I'd spend each one going through the motions: learning about disaccharides and Dickens, eating lunch with Libby and Greg, constantly looking out for Eden, and getting the familiar tingle of anticipation the closer four o'clock came.

The fencing, at least, was a pleasant way to take my mind off my relationship with Amy. It was ironic, I thought, as yet another day passed with us only sending one another a couple of texts, that just a while ago, both of us were convinced we could never live without the other.

I didn't read anything into it, of course. Just like I didn't read anything into our shorter nightly Skype calls, or that she was often out when I wanted to talk to her. What did I expect? That she'd be staying at home pining for me? It wasn't as if I was doing that, was I? Regardless of our guarantees to one another to be in constant contact, the simple truth of it was we both had things going on in our lives that prevented that.

Life went on. And my life went on with the help of Eden.

She was rapidly becoming my distraction, and the more I got to know her, the more I realized how nice she really was. If I didn't know any better, I'd say throwing off the shackles of Gabby and Beth made Eden far more light-hearted than she usually was during school hours.

Not that she ever spoke to me at school, you understand.

Outside of the gym where we met each week, Eden was still

much of a stranger to me. She would only briefly speak to me before or after the two classes we took together—biology and philosophy—and then only if Gabby and Beth weren't taking her attention away from me.

Libby had once said it would take a very special person to infiltrate the Gabby, Beth, and Eden clique. During school hours I'd agree with her; the three of them were watertight. But when I had Eden on her own, she transformed. She was as smart, funny, and attentive towards me as I was to her, apparently hanging on every word I said just as much as I clung to every tiny thing she said to me. I liked that. I told myself I just wanted her as a friend. Another new friend in my new life.

Her friendliness towards me was starting to tell me that she liked me, too.

One Tuesday, a few weeks into my fencing classes, I turned up to find Eden playful, jokey, and relaxed—a totally different girl from the one I'd seen just earlier in our philosophy class. We were practising parrying again, and Eden had collared me the moment I stepped from the changing rooms, telling me she wanted to "push me to my limits." That sent a pulse through my body. Meekly, I followed her onto the practice mat.

"So, okay," Eden said, flexing her foil and grinning at me. "Rob says he wants us to perfect our defensive moves tonight."

"Okay," I said warily, seeing a look in her eyes.

"So I'm going to come at you, and you've got to try and hit either the tip of my foil," she said, waving her foil in the air, and plopping her mask down over her face, "or the base, near the handle."

"Tip or base. Gotcha." I lowered my mask over my face, too.

We assumed our positions on the mat, and I gripped my foil tighter, holding it up slightly in front of me as Eden came towards me. I backed away, ungainly, seeing her suddenly lunge towards me, the foil in her hand jabbing more and more at me.

"Take it easy, Eden!" I laughed. "Those things can hurt, you know."

"So, parry." Eden lifted her mask up onto her head and raised one perfect eyebrow.

"Playing rough, huh?" I spoke from behind my mask.

"Not scared of a little rough, are you?" She laughed back. "Hmm?"

"Me? Scared?"

I thrust forward with my right foot, driving Eden backward again. Pleased to have gained the upper hand, I stupidly let my concentration slip long enough to allow Eden one final lunge towards me, her foil centimetres from my face. The second I jarred back on my left leg, I heard a noise come from my knee. I instantly dropped my foil. My leg buckled as a shooting pain ripped through it, and I landed in a clumsy heap on the mat. I groaned.

"Oh God, Tabby!" Eden ripped off her mask and was at my side in an instant, an anxious look on her face. "I'm so sorry! I misjudged that last one." She sank to her knees next to me.

"Yeah, big time."

I winced as I tried to move. Okay, that wasn't good.

"I'm so sorry, really."

Eden reached over and rubbed at my knee, her fingers spreading out across my skin, massaging it over and over. I watched her as she did it, her face a picture of worry, and felt my breath start to come in gasps behind my mask.

What was she doing to me?

"It's fine, really." I scrambled awkwardly to my feet.

I took my own mask off, then tested my leg, leaning gingerly over onto my left foot and screwed up my face as another jolt shot through my knee. I suddenly felt sick and faint, the gym appearing to close in around me, and sat down hard on the mat.

"Tabby?"

I lay on my back, groaning up at the ceiling. It seemed as if it was dropping down at me, then floating away again, ebbing and flowing in rhythm with the pain. Eden stood over me, looking panicked.

"I think I've broken my knee." I grimaced, the pulses of pain in my leg increasing with every heartbeat. "Soldier down." Another wave of nausea hit me.

The next thing I was aware of was Greg and Rob kneeling next to me. The pain was constant. Intense. Excruciating.

"Can you stand?" Rob's face loomed over me.

I shook my head. "I already tried."

"Is it bad, Rob?" Eden spoke from behind Greg, who was watching, his face anxious.

"Okay, that really hurts." I screwed up my face as Rob poked his fingers into the muscles around my kneecap. "You didn't have to do that, you know!"

"How the hell did this happen?" Rob swung around and looked at Eden, who visibly jumped at his words.

"I don't know...I just—" Eden looked like she might cry, her face crumpling. She beseeched me, and I smiled back.

"It wasn't Eden's fault," I said, trying to forget I'd only jumped back because Eden's foil had been so close to my face. "I stepped back and landed funny. It was more my fault, really."

The relief on Eden's face was palpable.

"Hmm." Rob stood, bending over and putting his hands under my arms. "Let's try and get you up, then."

I clambered to my feet and, with the help of Rob on one side and Greg on the other, hopped on my right foot, trying to get my balance. I put my left foot on the ground and gritted my teeth as a spasm ripped through my knee again. I was relieved when Rob and Greg lifted me between them and carried me to the gym's exit. Eden followed close behind us, occasionally reaching out and touching my arm, saying over and over how sorry she was.

There was a small part of me that wanted to turn to her and say, "Well, this is one helluva way to get to know you better, isn't it?" but instead I just told her it was okay, that accidents happened, and that at least I'd have a temporary reminder of how lousy I was at fencing. She laughed at that. Her laugh was like her voice, soft and sweet, and if my heart hadn't been busy pounding away at the pain in my knee, I think it would have flipped over at the sound of it.

After making a quick detour via the school's office, where my predicament was duly logged and numerous sympathetic looks were directed my way, we were instructed to head straight for the nearest hospital. I wasn't about to complain about that, despite knowing I'd no doubt end up being stuck there for the rest of the evening, putting paid to any thoughts I'd had of Skyping Amy that night. The pain in my knee had reached such an intensity that I knew if I didn't get some painkillers within the hour, I'd probably start trying to kill someone.

"Right, in you hop." Rob opened the passenger door to his 4x4, parked just outside the gym, and held my arm as I scrambled onto the seat, then walked around to the driver's side, his mobile clamped to his ear. "You, too." He gesticulated towards Eden, who was standing next to my window looking adorably lost.

She clambered into the back of the 4x4 and sat down, leaning forward between the passenger and driver seats to rub my arm, then leant back again and buckled herself in. We drove in near silence on the twenty-minute journey out to our local hospital, Rob occasionally asking me if I was okay, if I felt sick or faint, or if I wanted him to stop. I shook my head at each question, just wishing the traffic would hurry up so we could get to the hospital as quickly as possible.

The hospital's Emergency Department was unusually quiet. I was ushered more or less straight into a cubicle, where I sat on a bed, propped up with pillows, fighting the urge to cry. Or be sick.

Not the way I expected the evening to end.

"Why do hospitals always give me the willies?" Rob sat on the end of my bed and gestured for Eden to have the chair. "The minute I step into one, I feel ill."

"It's the smell." Eden sat down, looking around the cubicle. "Does the same to me."

"Can't say I'm feeling too hot at the moment either," I muttered.

The pain in my knee still hadn't subsided at all, and I fought hard not to show my increasing panic that I'd done some serious damage to it.

"Want a drink?" Rob stood up. "I can't stand all the waiting around in these places."

"Coke would be good. Thanks."

"Eden?"

"Same. Thanks."

I watched Rob disappear out of the cubicle, poking his head back in briefly to instruct both Eden and me to telephone our parents by the time he returned, before disappearing again. I looked over to Eden, but she wasn't looking at me. Instead, she was staring hard at the curtain, then the ceiling, then the floor—anywhere but towards me.

"How is it now?" she finally said.

"Still ragging, unfortunately."

"Thanks for saying it wasn't my fault, by the way."

I waved a hand. "S'okay. I don't think it was anyone's fault, to be honest."

"No, but if I hadn't come at you like a thing possessed, you wouldn't have jerked back."

"I guess."

"So, thanks."

"Bet we look dumb in these, huh?" I said, nodding at my jacket.

Eden smiled. "I think they look okay, actually. You look like a proper pro in yours."

"A proper pro with a busted knee?"

"Well, you know what I mean."

She leant over and rummaged in her bag, pulling out her phone. "Mum," she said. "Just letting her know where I am."

"This isn't keeping you from anything, is it?" I asked. I pulled my phone from my sweatpants pocket and fired the briefest of texts off to my mother, too.

She shook her head. "It's fine. Honestly."

I watched her from the corner of my eye as she wrote out a text, her fingers sliding quickly over the screen.

"So, who's at home waiting for you?" I asked.

"Mum, Dad," she said, not looking up from her phone. "Annoying brother."

"You, too, huh?"

"Hmm?"

"Annoying brother. I have one, too."

"Yeah, he's called Ben." Eden tossed the phone back into her bag. "Yours?"

"Ed. Is yours older or younger?"

"Older. Yours?"

"Same," I said.

Eden nodded.

The conversation ground to a halt after that, and I was grateful when I felt my phone buzz in my pocket. I retrieved it, flicking my eyes over it.

"Overreacting mother." I held my phone up. Then, noticing the time, I hurriedly wrote out a text to Amy: *At hospital. Busted knee. Long story. Don't worry if I don't Skype on time. I'll catch you later xxx*

"Bloody drinks machine was out of order, so I had to go across to the other ward." Rob flung the curtain of my cubicle back and stepped inside. He handed me and Eden a bottle each, then retreated back to the entrance to the cubicle. "Seen anyone yet?"

I shook my head, then unscrewed the cap on the bottle and took a long drink. I was thirstier than I'd realized.

"Tabitha Morton?"

I grimaced at the sound of my name and grunted a reply of sorts. A nurse in scrubs poked her head around the side of the cubicle curtain, then held it open so that Rob could make a discreet exit.

"So what have we here?" She read from a clipboard. "Knee injury, yes?"

"Mm."

"Right, if you can wriggle yourself out of those trousers, I'll take a look."

I put my bottle down and lifted my hips up from the bed, glancing self-consciously at Eden as I did so, and cursing the fact I'd chosen that very day to wear a pair of *Simpsons* boy shorts. I shuffled my sweats down to just past my knees and sat there, with Homer poking out from under the hem of my jacket, feeling stupid and embarrassed. Thankfully, Eden was being considerate and had turned to face the curtain.

"Can you bend your knee?" the nurse asked, shaking her head as I tried and failed to bend it. "I think you've probably just twisted it, but we'll X-ray just to be safe and make sure it's nothing more serious than that."

"So that means at least another hour's wait," I heard Rob mutter from outside my cubicle as the nurse left again. "I'm going for a wander." He poked his head through the gap in the curtains. "Be back in a mo."

"The wheels sure turn slowly in this place, don't they?" Eden stood up and yawned, linking her fingers and stretching her arms high above her head.

"If you have to go, it's cool," I said. "You really don't have to wait. My mum will be on her way soon."

"I want to, I told you," Eden said. "I'm responsible for all this—it's the least I can do."

"Well, thanks," I said. "I appreciate it."

I stared down at my skinny, bare knees poking out above my waistband and started to pull my sweats up again.

"Can I have a look?" Eden suddenly said. "It's sure swollen, isn't it?"

"Like a balloon," I said, mid-wriggle.

Eden came around to the left side of my bed and leant over, peering hard at my knee. She'd undone the top buttons of her protective jacket, so that the lapels flapped down. When she leant over I was acutely aware I could see a hint of cleavage and the satin of her bra. I swallowed hard, trying to stop my eyes, which had mysteriously taken on a life of their own, from staring down her front.

"Yikes." Eden grimaced. "Can I?" She waggled her fingers, indicating that she wanted to touch my knee.

"If you want," I said, my voice suddenly sounding strange.

It had been bad enough back at the gym when she'd massaged my leg through my sweats, but this? This was a thousand times worse. Or better. I wasn't sure. All I was aware of as she gingerly traced her fingers across my skin, occasionally looking at me, her cleavage tantalizingly close, was that it was absolutely fucking killing me.

"You have goosebumps on your leg!" She suddenly laughed. "Are you cold?"

Are you kidding me?

"I…uh…"

The abrupt buzzing of my phone on the bed next to me made us both jump.

Amy.

As her name flashed on and off my screen, Eden pulled away from me. My eyes followed her around the end of my bed, the intensity of having just had Eden touch my bare skin apparently rendering my brain completely unable to register that my phone was ringing.

"Aren't you going to answer that?" Eden flopped back into her chair.

I snatched up my phone, hoping that my hands weren't shaking too obviously.

"Baby." Amy's voice was fretful.

"Hey." I subconsciously shifted a shoulder so I was leaning slightly away from Eden.

"So what happened?"

"I just crocked my knee a bit, that's all." I glanced at Eden.

"How?"

"An overexuberant opponent." I dropped my eyes from Eden's. "Look, I better go. We're not supposed to have phones on in here, and—"

"Call me when you get home?"

"Sure." I killed the call and looked apologetically towards Eden.

"Parent?"

"No. Old school friend."

"Nice that they called." Eden studied me, a faint smile at the corners of her mouth.

The curtain to my cubicle was pulled back, and the nurse who'd seen me before came back in with a porter who was pushing a wheelchair.

I'd never been so grateful to see two people in all my life.

"You're in luck," the nurse said. "X-ray department's fairly quiet, so Frank here is going to take you on up now."

"Thank God," I said, with feeling, grateful to at last pull my sweats back up and get out of the cubicle.

The nurse turned to Eden. "You want to come with your friend?"

"If that's okay with you?" Eden looked at me.

I nodded weakly, by now beyond words, the memory of Eden's fingers on my skin still teasing me as Frank wheeled me from the cubicle and down the harshly lit corridor to X-ray.

Chapter Nine

The X-ray, much to my relief, showed a sprain to my knee ligaments but nothing more serious. By the time I left the hospital with some anti-inflammatories and a pair of crutches I'd never get the hang of, Eden had already left, collected by her mother a good hour before my mother turned up.

Of course, I spent the entire journey home in the car with my mother fending off inane questions from her, then having to go over it all again once my father arrived back from work, shortly after eight p.m. His reaction was exactly what I'd expected it to be: fencing was a sport for gentlemen and ladies, he thought I lacked the required sophistication needed to be good at it, and he could have guessed I'd end up getting injured within weeks of taking it up.

"I suppose you went at it like a bull in a china shop as usual?" he said, looking unsympathetically at my swollen knee, propped up on a footstool. "Trying to prove that you can beat everyone? Fencing takes patience and guile, Tabitha. Neither of which you're blessed with."

And that was all the sympathy I got.

I fared better with Amy, though, when I Skyped her later that same evening, needing to see her face, knowing I'd get the compassion I needed from her.

"You poor thing." Amy's face creased with concern as I held my iPad over my knee to show her. I was lying on my bed, my crutches propped up against the wall next to me. "Does it hurt?"

"Not so bad now." I waggled the pack of pills the hospital had given me. "Thanks to these."

"How did you do it again?" Amy asked. "You didn't get a chance to say much earlier."

"Meh," I said nonchalantly. "Just mistimed a step backward and *whoomph!* Bye-bye knee."

Amy pulled a face. "So no fencing for you for a bit, then?" she asked, peering at the screen.

"Guess not," I said, disappointment stabbing at me.

"You want me to come and kiss it better?" Amy raised her eyebrow.

An image of Eden bending over me in the hospital and rubbing my knee floated into my head, making the skin on my face feel warm. I tried to shake the image from my head.

"When are you coming down here?" I gazed at my screen, ignoring Amy's comment. "I miss you, Ames."

"I miss you, too." Amy comically jutted out her bottom lip. "I don't know when I can get down to see you, though." She shrugged. "Sorry."

"S'okay."

"You know I'd be down in a flash. It's just always a case of this"—Amy rubbed her index and middle fingers against her thumb, indicating money—"isn't it?"

"Yes. It always is," I agreed.

"I guess you won't be coming back up this way again for a while now, will you?" Amy said, motioning towards my knee.

"I guess not," I said simply.

Strangely, though, that thought didn't feel as awful as I thought it would.

❖

"Y'know, I thought you were gawky enough as it was," Libby said, walking slowly beside me down the corridor at school as I hobbled along on my crutches. "But you're a million times worse with these things."

I stopped hobbling. "You're a pal."

"Is it still really painful?" Libby walked ahead of me and

opened a connecting door to the next corridor, stepping aside as I went past her.

"Only when I try to run on it."

"You tried to run on it already?"

"No, Libby. I was kidding with you."

I slowed as I saw Gabby, Beth, and Eden just up ahead of me, waiting to go into the biology lab. Gabby and Beth were leaning against the wall, while Eden stood in front of them both, talking animatedly about something, waving her arms around. I wondered for a moment if she was telling them about what had happened the previous evening, but then I saw Gabby laugh, doubling over at something Eden had said, and immediately hoped she wasn't talking about me after all.

As we approached, Eden caught my eye. A meltingly gorgeous smile lit up her whole face. I returned her smile, a twinge pinching pleasantly in the pit of my stomach.

"What have you done to your leg, then?" Eden spoke before either Gabby or Beth had a chance to ask me. She bobbed her head towards my crutches, then implored me.

"I…" I frowned slightly, but the pleading look in her eyes told me to be vague. "Ah, I hurt my knee at my fencing class last night."

"Nasty." Beth looked at my crutches.

"You fence?" Gabby asked, witheringly.

I looked directly at her. "Yeah."

A look shot between Gabby and Beth.

"Who in the twenty-first century fences?" Gabby said.

"Me." I tried to stand taller. Not easy when you're on crutches.

"Loser." That was Beth. Said quietly, but loudly enough that I'd hear. "Doesn't that weedy little friend of yours do it, too? Greg?"

I stepped forward. Well, shuffled.

"Even I didn't know Tabby fenced." Libby draped an arm over my shoulder to stop me. She glanced to Eden and back again. "Did you, Eden?"

I knocked my crutch against Libby's leg.

"Ow!"

"How would I know?" Eden held my gaze. "Is it very painful?"

"Better now." I lowered my eyes.

"She was at the hospital all yesterday evening," Libby chipped in, rubbing her leg. "Weren't you, Tab? Just you and Rob, was it?"

"Mm." I looked back up. Eden was still looking at me.

"So, what have you done to it?" Gabby asked. The bored look on her face said she didn't care, but she thought she'd ask anyway.

"I've just twisted it, thassall," I said. "But I'll be back to normal in a few weeks."

"So no more fencing for Tabby for a while," Libby said, watching Eden.

"That's a shame for you," Eden said softly.

"It is, yes," I replied, turning my head as the door to the laboratory opened and the previous class came spilling out.

I shuffled back a bit to allow people to pass me, then lost sight of Eden as she disappeared inside with Gabby and Beth, getting sucked into the melee of students. Conversation over. Just like that.

"Why did she act so dumb?" Libby hissed as we settled ourselves on a bench at the back.

"I told you." I propped my crutches up against the back wall. "Beth and Gobby don't know she fences, remember?"

"Even though she spent pretty much the entire evening with you at the hospital?"

"She has her reasons."

"Despite the fact she practically caused it in the first place?"

"No one caused it, Lib," I said, getting my books out of my bag. "It was just an accident."

"Well, at least she had the grace to look sheepish." Libby fired a look towards Eden.

"You think she did?"

"Yeah. And rightly so, too."

I looked over to where Beth, Gabby, and Eden were sitting and stared at the back of Eden's head. I willed her to turn around just so I could see her face, but she remained looking at the front, watching as Mrs. Hamilton strode up to her bench and placed her laptop onto it.

"Today, photosynthesis," she said, flipping open her laptop. "Pigmentation and the absorption of light."

Reluctantly I dragged my eyes away from Eden, then opened up my notepad. I clicked the end of my pen with my thumb, ready to begin.

Somehow I knew Eden would still be on my mind by the end of the lesson.

❖

"I'll catch up with you guys down there," I heard Eden's distinctive voice say from nearby as Gabby and Beth gathered up their books and disappeared out the lab door, chattering away to one another.

I slowed down the packing away of my own things and glanced back over to where Eden was, hoping that if I timed it just right, I might be able to walk—or in my case, hobble—back down the corridor with her.

"I'll leave you to it." Libby bumped my arm with hers and tipped her head towards Eden. "I know when I'm not wanted."

I grinned. "See you in chemistry this afternoon, yeah?"

"Good luck," Libby whispered in my ear as she picked up her bag and left the lab.

I leant down from my chair, holding on to the bench for support, my damaged leg poker straight, and tried to grab my bag. I cursed my stupidity for not only dropping my rucksack on the floor before the lesson, but for also not thinking to ask Libby to pick it up for me as I balanced precariously on my chair, my hand flailing and repeatedly missing the handles.

"Let me."

I looked up and saw Eden standing next to my bench, her own bag slung diagonally across her shoulders. She bent over, picked my rucksack up, and placed it in front of me.

"Thanks." I pulled it towards me, putting my books inside it.

"You want these?" Eden pointed to my crutches, still propped up against the wall behind me.

"Won't be going very far without them," I said. "Thanks."

She stood back as I slotted my arms into the crutches and gingerly stepped down from my chair.

"Still not quite used to them." I pulled a face as I leant over to pick up my rucksack from the bench and wobbled slightly. I put the rucksack on my back, jiggling my shoulders up and down a few times until I felt more comfortable. "Okay, we're good to go."

I followed Eden out of the lab and turned left, walking with her back down the corridor.

"So, how is it?" she asked, waving a hand towards my knee.

"Stiff and painful. But I'll live," I replied.

"You'll still come along to the meets, won't you?" Eden asked. "Even though you can't fence for a bit? I mean, it would be a shame not to see you there," she added hastily.

"I guess I could," I said, catching her eye.

"Actually, I'm glad I got a chance to see you alone," she said, slowing her step so I could keep up with her. "I wanted to say sorry for before."

"Sorry?" I faced her. "What for?"

"For acting like I didn't know what you'd done to your knee."

"Ah. It's okay."

"It's just…well, like I said before. They don't need to know I go to fencing classes," she said. "You saw what their reaction was just now, didn't you?" Her face fell. "It's not worth the piss taking, trust me."

"You don't ever worry that someone else from the class might tell them?" I asked.

"No one in the group knows them. Only Greg, and he'd never say anything," Eden said simply. She thought for a moment. "My fencing is something I can do for myself, you know?" she said. "Without the pair of them."

"Libby reckons you three are joined at the hip," I said.

"Sometimes it feels like we are, yeah," Eden said. "Don't get me wrong, I love the pair of them. It's just—"

"Sometimes it's good to do something that doesn't involve them?" I offered.

"Exactly."

"You have your fencing, Beth has her singing, and Gobby has her men," I said. "It's healthy for people to do things independently sometimes."

"Gabby," Eden corrected.

"Sorry?"

"You called her Gobby."

"Did I?"

"Yeah."

"Gabby. I meant Gabby." I looked away, trying not to laugh.

Eden stopped walking. She appraised me, eyebrows raised. "Gobby, hey?"

"Slip of the tongue," I said, chewing on my lip in an attempt to avoid the smile that was trying to get out.

"I think it kinda suits her," Eden said. Her expression was poker straight.

"Mm-hmm?" I clamped my lips shut.

The poker face broke. A broad grin spread across Eden's face, followed by laughter from both of us.

"Don't tell her, will you?" I said, still laughing.

"What's it worth?" Eden winked.

I stopped laughing at her wink and looked away. My face flushed hot. I gazed out of the corridor window, hoping that Eden hadn't seen that I'd gone bright red.

"I won't tell her, don't worry," Eden finally said, bumping my arm with hers.

We carried on walking down the corridor a little further, neither of us speaking this time. We stopped just next to the canteen, and I looked at my watch. I had forty-five minutes until my next lesson.

Enough time to hang out some more with Eden. I could buy her a coffee, right? Splash out even—go for a cappuccino. She always left straight away after fencing because her dad picked her up from outside school. How awesome would it be to spend some time alone with her in the canteen right now?

Eden pulled out her phone. Looked at the clock on it. She was stalling for time. Or was she desperate to get away?

But if I didn't ask her, I'd regret it. I just knew it. If only my brain would connect with my mouth. Bit difficult to talk when your heart's floundering in your throat, though.

Quit being so chickenshit, Tab. Ask her.

I swallowed. Was it hot in the corridor all of a sudden?

Do it.

"I'm kinda at a loose end for the next half hour or so," I said. I put both crutches in one hand and rested my left foot on top of my right one. "Fancy a coffee?" I kept my voice light. If I didn't, it would tremble. I was sure of it.

Eden looked towards the canteen door. Her face flickered. "I can't, sorry," she finally said. "I have a report to write for my Spanish class this afternoon, so I'd better head up to the library and finish it."

Deflated.

"Of course." I looped my arms back into my crutches. "No worries." I stepped back, my arms stupidly shaking. A conflict of emotions—relief at actually managing to get the words out to ask her in the first place, followed by crushing disappointment.

Eden started to walk away from me. "Another time, though? I'd like that."

"Sure." That was definitely a positive, right?

And then she was gone.

Guess I was having that coffee alone, then.

Chapter Ten

The following week was half-term, which meant one whole glorious week away…from school, from the grubby Tube train grind, from nightly homework.

Unfortunately for me, it also meant one not-so-glorious week away from Eden.

Out of the nine total days I had off, I can confidently say, if I grouped all the minutes and hours together, I probably spent at least four of those days thinking about her.

Where was she?

Had she gone away?

Would I perhaps bump into her if I went out?

Of course I wouldn't. But that didn't stop me going to bed each night with Eden on my mind, or waking up thinking about her. My constant craving for Eden was eating away at me, though. I had a girlfriend, right? A girlfriend who loved me very much and who was missing me nearly 300 miles away. Yet all I could do was think about some girl I still barely spoke to outside of our fencing classes, but whom I just couldn't get out of my mind. The only way I could possibly think of at least trying to forget about Eden, if only for a few hours, was by either going to visit Amy or speaking to her on Skype.

But, almost as if to deliberately thwart my plans, Amy's school wasn't on holiday the same week mine was. A few brief conversations when she came home from school in the afternoons, a daily text message, and a couple of e-mails were all we managed the entire week.

I had another trip to the hospital during my time off as well. All I could think about while the doctors were telling me that my knee was healing nicely and that I didn't need my crutches any more was how the last time I'd been there, it had been with Eden, and not with my mother. More precisely, the last time I'd been there had been with Eden and her cleavage—the image of which had refused to leave my head since I'd seen it and kept floating back in at the most inappropriate moments. Like when one of the female doctors was inspecting my leg. Awkward.

With a week away from school, and only Libby to play with on a couple of days, I had far too much time to think. And at times, I thought my longing for Eden was getting too much. She infiltrated my every thought, my every move, and I knew I needed Amy right now to help me get my head straight and remind me that I was being not only stupid, but totally unfair to her. I'd made a vow to her that we would be together again soon, and I wasn't about to break that. Nothing was ever going to happen with Eden. Amy loved me, and I loved her, yet I was treating her like she didn't matter to me at all. If I was to make sure I didn't get completely obsessed with Eden, then I needed much more than the occasional Internet chat with Amy.

I knew, more than ever before, that I had to make plans to get Amy down to see me before I went out of my mind. I'd been in London for three months already. Three whole months without seeing my girlfriend. If ever there was an ideal time to chase Eden out of my head and bond with Amy again, it was now. Besides, I needed to give her the attention she deserved, and to remind myself the promise I'd made to her wasn't just made on a whim.

It was time to reconnect with Amy.

CHAPTER ELEVEN

God, I've missed you *so* much!" I wrapped my arms around Amy and held her tightly, remembering how good she felt to hold.

"The train was a nightmare." Amy pulled away. "Signalling problems at York, and it all went crappy from then on."

It was Saturday. The last one of my holiday. In two days' time I'd be back at school, and back in Eden's sphere. But for today, Amy was my priority.

"You're here now," I said. I took her rucksack from her and carried it. "That's all that matters." I'd never meant something so much in all my life.

We walked away from the barrier and towards the station exit.

"How's your knee?" Amy asked as she saw me limping slightly.

"Better," I said. "At least I'm off the crutches, so that's something."

We walked in silence for a bit, both of us acting stupidly shy all over again in one another's company. It was madness, I thought, as we walked down the steps outside the station and into the morning sunshine, that we'd known one another for years, yet still felt somewhat hesitant towards each other.

That's what distance does to a couple, I guess.

"So what do you want to do?" I asked as we sauntered down the road away from the station.

"I dunno." Amy shrugged. "Coffee, then show me some sights?"

"There's a Starbucks just around the corner," I said, taking Amy's hand, feeling a stab of hurt when she casually let it drop again a few seconds later.

We went into the Starbucks I'd suggested. It was already beginning to fill up with the Saturday morning crowd, but we found a small table by a window. I ordered us a cappuccino each, Amy shaking her head at my offer of a blueberry muffin to go with it. I ordered, then returned to her, a steaming drink in each hand.

"So," I said, sitting down. "Any other news from home?"

Amy stirred sugar into her coffee. "No, not really."

"Your mum and dad okay?"

"Fine, yeah," Amy replied. She sipped at her coffee. "Thanks."

"And you handed your assignment in on time yesterday?" I asked.

"Assignment?"

"The one you were stressing over the other night," I said. "You told me about it on Skype."

"Oh, that," Amy said dismissively. "Nah."

"And Smith didn't kill you?"

Amy laughed. "I didn't go in all day, so she didn't get a chance."

"You skipped school?"

"Why do you sound so surprised?" Amy came back, quick as a flash. "We used to do it all the time."

"Yeah, but you still do it?" My brows pinched into a frown. "Even now?"

"You're telling me you don't do it?"

An image of Eden flickered and then faded in my mind.

"No," I said. "I don't."

"So your boasting to me about behaving so badly they'd boot you out of your la-di-da school was all bollocks?"

"No, I—" I sat back in my chair. "Let's not argue, Ames. I'm sorry." I skimmed the froth off the top of my cappuccino with my spoon. "I've missed you," I repeated. "It's been horrible being down here without you." I reached across the table and took her hand in mine, turning it over and rubbing my thumb across her palm. "But every day apart just takes us closer to when we can both finish school and be together again," I said, looking down at her hand in mine. "It'll just take longer than I first thought."

"I know," Amy said, pulling her hand slowly from mine and glancing around her.

"You don't have to be shy about showing your feelings, Amy," I said, my hand still outstretched towards her. "This is London. No one gives a fuck about PDAs here."

"It just feels weird," Amy said. "I'm not used to it, that's all."

"But that's what's nice about here," I said. "I don't really feel like I have to hide who I am as much as I did at home. People are so much more broad-minded in London." I studied my hands. "Remember I told you I'd come out to Libby and Greg a while ago? That felt fabulous."

"That's nice for you," Amy said sarcastically. "But I'm still a small-town girl, remember?"

"Don't be prickly," I said, seeing the look on her face. "I'm sorry. I didn't mean anything by it." I tucked my hands in my lap, well away from her.

Two arguments already.

Not good.

"No, I'm sorry, too," Amy said. "I didn't come down here so we could bicker."

I thought she might reach out for my hands but she didn't. Instead she took another sip from her coffee and, grimacing, opened another sugar packet and poured it in.

"So tell me about school." She stirred her coffee and smiled across at me. "Other than what you've already told me, I mean. It must be all right if you're happy to be there every day."

"Well," I began, "the school's posh, but you already know that. But that's not to say all the students are posh. Okay, some are, but mostly they're pretty middle of the road like me and you." I considered for a moment.

"Middle of the road but with rich parents?"

"Rich parents who don't want their kids going to an inner-city school where they might get enticed into joining gangs, yeah." I laughed.

"Like your parents?" Amy said.

I thought I noticed a hint of bitterness in her voice. I chose to ignore it. "The most violent thing our school can offer is the fencing class," I said. "Did for me, anyway." I lifted my injured leg.

A crystal clear image of Eden gatecrashed my head the second I mentioned fencing, swiftly followed by the memory of her touching my knee in the hospital. It was so intense it gave me shivers just to think about it. I looked away, my face warming.

"I suppose you have debating classes and chess classes and posh things like that, too?" Amy said.

"I'm sure." I looked at Amy over the top of my coffee mug, still trying to shake away the image of Eden. "Not for me, though."

We talked on for a while after that. Just tittle-tattle: school, Cragthorne, Amy's dog, my parents. Nothing profound or really meaningful.

We finished our cappuccinos and left.

"How about a tour?" I grabbed Amy's hand and hopped onto the first tourist bus that happened to come past us. It was a beautifully crisp, sunny day, so we sat up on the top deck, giving us the perfect view of all the landmarks as the bus trundled slowly around the roads.

I glanced at Amy in the seat next to me, the wind blowing her hair around her face as she put her elbows on the barrier around the top of the bus and leant over, straining to see certain things better. The look of excitement on her face as she spotted landmarks that she'd seen a hundred times on the television—Big Ben, the Houses of Parliament, Buckingham Palace, Trafalgar Square—made my heart pull towards her. I'd been so wrapped up in my confusion over Eden that it hadn't really occurred to me just how much I'd missed Amy. But now, sitting next to her on the bus, I missed her all over again.

"Lunch," Amy said firmly as our tour finally finished. "I'm starving."

We found a reasonably priced pizza restaurant near to where

the bus had dropped us off and managed to bag the last seat outside. We settled ourselves, chose and ordered drinks and pizzas, then sat back to watch the world go by on the busy side street.

"This is nice," Amy said, lifting her face to the weakening autumn sun. "I think I could get used to this."

"You sure you have to go back home tonight?" I asked. "You could sleep on my floor. I 'spose my parents wouldn't—"

"No, I'm sure." Amy cut me off. "I've got things I need to do tomorrow."

"You know, if you chose a university down here, we could do this all the time." I pushed my sunglasses up onto my head and squinted against the sun at her. "If you think you could get used to London life."

"I meant the sun," Amy said. "I'm not sure I could cope with London all the time."

"Oh," I said, disappointed. "But what about everything we'd talked about before I left?"

"About you doing everything you could to get back up to me?"

"Mm."

"Well, I still want you to." Amy looked confused. "Of course I do."

"And then we'd find a university together?" I prompted.

"In the North."

"We never said the North," I said. "I said I'd come back to you, but we never talked about settling in the North."

"But it's where we're from, Tab," Amy said slowly. "I don't want to live anywhere else."

I pushed my sunglasses back down and stared out across the street, trying to stem my frustration. "But I thought when we spoke about it before, we kinda said we'd both like to go to a large city together," I said, not looking at her. "I thought you meant somewhere like London."

"Maybe I changed my mind."

Annoying. Deeply annoying.

"Hey, who's to say we'll even get the grades to go to university anyway?" She looked at me. "Our first goal is just to be together again, isn't it?"

"Of course," I said. "I just assumed..." I leant back as the server brought our drinks out and laid out cutlery and napkins. "Never mind. I guess it doesn't do to assume."

"Don't look so sad." Amy glanced at the retreating back of our server, then at the tables around us. She reached over and took my hand.

"You're getting brave," I said, smiling.

"Very brave," Amy replied, taking my other hand, too.

"How long do you suppose for the pizzas?"

"You're that hungry?"

"No, but I need the loo." I grinned and released her hands. "Be right back."

I scraped my chair back and ambled into the restaurant, allowing my eyes to adjust from the sunshine to the gloom inside. Looking around me, I located the door just as a person inside came out. I stepped back when our eyes met in the doorway, my heart thudding in my neck, my stomach doing somersaults.

Eden.

Chapter Twelve

"Tabby!" She looked pleased to see me. I was sure of it.

"Hey. How are you?" A curious rush of blood pounded inside my ears.

"Good, yeah."

We stood in a small corridor that was visible to the rest of the restaurant.

"How was your week? I mean, break? Away from school?" I asked, practically swallowing the last few words of that sentence in my nervousness.

"So-so. You?"

"Same." I nodded far more than was necessary.

"How's your leg?" Eden asked. "All mended?"

"Good as new."

Eden leant against the wall of the corridor, as relaxed as I was tense. My pleasure at seeing her, however, was tempered by the thought of Amy waiting for me outside.

As if reading my mind at that precise moment, Eden looked over my shoulder. "You here with friends?" she asked. Her eyes scanned around us.

"Just the one. You?"

"My dopey brother." She pulled a face, but it was still kind. "You with Libby?"

"No," I said. I dug my hands into my trouser pockets and stared down at the floor. "Someone else." I looked back up at her. "You're not with Gabby and Beth, then?"

Eden laughed through her nose. "Funnily enough, no," she said. Her face flickered. "I saw them the other day," she continued airily.

Her gaze drifted around again. If I didn't know any better, I'd have said she was searching to see who I was with. I shifted my position slightly, not wanting to leave her, but knowing that I had to get back to Amy.

"I better go." I swivelled my feet around, making my shoes squeak on the floor. "My pizza will be coming soon, I guess." I turned to go.

"Weren't you...?" Eden pointed at the loo door.

"Of course." My face flushed as I squeezed past her in the corridor and placed a hand on the door.

"Awesome seeing you, Tab." Her eyes skimmed mine.

"You, too." I practically fell in through the door, my face burning both from my proximity to her and the look on her face as she'd just spoken to me.

❖

"Everything okay?" Amy leant her head to one side.

"What? Yeah, fine." I flopped down in my seat.

"You were ages." Amy sipped at her drink. "Who was that you were talking to?"

A clamminess prickled at my palms.

Amy had seen us? From outside?

"Just someone from school."

Amy leant closer. "She looked posh." She winked. "Are you moving in high-class circles at last? Your father will be so pleased." She collapsed back in her chair, pleased with her joke. I didn't smile.

Just as Amy was about to speak, presumably to make another quip, the server came out with our pizzas, a plate in each hand.

"Pepperoni?" He placed my pizza in front of me when I answered him, then Amy's in front of her.

"Black pepper? Parmesan?" he asked, smiling and returning inside when both Amy and I shook our heads.

Suddenly I didn't feel as hungry as I had when I'd ordered the pizza. Eden was inside the restaurant. I wanted to be with her. I wanted to be sitting across a table from her, eating pizza with her. I looked across at Amy. I wanted to be with her, too. I was happy to be with Amy, for goodness' sake! I hadn't seen her in ages, and yet my mind constantly tugged, like it was on a leash, to be allowed to go back inside and see Eden again.

I picked up a slice of pizza, the end sagging so much as I brought it to my mouth that I had to scoop it up with my tongue in order to eat it. I wanted to be with them both. How fucked up was that? Two girls I really liked were within feet of one another, and neither knew of the conflict inside me over them.

The knot in my stomach resisted a second slice.

"Not hungry?" Amy asked me through a mouthful of her own pizza.

"Yeah, I..." I shook my head. I was being an idiot. "Yeah, starving. Let's eat up and then head over to Hyde Park, okay?" I said, beginning to eat the rest of my food.

Anything to get as far away from Eden as possible.

Chapter Thirteen

I'd dropped Amy back off at the train station on the Saturday evening, the tears we'd cried when I'd first left her all those months ago no longer present. Heartbreak and the numerous blind, irrational declarations we'd made that neither of us could ever live without the other had been replaced with a long, loving hug just before the train doors closed.

That, and a resigned acceptance that this was the way things had to be for now.

Now it was Monday. And although part of me was dying to see Eden again, the other part was dreading it. Why, though? Was I afraid she'd question me over who I was with at the pizza place? Eden was just a friend to me—okay, a friend that made all rational thought go out of the window the second I saw her—but why would I be shy in telling her who Amy was? Libby and Greg knew, and they were my friends. Why shouldn't Eden?

I'd eaten my lunch at school alone, choosing to sit on the wall outside and make the most of the last burst of late-autumn sunshine rather than take up Greg and Libby's offer to hang out in the canteen. I'd just hopped back off the wall and made my way over to a classroom at the far side of school for my afternoon's philosophy lesson when I saw Eden. She was alone, too, walking in the same direction as me, but a good few feet ahead. She was walking and texting at the same time, her head bowed in concentration, making her walk so slowly I knew it would be impossible not to catch up to her.

I hung back, trying to allow her to keep ahead of me, thinking how absurd it was that I was reluctant to talk to her when really everything inside me was yelling at me to go up to her, walk with her, and just *be* with her. Finally, still texting, she looked behind her, straight at me, then turned away again. My heart plummeted. So she didn't want to talk to me, either? I shoved my hands deep into my trouser pockets and carried on walking, staring down at the ground as I did so. When I looked up again, she'd stopped walking and was waiting for me.

"Hey." A grin spread across her face, instantly lighting it up.

"Oh, hi!" I did that stupid thing of pretending you haven't seen someone, then acting all surprised when they speak to you. So dumb.

"You heading to class?" she asked.

"Mm-hmm. You?"

"Yup. Mind if I walk with you?"

"Of course not," I said, trying to sound as casual as possible.

"So how was the pizza?" Eden pressed herself flat against the wall as a swarm of little year sevens came rushing down the corridor, presumably late for a lesson.

"Not bad," I said. "Yours?"

"Same." She pulled herself from the wall and fell into step with me again. We entered the classroom, and she pointed to a desk by the window. "Can I sit with you?" she asked.

My insides fizzed. This was a first: Eden wanting to sit with me. "Sure," I said, looking around. "But what about Gabby and Beth?"

"They're skipping class," Eden said, sitting down. "Well, not exactly. Beth has a rehearsal for the school play and Gabby's gone with her on the pretence of being a moral support," she said.

"When in reality...?" I asked.

"She's skipping." Eden grinned. "So you had a nice time?" she asked, opening her bag and peering inside it.

"When?" I asked, deliberately being vague.

"At the pizza place." Eden pulled two books from her bag and put them on the desk in front of her.

"Yeah. Good pizza." I pulled my rucksack open and looked

inside, searching for a pen. "I can recommend the pepperoni," I said. "It was awesome."

"I know. Pepperoni's, like, my most favourite pizza ever," Eden said, her eyes wide. "It's the only pizza I ever order."

"No kidding?" I looked up from my bag. "Mine, too."

Could she be any more perfect?

"And your friend?" Eden persisted. "Is she from here? I've not seen her around before."

"Amy?" My voice wobbled. "Nah, she's from back home. She just came down for the day to visit."

So she had seen her, too?

"Just for the day?" Eden shrugged her jacket off and hung it over the back of her chair. "She been to London before?"

"Nope," I said. "First time."

"Did she like it?" Eden asked, turning her head as Mrs. Belling, our philosophy teacher, entered the room and closed the door behind her.

"Yeah," I said quietly. "She loved it, I think. We did all the touristy things, you know?"

"Bus? Buck House? The Eye?"

"Not the Eye. She doesn't like heights."

We'd had an argument about it.

Another one.

The classroom quieted as Mrs. Belling entered the room and started talking. I didn't really take in what she was saying, though. My mind was replaying the conversation I'd just had with Eden about Amy and constantly questioning whether I ought to just tell her everything once the lesson was over.

Why shouldn't I tell her? Wouldn't it be better for her to—

"Sometimes"—Eden leant over and whispered in my ear, sending my thoughts scampering from my head—"I think Mrs. Belling likes the sound of her own voice. I thought she was never going to stop talking."

The lesson was over? I'd had no idea.

"I was with her up until Descartes, then I drifted off," I said, standing up.

"I thought I noticed your eyes glazing over." Eden looked up at me from her chair and winked, making me drop my pen on the floor in a fluster. I spun away, reaching down to pick up my pen and my rucksack, and turned my back slightly to her as I stuffed my things into it, hoping that by the time I turned around my face would have returned to its normal colour.

We exited the room along with the rest of the class and headed back down the corridor to the main exit door, just as we always did after our Monday lesson. This time, though, I hung back, my mind wandering to the subject of Amy. Eden opened the door. She stepped outside and held it open for me, waiting as I joined her and then walked with her down the covered walkway that led to the school gates.

It was now or never.

"Eden?" My voice sounded thick. I cleared my throat, embarrassed.

She lifted her chin and smiled.

"The girl I was with on Saturday," I began.

"Amy, you said?"

"Amy, yeah."

"What about her?" Eden asked, slowing her step.

I took a deep breath. "She's, uh, she's more than just a friend," I said. "I lied before." My face burned hot again at my words.

Eden stopped walking and leant against the wall of the walkway, watching as some other girls came past us. She looked at me for a moment. "So…Amy's your girlfriend?"

I nodded shyly.

"Sweet," she said. "Have you been together long?"

"A few years." I stepped closer to Eden to allow two girls to pass us, then stepped back again.

"But she still lives up North, I take it?"

"Yeah."

"Must be horrid."

"It is," I said.

"It's nice, though." Eden breathed out slowly and shifted the weight from one foot to the other. "Long-distance love."

"Yeah, but…"

"But?"

"Sometimes I wonder if it's all worth it, you know?" I said. "Her up there. Me down here."

"I'm sure those kinds of relationships can work if you're really into one another." Her eyes roamed mine. "Are you?"

"Am I what?"

"Really into her?"

"Yeah." I looked away. "And kinda counting the days until I can leave this place and be with her again." I slid my eyes back to her. She was still watching me, so I looked out of the window.

"Only kinda?"

Was she sounding me out? Questioning my loyalty to Amy?

Of course she wasn't.

"We made a pact," I said, "that I'd be as horrendous as I could at Queen Vic's so I'd get sent home." I shrugged. "Three months in and I'm still here."

"Because you're not an horrendous person," Eden said softly. "Or is it more like now you're here, you realize it's not as bad as you thought?"

More like now I'm here, and I've met you.

Eden looked out of the window, too, so we were now both facing in the same direction.

"So who else knows?" she asked.

"About me?"

"Yeah."

"Libby and Greg," I said. "That's all." I hesitated. "It's no secret, really. So as vacuous as Beth and Gabby can be, I don't care if they know, either."

"It's nothing to do with them." Eden bristled.

"No, but they're your best friends. If they ever ask you, just tell them."

"I don't know," Eden said, sighing. "They're so shallow sometimes, it does my head in. Boys are everything to them, but boys aren't everything to everyone, are they?"

"Not to me." I grinned.

"No." Eden stared straight ahead for a few moments, thinking. "Anyway, I'm glad you felt like you knew me well enough to tell me," she finally said.

"Me, too," I said.

"I better go," she said. "You're coming to fencing tomorrow night, aren't you? Knee permitting?" She signalled towards my leg.

"Wouldn't miss it for the world," I said.

I meant that, too. Every word.

CHAPTER FOURTEEN

I was thinking," Eden said, stepping back from me and lifting her mask. Her face was shiny with sweat, her hair sticking up. "About what you said about sightseeing with Amy."

It was the next night. Tuesday. Fencing night. I was still buzzing from the day before when I'd come out to Eden. Although I knew I probably shouldn't have fenced that night, considering I'd only busted my knee a few weeks earlier, I also knew nothing was going to stop me. My euphoria from having told Eden would see me through any pain barriers, I guessed.

"And?" I replied, pulling my mask off and running my hand through my hair.

"Well, I couldn't believe it when you said you didn't go up in the Eye," Eden said slowly.

"Yeah." I laughed. "Just about the one thing we didn't do, but it would probably have been the best thing." I declined to tell Eden about the row Amy and I'd had over it.

"So there are still parts of touristy London you've not seen?"

"I guess." I put my foil on the mat by my feet and took my glove off, wiping my hand down my sweats. "It's so hot in here, don't you think?"

"Boiling." Eden took her glove off and did the same thing. "So, yeah. I was wondering if you fancied doing the Eye experience thingamabob with me this weekend? I mean, it's been ages since I've done it myself. It'd be good to—"

"The London Eye?"

"Yeah. Or is that too nerdy, like you thought fencing was nerdy?" Eden grinned.

"No!" I blurted. "No, I'd love to. Thanks."

"London's an awesome city," Eden went on. "It would be a shame if you didn't see all its best bits. From the Eye you can see, like, everything."

"And...you want to bring Beth and Gabby, too?" I asked hesitantly.

Please say no.

"Well..." Eden bent down and picked up her foil again. "I was kinda thinking just me and you. Is that okay?"

"Yeah, sure. Thanks." I tried to keep my voice measured, when inside I was jumping around with happiness.

"I mean, Beth and Gabby have lived here all their lives," Eden said. "I'm sure they wouldn't want to come, even if I asked them." She paused. "But if you want to ask Libby or Greg...or Amy, if she can come down again so soon?"

I felt the usual wave of guilt. The thought of spending an entire day with Eden on my own was too good an offer to turn down. There was no way I'd ask Amy to come, despite knowing it was wrong to think like that.

"No," I finally said. "She wasn't keen on the idea on Saturday. I don't think she'll have changed her mind in a week."

Lame.

"So, you fancy it, then?" Eden twiddled the handle of her foil in her hand and considered me.

"Well, it's either that or go watch my brother play football this weekend." I grinned. "So, yeah. I'd love to."

❖

"She's taking you where?" Greg leant past me and grabbed one of my pens, waggling it in my face. "Can I?"

"Do you ever have a pen with you?"

"I do! I have lots." Greg opened up his messenger bag and showed me a pile of pens inside. "Just none that work."

"Handy."

I fished in my rucksack and pulled out another pen to replace the one Greg had just taken from me. I pulled the lid off and scribbled some circles on my notepad to make sure it worked.

"So? Saturday?" Greg asked. "The Eye, huh? Nice."

"Yeah," I replied. "I told her I hadn't done it yet, and she said it was the only way to see this fair city of ours."

"Ours?"

"What?"

"This fair city of *ours*?" Greg repeated. "Are we converting you at last?"

I didn't answer.

"And then maybe drinks afterwards? Perhaps a little dinner? Sharing a plate of spaghetti?" Libby bumped my arm. "A romantic stroll down along the Thames?"

I gave her a withering look. "You forget two things," I said. "One, she's straight, two, she's just being friendly, and three, I'm dating Amy."

"You said two things."

"Whatever."

"Well, you never know," Libby said, watching as Dr. Thompson entered the room. "After this weekend, you might have a better idea of whether you really do like her or not."

"I do like her," I stressed. "That's becoming clearer and clearer the more time I spend with her." I lowered my voice as Dr. Thompson began to set up his laptop on his table to the front of the lab. "Despite me telling myself she's just a friend, well—"

"It's clear you want her to be a helluva lot more than that?" Greg offered.

"And then I come back to Amy," I said, lowering my voice even more as Dr. Thompson began to speak. "So, yeah. I like Eden too much, but there's not a damn thing I'm going to do about it."

Chapter Fifteen

Eden was waiting for me on that Saturday, just as we'd arranged, outside Bond Street station, having come down the line from her house in Kilburn. She was leaning against the wall outside the Tube station, gazing around her and looking so captivating, it made my heart ache just to see it. I loved how she was dressed: hands dug deep into a dark blue hoodie with *I'm Not Getting Smaller, I'm Just Backing Away From You* written on the front of it in white letters, faded jeans, and a pair of Airwalks that gave mine a run for their money in the battered-up stakes.

Her hair was gathered up and held in place with a large grip. She only occasionally wore it like this at school, usually preferring to have it loose. I loved it either way, but today she looked especially cute.

"You're early." Eden pulled herself away from the wall and approached me. "My train got me here quicker than I thought it would. I thought I'd be standing here for ages."

"Am I?" I looked at my watch. I knew I was early. That had been deliberate.

"Nice top." She nodded. Her eyes lingered briefly on it, making me self-consciously smooth it down.

"Thanks. Yours, too."

We walked mostly in silence towards the Eye, stepping out of the way of the people walking towards us, occasionally making a comment about something we'd seen in a shop window or across the other side of the road. It didn't matter how inane the stuff we were chatting about was—I was just happy to be in her company, to be near her, and have her walking so close next to me.

I felt easy in her company, too. The nerves I'd felt on my way over to meet her had disappeared the second she'd spoken to me, and now I felt relaxed and contented. We rounded the corner and mingled with the small crowd that was gathered next to the Eye, my ears picking up snippets of different languages—Spanish, French, Japanese—as people chattered excitedly amongst themselves.

Now that I was standing right next to it, the huge scale of the London Eye was jaw-droppingly apparent. It rotated much slower than I thought it would, giving the uniformed guides below plenty of time to herd groups of tourists into each capsule. I stood rooted to the spot, gazing up at it, my eyes wide in wonder, my mouth slightly open, thumbs hitched firmly into the pockets of my trousers.

After a few moments, I became aware of Eden standing next to me and hastily looked away, glancing at her as I did so. She was smiling.

"You look like a kid who's watching fireworks for the first time," she said.

"Sorry," I said. Warmth flooded my cheeks. "I didn't realize just how big it is. I mean, it's huge, isn't it?"

"Biggest in Europe." Eden looked up at the Eye. "And you don't have to apologize, you know. It was nice to see. The look on your face, I mean." She glanced down at me and held my gaze awhile. "Not gonna be scared, are you?"

I pulled my eyes away from hers and looked back up to the sky. "Scared?"

"Because it's so high," Eden said. "Now's not a good time to remember you don't like heights!"

"*Pff!*"

"Good, 'cos I don't want us to get up there and have you pass out on me. C'mon." Eden took my hand and pulled me away from where I was standing, leading me over to the ticket office.

The feel of her hand in mine sent tingles through me, the warmth of her skin and the occasional squeeze of her fingers making me light-headed. As we joined the end of the queue just inside the office door, she slowly let go again, the brief brushing of her fingers against mine the last lovely reminder of how it had just felt.

We bought our tickets and made our way back out of the busy office, this time joining the end of the queue of people waiting to board. I looked idly around me, staring at the nameless faces in the queue. I wondered if any of them were with someone they really liked, desperate to make a good impression, like I was with Eden. I glanced across at her and watched while she gazed ahead. Her profile was illuminated by the midmorning sunshine, the sun radiating from her honey-coloured skin, giving her a fresh, beautiful glow. I occasionally glanced away but kept looking back, unable to pull my eyes away from her for more than a second.

"Remind me to show you St Paul's when we get to the top." Eden's voice made me immediately look away, worried that she'd see me staring at her yet again. "On a clear day like today it'll really stand out."

"I'll have my phone ready." I put my hand into my pocket and pulled out my iPhone, waggling it in the air.

"I can't believe you didn't get to bring Amy here, y'know," Eden said as the queue finally started to move.

"Yeah, I know." I took a few steps forward. "But she wasn't keen."

"Seriously? I mean, the tour bus is great, but to see the real London you really have to come up here." Eden jerked her chin towards the Eye. "At the top you can see for miles. It feels magical up there."

"Do you have shares in it or something?" I joked. "You keep telling me how good it is. It's like you have money tied up in it."

"No." Eden's face fell. "I just know how good it is 'cos I've been on it myself."

The look of hurt on her face made me feel like I'd just kicked a puppy. I felt like the biggest jerk in the world for mocking her when all she was doing was trying to be friendly.

"Sorry," I said. "That came out wrong. I didn't mean to—"

"I thought it'd be a cool way to show you the best of London, thassall," Eden said, still looking crestfallen.

"It's perfect, and I'm sorry." I reached out and ran my hand up and down Eden's arm, making her look at it, then back to me. I dropped my hand and deliberately took a small step away from her, afraid I might have freaked her by touching her arm.

"Am I being a bit full-on?" she said. "Gabby's told me I have a habit of being in people's faces."

"I like full-on," I said. My face heated when I realized what I'd said. "I mean, not that you are. But if you were—which you're not—I'd like it because I like people who are like that."

Quit gabbling, Tab.

"So," Eden said slowly, "if I wasn't full-on, you wouldn't like me?"

"No! I mean, yes," I blurted out. "I'd like you whatever. I mean I *do* like you whatever."

"Good," Eden said, a look of mischief on her face. "I like you, too. So we're sorted."

We advanced in the queue while my face returned to its normal colour, and my heart started to slow back to its regular rhythm once again.

"You're a breath of fresh air at school, you know that?" Eden turned and looked at me.

"Really? That's nice."

"Yuh-huh. With your funny quips and funny ways." Eden glanced at me again. "And your funny accent." She caught my eye, making us both laugh.

"Well, I aim to please." I poked my tongue out at her, suddenly feeling overwhelmingly happy.

I gathered my thoughts, desperate to talk more with her, wanting to hear her laugh again. It was a nice sound, and I suddenly thought I could quite happily listen to Eden Palmer laugh all day.

"Won't Gabby and Beth be insanely jealous that you've found yourself a new friend now?" I raised my eyebrow mischievously.

"Tsh." Eden looked out into the distance, a flash of disdain on her face. "Like I just said, you're a breath of fresh air around here."

"I thought you three were watertight?" I arm bumped her.

"Sometimes that's not always healthy," Eden said.

We moved forward another step, closer to the entrance to our capsule.

"But you get on okay with them, don't you?" I persisted. Libby, I thought with a wry smile, would love the way this conversation was going, if she was here.

"Oh yeah, I get on fine with them," Eden said hastily. But then she faltered, choosing her next words carefully. "But sometimes... you know?"

"You feel like a change?"

"Precisely," Eden replied. "Sometimes, I don't know, sometimes it feels as though I can't do anything without them wanting to know about it. I feel suffocated by them, which isn't fair of me because they're my oldest friends."

"But you've managed to keep your fencing secret."

"So far." Eden smiled tensely.

We took another two steps forward, then stopped again.

"Were they always like that?" I asked. "Overbearing, I mean."

Eden shook her head. "I guess people can drift apart, can't they?" She looked at me. "We seem to have different interests these days. I mean, neither of them are into the same things as I am."

"Such as?" I asked.

"They think we're still thirteen," Eden said. "And that we're all still into the same music, the same clothes, the same boys..." She sighed.

"And they don't understand people change?" I offered, thinking about Amy and the comments she'd been making to me recently about her still being small town while I was beginning to feel like I was moving forward. "It happens a lot. People grow up and find other things in life that they want to do. It's the natural progression of growing older, I guess."

"Nope. They don't understand that." Eden took another step and I followed. "And...oh, I don't know...then someone else comes along..." She looked at me. "And that person clicks and feels more like who you are yourself, and then you look at your old friends and begin to see strangers."

"Do you mean me?"

Eden nodded. "You're more like me than Gabby and Beth are these days," she said. "I feel like I've got a lot more in common with you than I do with them." She stopped. "And I've started to feel recently like I want to spend more time with you than them," she suddenly said. "What with fencing and everything, you know?"

"Ha!" I laughed. "Don't tell them that, will you? I think they already don't like me very much. If they think I'm taking you off them, that'll give them even more reason to dislike me."

"I don't think they dislike you, Tabby," Eden said. "I just don't think they get you. Because you're different. They don't quite know what to make of you, your sense of humour, your quirks and put downs."

"And they don't even know I'm gay yet, do they?" I asked. "That's going to be something to look forward to." I laughed hollowly.

"No," Eden asserted, "they don't know."

"But you get me, don't you?" I said, catching her eye.

Eden didn't answer at first, and I wondered if she'd actually heard what I'd said. Then finally, "I totally get you," she replied slowly, returning my look and holding it.

Chapter Sixteen

O kay, next!" A deep male voice broke our gaze. We reeled away from one another. We were now at the front of the queue, something that neither of us had realized as we'd been so deep in conversation. The door to our capsule was opened and ready for us.

We showed our tickets and stepped inside, me going to one side, Eden to the other. In the brief moment while the people behind us discussed a problem with their tickets with the uniformed guy outside, Eden and I were alone inside the capsule. I leant against the railing by my window and looked across at Eden, who was staring back at me, smiling. Neither of us spoke—instead, we looked around the capsule, occasionally glancing back to one another and smiling, before glancing away again.

The few seconds it took for the tourists behind us to sort out their tickets felt like hours. I could feel tension beginning to rise the longer the silence went on, and then it got worse, little by little. I busied myself by looking everywhere I could—around the capsule, to the floor, the ceiling, out of the window—anywhere but over to Eden, because I sensed she'd be looking at me, and I didn't know if I could cope with that after what she'd just said to me.

Or the way she'd said it.

I totally get you.

What did she mean? Had I imagined the look on her face when she said it? Of course I had. Just because I liked Eden didn't mean she liked me like that, did it? So she got me. Good. She liked me as a friend and that was fine with me. What was it she'd called me? A breath of fresh air. She'd grown apart from Gabby and Beth and was looking for another friend. That friend was me, and I was stoked about that.

The other tourists finally hopped inside with us. Eden pushed herself away from the railing opposite and joined me as the capsule quickly filled up with other people, eager to get inside and get going.

"Got your camera ready?" Eden casually draped her arm around my shoulder and pointed to a landmark in the distance. I immediately tensed, patted my pocket, and nodded my reply. I didn't want to speak in case my voice reverted to its usual strangled squeak, which it seemed to do whenever Eden was close to me. Her arm around me didn't help one little bit. It felt nice there although I was sure it meant nothing to her. But her proximity was making my heart thump so much, I was sure she'd be able to see the pulse beating in my neck.

"Apparently on a clear day you can see right down the Thames towards Berkshire," Eden said, lifting her hand from my shoulder again and pointing lazily at some point in the distance, before letting it drop back where it had been. "Don't know if you can see Eton College or anything like that, though."

I looked down at her hand, slung around me, and realized I was still standing stiffly. I so wanted to reach up and touch her hand but knew that I couldn't.

Finally Eden moved her hand so that she could retrieve her phone from her bag. Our capsule gradually began to climb higher. London was spread out below us, a vast patchwork of water, streets, and buildings. People either meandered along the banks of the Thames or scurried like ants up and down the streets, and in and out of Tube stations. Red London buses snaked their ways up congested roads, black taxi cabs weaved expertly in and out of traffic, and high up above us, visible through the clear ceiling of our capsule, an aeroplane flew over, its fuselage glinting in the sunshine as it made its way across towards Heathrow.

It was the perfect day.

"So, tell me about Amy," Eden's voice sounded softly beside me. She had come closer again, and now stood right next to me, facing the same way as I was.

"What do you want to know?" I asked, slightly flustered by her request.

"The usual." Eden rested a shoulder against the glass of the capsule. "What's she's like, how you met."

"Well," I began, "she's lovely. Very kind, very funny."

"Do you miss her?" she asked.

I didn't miss a beat. "I do," I said. "When you've known someone for such a long time, and hung out with them every day, you're bound to miss them when they're not around."

Was that the right answer?

Apparently so.

"That's nice," Eden said. "I wish someone would miss me."

"No one special in your life, then?" I asked slowly. I wanted to tell her I knew she was seeing this William guy that Libby had told me about ages ago, but how could I? I didn't want her to think I'd been talking about her, that's for sure.

"Nah." Eden pulled a face. "Not for a while now, if I'm honest." She turned and looked at me. "How sad is that?"

"The right person will come along when you least expect it," I said, pleased that she was single again. "Isn't that what they always say?"

"I was seeing a guy not so long ago," Eden said.

"Oh?"

"William. He was cute."

"But not any more?"

"Nope," Eden said, emphasising the *p* with a pop.

"Sorry," I said, unsure what else to say.

"Nah, don't be." Eden traced a pattern on the handrail with her finger. "He was nice, but it just kinda fizzled out. You know how it is."

"No one else on the horizon?" I asked, knowing exactly what I wanted her answer to be.

"There's this guy, Marcus, in our French group that Beth and

Gabby want to set me up with." Eden wrinkled her nose. "But I'm not so sure." She looked at me. "Apparently he fancies me. And Beth and Gabby being the troublemakers—sorry, matchmakers— that they are, they're trying to get us to hook up."

"Do you fancy him?" I asked. I sensed my voice catch a little.

"Dunno. Maybe."

I felt a stab of jealousy right in the centre of my chest at the thought of Eden fancying some guy from her French group. I was being unfair, I knew. But I just couldn't shift the feelings of gut-clawing envy and resentment—both at Eden for admitting she might like this guy, too, and at Beth and Gabby for trying to set her up.

"Hampton Court." Eden touched my arm, shaking me from my thoughts, and pointed in the distance to a striking, rusty-bricked building with perfect lawns spread out around it.

"It looks amazing." Realizing I hadn't taken any photos yet, I pulled my iPhone from my pocket and rattled off five or six photos through the window.

"And we have to have one of us," Eden said as I took the final picture. She took my phone from my hand, her fingers briefly grazing against mine, and held it at arm's length in front of us.

"Say cheese," she said, leaning her head towards mine so our foreheads touched and her hair tickled the side of my face. "Sweet!" She looked at the picture, then showed it to me, before finally handing my phone back.

"And one more on my phone as a reminder of an awesome day." Eden held her own phone out at arm's length and leant her head to me. This time, she placed her left arm around me, pulling me even closer, allowing her cheek to touch mine, the warmth and softness of her skin against mine making me involuntarily hold my breath.

After what felt like an age, she took the photo and immediately moved away again. She showed me the picture, then put her phone back in her bag once she was satisfied I'd had long enough to see it properly.

"The sunlight catches your hair, you know," she said, looking at me. "It looks nice."

"Thanks," I said, flustered. "Amy always says it's a nondescript colour. A sort of browny, fairish, mousy mess. It's never been described as nice before."

"Amy's wrong." Eden shrugged, then turned to look out of the window. I wondered if she might say something else, but she didn't. Instead, we stood mostly in silence, looking out the window, occasionally pointing out something interesting that one or the other of us had seen.

The Eye was, by now, beginning its descent. I took the opportunity to take some more photos of landmarks on our way down, wandering to the other side of our capsule and capturing Big Ben, the Houses of Parliament, plus a few random ones of buses, and boats going up and down the Thames. I wanted to send them to Amy when I got home, then had a sudden pang when I wondered if she'd be interested in seeing them, or whether, as I'd sensed from her when I'd left her at King's Cross the previous Saturday, she couldn't care less about London any more.

Or possibly even me.

Chapter Seventeen

"A re you hungry?" Eden's voice sounded in my ear. "It's gone twelve already."

"Starving," I said, wanting to add that I'd been trying to ignore the rumbling of my stomach for the last half an hour.

We'd arrived back at ground level, our capsule slowly approaching the platform, where we stepped off before the next batch of tourists stepped on and began the whole process all over again.

"Good," Eden said. "There's a place I know not far from here that does awesome tapas. You like tapas, don't you?"

"Well," I replied, following Eden from the capsule, "there weren't many tapas places in the village where I used to live, but I'm partial to a bit of Spanish omelette, so I'm sure I'll cope."

"Funny." Eden slapped my arm, then, pulling me playfully to her, linked her arm in mine. We walked together from the Eye, making our way to the nearest Tube station, hoping that we could get on the first train that would take us across to Leicester Square and on to the cafe that Eden knew.

Rounding the corner towards the station, our arms still linked, I felt Eden freeze. I followed her gaze over to the station entrance and spotted what she'd evidently seen: a girl we both knew from our biology class with some tall, muscular boy I didn't recognize.

We slowed our steps, and I sensed Eden fighting a dilemma with herself. She unhooked her arm from mine, all the while her eyes on the girl, who was oblivious to our presence. Then, without warning, Eden grabbed my hand and pulled me in the opposite direction, away from the girl and her potentially prying eyes.

And, presumably, away from having to face any awkward questions in front of Gabby and Beth on Monday about why Eden had been hanging out with me in town.

We ran, still hand in hand, back down the street. Eden was just in front of me. I had to stretch my arm out straight to keep up with her as she negotiated the crowds on the street, occasionally turning to look at me. All the while she laughed, making me laugh. It was as though she was turning it into a game, rather than what I knew it to be: fleeing from a situation she didn't know how to handle.

Finally we stopped running. With our sides heaving from the effort, we leant against the window of a department store, looking at each other and laughing. I wanted to be angry with her, but how could I? How could I be upset that she'd hauled me away rather than having to explain to anyone why she was with me? No, rather than being hurt and upset by her apparent embarrassment at being with me, I was instead mesmerized by her laughter, her exuberance, and the look of sheer mischief on her face.

"You know we're miles from the Tube station now, don't you?" I eventually gasped.

"So we'll walk to the next one along," Eden said casually. Her eyes though, I noticed, still darted back down the street. "Come on." She shoved herself away from the window and beckoned me to follow her. "I'm starving after all that running."

The tapas bar was a smallish, smart-looking place, sandwiched in between a florist and a delicatessen. As we arrived I wondered briefly if I was dressed appropriately enough, bearing in mind my scruffy jeans and scuffed boots.

I glanced across at Eden. Seeing her fabulously mussed-up hair, hoodie with sleeves at least two inches too long, and jeans with a small hole at the back (yes, I'd been looking), I figured if I was going to go into a place looking scruffy, Eden Palmer was the best person to go with.

We entered and chose a table close to the window, Eden ordering a glass of sparkling water while I opted for cloudy lemonade. I picked up the lunchtime menu and ran my eyes over the choice of food while we waited for our drinks, wondering with a pang whether Amy would have liked to have come here when she'd visited at the weekend, rather than the pizzeria we ended up in.

"So, what do you fancy?" Eden asked. "There's an omelette," she added with a mischievous grin.

"So then I'll have that, and...let me see," I said, leaning back slightly as the server brought our drinks. "Chorizo. I like chorizo."

"And paella? Do you like that?"

"I do, yes."

"So let's have that. We can share." Eden sipped at her water.

"Sure," I said. I took a gulp from my drink.

"What about"—Eden's eyes scanned the menu in front of her—"*patatas alioli?*"

"I'm sorry?"

"Patatas alioli."

"Ally-what?"

"Oli. It's potatoes with a sort of garlic mayonnaise over them."

"Why didn't you say so?"

"I just did, didn't I?" Eden grinned. "And some ciabatta too. Just love me some ciabatta." She folded her menu back up and placed it on the table. "Sound good to you?"

"Perfect."

I looked across at Eden, sitting with her back to the window so she was able to see out across the restaurant, and watched as she lifted her head higher and searched out a server. Her eyes moved slowly as she tilted her head this way and that slightly until, at last, she caught the eye of the guy who'd brought us our drinks. With a small nod of her head and a raise of her eyebrows, she confidently summoned him to our table, where she effortlessly ordered our food in Spanish, once she'd found out that he was Spanish.

I watched in awe, admiring both her confidence and natural friendliness, and the ease with which she spoke to our server. It made her previous lack of confidence out on the street seem even weirder. "My Spanish teacher will be pleased when I tell her I ordered us lunch in the lingo." Eden watched as our server walked away from the table. "She's always telling me to practise more."

"You're good," I said truthfully. "You lost me, anyway. You could have been asking him on a date for all I know."

"Mm, tempted," Eden said, glancing over at the server. She looked back at me and promptly poked her tongue out, making my stomach flip over. "But not tempted enough."

She looked down into her glass, idly popping a few bubbles with the tip of her finger, then back up at me.

"Why did you run away from that girl?" I asked.

Eden stopped her bubble popping.

"Dunno," she said. "Spur of the moment thing."

"She's your friend." A statement. Not necessarily one that needed an answer, but one she needed to hear.

"I know she's my friend," Eden said. "I just figured if she saw us, we'd never get away."

I grinned. "True."

"Tell me some more about Amy," Eden said.

She was changing the subject. Not too obvious, then.

I took a long drink of my lemonade, then put the glass back down on the table.

"I think I've told you most things," I said.

"You've hardly told me anything!" Eden laughed. "What does she look like? What subjects is she doing at school?"

"Why are you so interested?" I asked slowly.

"Sorry—shouldn't I be?" Eden asked. She looked hurt, and just like when she'd looked hurt back at the Eye, I instantly felt bad that I'd said anything.

"Of course. I'm sorry, too," I said finally. "Well, she looks like this." I fished my phone out of my pocket and scrolled through my photos until I found a picture of her on her own. "This was taken just before I left for London." I held the phone up to Eden.

"She looks nice."

"She is," I said.

"It must be nice to be so in love with someone," Eden said.

"It is," I replied. "It's the nicest thing, but it's also the worst thing at the same time. Especially when you're not with them. Then it's shit."

"I hope you don't feel like shit at the moment," Eden said softly.

"God, no." I looked straight at her. "I feel amazing right now. I mean—"

"Good," Eden said, just as softly as before.

I grabbed my glass and took another long drink, hoping the cold lemonade would steady the nerves that were creeping back again. Eden's velvety-soft voice, so quiet and gentle, and the way she looked right at me when she spoke, holding my eyes for a second too long, all conspired to make my hands sweat and my insides dissolve.

Thankfully Eden didn't ask me any more questions about Amy that day. I was relieved. Talking about Amy in Eden's company made me uncomfortable. Crazy. Amy was my other life. My Cragthorne life, if you like. This was my London life, and the two seemed a million miles apart right now.

If that makes you think I'd put Amy to the back of my mind all day, you'd be wrong. When Eden left the table to visit the loo, I felt compelled to text Amy to ask her how she was, and to tell her I loved her. I kinda hoped she would have replied by the time Eden returned. She hadn't. Pretty standard these days, I'd say.

Our tapas were fabulous. We spent hours in the restaurant, taking our time over our food, ordering more drinks, then desserts, then coffees. And we talked and talked, until I was sure we'd have nothing left to talk about. I was wrong. After we finally left the restaurant, we spent the rest of our time just walking and chatting more, ending up sitting on a bench along the South Bank. There we sat in the fast-approaching dusk and watched the last of the day's glass-topped tourist boats plough up and down the Thames.

We spoke about everything: school, fencing, music, politics, our families, likes and dislikes. Eden was such easy company, and I realized with a jolt that I laughed more with her that day than I'd done with Amy the previous weekend. I was spellbound by Eden's intelligence, too. I loved that I could have a conversation with her about politics and current affairs without her talking me down or storming off in a huff. That was a favourite trick of Amy's whenever we attempted to have a conversation about anything with any depth.

I knew I could have sat with Eden talking to her until the first rays of sunshine rose up again the next morning, but I couldn't. Finally, reluctantly, I told her I ought to head home.

"My parents stress about me travelling home alone on the Tube after dark," I said, pulling an exasperated face. I felt like I needed to explain.

"No worries." Eden stretched her long legs out in front of her. She linked her fingers together and stretched her arms high above her head, suppressing a yawn. "I should get going, too. We've been out nearly ten hours, you realize that?"

"I haven't bored you, have I?" I said, suddenly worried that I might have kept her, and that she'd been too polite to say anything.

"God, no." Eden stopped stretching and swung around to face me. "I've had an awesome day." She paused. "Have you?"

"I think," I said, choosing my words carefully, "this has been the most fun day I've had since I came to London. And I really mean that."

Eden stood and held out her hand to me. I took it, letting her haul me to my feet. I quickly dropped it again and stuffed my hands into my pockets.

"Then we should do it again sometime," Eden said, walking away from the bench.

I followed and fell into step with her. I didn't know which was stronger—my happiness about having been with her, or sadness about leaving her. It would be over a day before I'd see her again at school.

What was it about Eden that had hooked me so quickly?

No idea.

We said our goodbyes at Covent Garden, and as I watched her get swallowed up by the throng of people inside the station, all I knew was this: after ten magical hours together, I missed her the second she disappeared from view.

Chapter Eighteen

The Girl.

That's all she'd been to me at the beginning. Just the nameless girl who I knew I wanted to get to know better the second I set eyes on her.

I sat on the Tube taking me back home, looking at the dead, expressionless faces of the people sitting opposite me. I imagined Eden heading home on her train, too. What was she thinking? Had she really meant it when she said she'd had an awesome day, or was she just being polite? Spontaneously, I reached for my phone and opened up the photo she'd taken of us on the London Eye.

She was gorgeous. The sunshine in the capsule made her eyes look even brighter than they normally did. I looked at her soft hair, her lovely upturned mouth, her freckled nose, her long, dark eyelashes. Then I ran my thumb over the screen and scrolled through until I found the photo of Amy that I'd shown Eden. I gazed down at her smiling face and realized with a pang that she still hadn't replied to my text from hours earlier when I was in the tapas bar, telling her I loved her.

My confusion intensified.

Undivided attention from Eden for the last ten hours.

Silence from Amy.

Finally the train arrived at my station. Fighting the urge to text Eden to thank her for an amazing day, I switched my phone off and made for home. I was cross with Amy for still not having replied but accepted that I didn't really have the right to feel like that.

I knew the second I put my key in the door I'd get grief for coming home after dark, and I wasn't wrong.

"I'm not sure what part of *Be home before dark* you don't get." My mother was waiting for me in the hallway, tea towel in her hands, usual pissed-off expression on her face.

"I didn't realize the time." I took my jacket off and flung it onto the stairs.

"Please, Tabby"—my mother wiped her hands on the towel— "if we ask you to do something, it's for a good reason, okay? We just don't like you to be on your own after dark. Not around here. It was different at home, but here—"

"I'm seventeen, you know," I interrupted. "I'm not a kid any more."

"Do you think that makes a difference if someone wanted to mug you out there? Knife you?"

"Knife me?" I scoffed. "No one's going to knife me."

"You hear about it all the time." My mother persisted. "And don't say it's our fault for making you move to London. I've heard it all before."

"I'm not going to say that," I said truthfully. "But you're right, I should have been home earlier." I looked down at my feet. "And I also know it's not as safe as Cragthorne here, and I'm sorry," I said. "I should have thought."

My mother drew her breath in, ready to retaliate. When she realized she didn't have to fight back, she wavered. "Right. Okay," she said, looking at me uncertainly. "You want anything to eat?"

"I'm going to Skype Amy, then I'll come down afterwards, if that's okay?" I started to walk up the stairs, pausing to wait for my mother to acknowledge what I'd said, then carried on up to my room.

Kicking off my boots, I propped myself up on my bed. I nestled my iPad on my knees and rang Amy. Habits were sometimes hard to break. Plus, I guess a small part of me wanted to know why she hadn't messaged me all day.

She answered on the third ring, her face flickering into life on the small screen in front of me.

"Hey!" She looked pleased enough to see me.

"You okay?" I shuffled myself down slightly to make myself more comfortable.

"I'm good. You?"

"Yuh-huh, fab. You had a good day?"

"Meh, not bad," Amy said. "I met up with some friends from school. Hey, you know that cafe we used to go to? Down by the river?"

"Yeah. Owner was Italian?"

"Yeah, well, it's gone. Can you believe it? After all these years." She pulled a face. "Went to get a cappuccino this morning and it was all closed up."

"Right. Shame." I nodded. "What friends?"

"You don't know them," Amy said. "Well, I say friends, but it was just one."

"I see."

"The others bailed on me." Amy ran her hands through her hair and looked away from the screen briefly. "Anyway," she finally said, "how was your day? What've you been up to?"

"I've been in London all day," I said happily. "Went on the Eye, walked around town a bit, sat down by the river. It was nice."

"So you got to go on the Eye," Amy said, "just like you wanted?"

Did I detect a tone? Maybe. Maybe not.

"I did." I left it at that.

"Sounds neat." I heard Amy's phone make a noise and waited as she leant away to look at it.

"It was," I said when she reappeared on the screen. "I texted you while I was out. You didn't reply." I tried to sound pissed off. Evidently I should have tried harder.

"Oh yeah." Amy dismissed. "Sorry. Busy day and all that."

"S'okay," I said, thinking Amy might elaborate. She didn't. "Hey, you'll never guess what I had for lunch as well." I laughed, remembering.

Amy raised her eyebrows.

"Tapas. It was epic. Really nice. Very garlicky." I wafted my hand in front of my mouth.

"Tapas in London, hey?" A forced smile. "Sounds a million miles from anything we've got here."

"I'm sure there are places in Durham we could go to—"

"If you still lived here."

"Which we can go to when I visit," I corrected. "Or I can take you to this place next time you're down."

"I'm not sure Spanish food's my thing," Amy said, wrinkling her nose. "You know me. Pie and chips."

"Then maybe it's time you broadened your tastes." I laughed. I wasn't laughing inside.

"Like you have?"

"No, I didn't mean—"

"I know what you meant," Amy said. She contemplated for a moment. "So, when are you coming back up here?" she eventually asked. "You've been gone from Cragthorne nearly three months."

"When I can squeeze the train fare out of my tight-arse father," I said. "He's finding London—now what did he call it?—pricier than he remembered."

"So no time soon, then?"

"You'll have to come to me if you can't bear to be apart from me." I grinned and pulled a silly face.

"There's the small matter of a train fare to London, though." Amy looked slightly irritated, I thought.

"Which you'll find a lot easier getting out of your parents than I will mine." I wavered. "Anyway, isn't it more fun if you come down here? I mean, there are more things to do here, and it's all new for you. It's not like I don't know what home looks like, is it?"

Amy's look of annoyance increased. "I don't want to keep coming down to you," she said. "If I want to know what London looks like, I'll Google it. I want to see you, not the Houses of bloody Parliament." She looked at me for a moment before speaking again. "Don't you want to come home?"

"Of course," I said, without much enthusiasm. "I just thought…

it doesn't matter." I took a breath. An argument was looming. "Let's not fight, huh? I've had an awesome day and I don't want to finish it with a fight."

Amy leant back. "So who did you hang out with today?"

"Oh, a mate from school."

"Libby?"

"No," I said. "Someone else. Eden. You saw her at the pizza place last week."

"The posh girl?"

"If that's what you want to call her."

"You didn't say you two were close."

"We're not, we just hung out today."

"So a new taste in posh friends and a new taste in posh food." A dig at me. Again.

"It's no biggie. I like all foods. Spanish, Italian, Indian…you know me."

"We only ever had chips or Chinese from the bloke on the corner when you lived at home," Amy said. "I didn't know you had a more sophisticated taste than that."

"Even after two years of dating?" I laughed.

"Seems not." Amy looked away as her phone made a sound again. She picked it up, looked at it, her expression never changing, then placed it back down again.

"I better go," she said at last. "I've got some work to get done for school tomorrow."

"Okay." I tried to sound disappointed, but suddenly I was really hungry. Now all I wanted to do was go downstairs and eat.

"I'll text you later, yeah?" Amy waved goodbye at the screen. "I'm glad you had a good day."

And then she was gone, leaving me staring at an empty screen, but with a head full of questions and doubts.

Chapter Nineteen

"One whole day in the company of Eden, and you're acting like a lovesick puppy." Libby linked her arm with mine as we walked down to the laboratory for our first lesson of the day. "And I think if you look at that photo one more time, you'll go blind."

It was Monday morning. Thirty-six hours, four minutes, and too many seconds since I'd last seen or heard from Eden. I'd spent most of Sunday in my bedroom, effortlessly avoiding my mother, father, and Ed, and trying—but failing—to speak to Amy. She'd been out all day, at work I assumed. I felt like we'd left on bad terms the night before. I wanted to clear the air, but her absence meant I had nothing to do but spend hours lying on my bed trying really hard not to think about Eden instead.

"It was awesome, Lib," I said, stuffing my phone back into my trouser pocket. "She's awesome."

"When I was younger," Libby said, her arm still linked in mine as we sauntered down the corridor, "I used to like to watch old cartoon reruns on the Cartoon Network."

"Fascinating."

"And my particular favourite used to be Pepé Le Pew. Do you remember Pepé Le Pew?"

"Strangely, no."

"He was this French skunk who was madly in love with a cat," Libby said, "and he'd go around with this soppy grin on his face and little red hearts popping around his head every time he saw her."

"Does this have a point? Or are you just reliving your childhood?"

"You remind me of Pepé," Libby said, waving to someone she knew further down the corridor.

"I remind you of a French skunk?"

"No." Libby squeezed my arm. "Only the lovesick bit. I imagine you having little red hearts popping around your head every time you see Eden."

"Thanks," I said. "I think."

"Anytime."

Libby unzipped her bag and pulled out a textbook. "So, she was awesome, huh?" she asked as we arrived at the lab and made our way inside.

"Totally and utterly," I said. "She said I was like a breath of fresh air, too. How amazing is that?"

She glanced at me as I sat down. "You really like her, don't you?"

"Mm." I pulled my notepad from my rucksack. "She's not seeing William any more, by the way."

"And you're telling me this because…?"

"Just making conversation."

"Did she say why?" Libby asked.

"She didn't, no," I said, taking the top off my pen. "Maybe William was a prat."

"Or maybe she catches a different tram into town," Libby said, still grinning. "You can dream."

"Different tram?" I looked at her incredulously. "What is this? The 1800s?"

"My gran used to say it about my cousin," Libby said airily.

"The cousin that *dabbled*?"

"The very same."

"Sometimes I have no idea why we're friends."

"Can I gatecrash your conversation?" Eden loitered uncertainly a little way from our bench.

Cue flashback, superfast: London Eye, tapas, Eden sitting barely feet from me.

"Sure." My voice was controlled. I was pleased.

Eden threw a quick look back behind her and came closer. "I

just wanted to say again how neat Saturday was," she said. "And that we should do it again…so I can show you some more of London, I mean."

Libby busied herself with her books, focusing on them as if her life depended on it.

Way discreet, Lib.

"It was good, wasn't it?" I blinked. Pulled my eyes from hers.

We both heard Beth before she'd even entered the room, her voice reverberating hollowly outside in the corridor.

Eden stepped back from my bench. "Better go." She smiled and retreated from us just as Beth entered the lab.

Libby practically bubbled next to me.

"Don't," I said. "Just…don't."

Chapter Twenty

I'd had a long conversation with Amy on Skype earlier in the evening. Less conversation, more of her frustration that I "hadn't made any effort to see her." I'd promised I'd speak to my father about it, which is how I now found myself arguing my case with a man who, just lately, was grumpier than I'd seen him in years. And that was saying something.

"I've told you no, and that's an end to it." My father picked up his newspaper and started reading. Discussion over.

It was late Wednesday evening—around ten p.m.—and my father had just come home from the office, tired, hungry, and irritable. My insistence that I go visit Amy that weekend was only shortening the fuse of his bad temper. He looked dog-tired, the seventy-plus hours he'd worked that week showing starkly in his face. I stared at him, trying to find a speck of sympathy, but I couldn't. He chose to accept a job where a nine-to-five day didn't exist, so what did he expect?

He glanced over the top of his paper and, seeing me still looking at him, frowned. "And you can stop glowering at me as well," he said. "You've got schoolwork to do this weekend, so Amy can wait for another weekend when you don't have schoolwork." He looked steadily at me. "I'm sure she'll cope."

"But I haven't seen her for ages," I protested. "And I found a train that's reasonable, and I can do my schoolwork on Sunday when I get back."

My father put his paper down. "Do you know how much I pay for you to go to that school? Hmm?"

And do you know how much grief I'm getting from Amy about not visiting?

"No," I said, "but I have a feeling you're about to tell me."

He raised his eyes upward and muttered under his breath, calculating. "Let's say roughly two hundred pounds per day."

"You're not an economist for nothing," I mumbled sullenly.

"Now. Do you think I pay two hundred pounds a day for you to attend one of the best schools in West London just so you can cram your homework into a Sunday night?"

"I'm thinking no," I said, looking at my nails.

"No." A self-satisfied look. "So when I say you can't go visit Amy, I mean it."

My father continued to look at me. I remained slumped on the sofa, inspecting my nails as if my life depended on it.

"I know you think I'm the worst father on the planet," he now said, "but it's important you do well at school." He folded his paper up. "You have a tendency to drift."

"I like Queen Vic's," I said. I'd told Amy that before; I was surprised I was now admitting it to my father. "And I want to do well there. I just didn't think having a weekend away so early in the term would be such a biggie."

"You like it?" My father looked surprised—shocked, even. "Well, that's good."

"I do," I said truthfully. "It's a good place. The teachers are cool, the people in my classes are nice."

"So where's the punchline?" he asked.

"I'm sorry?"

"The glib remark you always come up with to counteract the positive thing you've just said."

"There is no punchline," I said. "I like the school. That's it."

"Well...that's good to hear." I saw my father's face soften for the first time in our conversation. "I'm pleased."

He placed his newspaper on the coffee table. "And will that feeling last?" he asked. "Or will you spend half your time skipping classes? Spending your days around at your mates' houses like you used to in Cragthorne?"

I shifted my position on the sofa and curled my legs up beneath me. How would I answer that question without blushing?

"The atmosphere at Queen Vic's is different from what it was at the High," I said, thinking. "Everyone wants to do well, so it kinda pushes you to do well, too." I looked at him. "So, no. I won't be skipping classes."

Of course, I wanted to add that nothing in the world would make me want to be anywhere Eden wasn't.

"And yet you still think you can cram your homework into a Sunday night and make a good job of it?"

"No," I said. "Perhaps not."

I caught his eye and saw that he was smiling. My father hadn't had any expression other than impatience on his face for a long time—certainly towards me, anyway. This made a pleasant change.

"I always hoped," he said, "that I'd find you a school which would inspire you to do better. Maybe Queen Victoria's is it."

It was Eden that inspired me, not the school. But how could I tell him that?

"Maybe," I finally said. I looked at my watch: ten past ten. "I'd best get off to bed. I'll tell Amy I'm not coming to visit."

"There will be other weekends, Tabitha." My father looked at me as I got up from the sofa. "And half-terms and holidays. You have your whole life to go back and visit old friends, don't you? And if they're true friends, they'll understand."

I nodded, wishing him goodnight, then left the room. I went up to my bedroom, changed from my clothes into my PJs, then lay out on my bed. I linked my hands behind my head and stared up at the ceiling, wondering how I was going to tell Amy I wasn't coming to see her. I wanted to tell her I'd fought and argued and screamed at my father, that I was devastated I wasn't coming. I wanted to tell her I hated him for keeping us apart, that I'd cried myself to sleep when he'd told me. I wanted to tell her I missed her and I loved her and I'd do anything to see her again.

But that would all be one big fat lie, wouldn't it?

❖

"And when my tyrant of a father says no, he means no." I pushed the door to the corridor open, hearing it hit the wall with a satisfying crash.

"And you're gutted because...?" Libby began.

"Because now I have to explain to my girlfriend that I won't be coming up this weekend," I said. "Which will make her hate me more than she probably already does."

"Amy doesn't hate you," Libby said kindly. "But she'd be a strange girlfriend if she didn't care, wouldn't she?"

"I guess."

"Tell me the truth," Libby said. "Would you care if Amy didn't like you any more?"

I stopped walking and leant against the wall, a little way down from the lab.

"What?"

Libby leant against the wall with me. "Well, don't you feel like you're two-timing her as it is?" she asked. "With all these thoughts you're having about you-know-who?"

"You know I do," I said miserably.

"So if she didn't like you any more, then..."

"And what sort of a person would that make me? Dumping a girlfriend on the off chance I might..." I stopped talking as Gabby appeared around the corner. Instead, I pulled my bag open and looked inside for my planner. "What is it we're doing today?"

"Stem cells." Gabby's voice sounded louder as she approached us. "And whose girlfriend's getting dumped?"

"Have you been listening to our conversation?" Libby spun around and glowered at her. "That was private."

"If it was private, then you should have kept your voices down," Gabby said snootily, coming to lean on the wall next to me.

"Like you always do, you mean?" I muttered under my breath.

"So whose girlfriend?" Gabby raised an eyebrow. "Yours?" She waved a cursory hand at Libby. "Or you?" She pointed to me. "I'm thinking you."

I narrowed my eyes. "Butt out, Gabby." I watched, panicked, as Beth and Eden approached us from further down the corridor.

The last thing I wanted right now was a conversation about Amy, especially not in front of Eden.

"This one's having girlfriend trouble." Gabby turned and grinned at Beth as she drew nearer. "Who'd have thought it?"

"Who'd have thought what?" Eden's soft voice drifted down towards me.

"Who'd have thought Tabby was a lesbian?" Gabby looked at me. "I mean, you'd never guess just by looking."

"Did she say she was gay?" Libby stepped up in front of Gabby, her eyes level with hers.

"She doesn't need to," Beth said witheringly.

"She advertises it well enough on her own," Gabby said. "I figured she was a lesbian the first time I ever met her."

"And you have a problem with that?" I asked. "Me being gay?"

Gabby and Beth looked at one another. A shared snigger, but no reply to my question.

"Because I don't have a problem with it," I said.

"Well, maybe I do," Gabby said slowly and clearly.

"So we have a lesbian in our midst!" Libby threw up her arms. "Ooh, the crops will be late this year. 'Tis against the will of God and nature." She looked Gabby slowly up and down, a look of pure disgust on her face. "Puh-lease."

"You can look at me like that," Gabby said, fixing Libby with a stare. "I'm not the one who's weird, am I?"

"Weird?" Libby leant her face in closer to Gabby's. "You think Tabby's weird?"

"You think a girl strutting around school with her hands in her pockets the way she does isn't weird?" Beth chipped in. "It's not right, that's for sure."

"So Tabby's gay." Libby rolled her eyes. "Big, fat, hairy deal." She glared at Gabby. "At least she has character, unlike some around here."

"She looks like a boy, she walks like a boy," Gabby drawled. "Maybe she just should have been born a boy, huh?"

"Girls aren't meant to go with girls," Beth said piously. "Just like boys were never designed to be with other boys. It's disgusting and it's against evolution."

"Evolution?" Libby's voice rose, so that it was beginning to echo embarrassingly down the corridor. "You want to talk about evolution? Let me tell you something."

I stood, my face burning, listening to the pair of them spar. Occasionally I slid my gaze around to see what expression Eden had on her face. She was staring at the ground, giving nothing away.

Libby leant against the wall, placing one hand to the side of Gabby's face.

"Fascinating fact," she said. "Did you know that homosexuality was practised by the Romans? No? Thought not. The Romans were cool with being gay. Does that mean our level of intelligence hasn't progressed, even after two thousand years?" She glared at Gabby. "Imagine that! This could threaten humans' whole position on the evolutionary scale, couldn't it? Although looking around me," she looked from Gabby to Beth and back again, "I'm starting to doubt the whole theory of evolution if you two are the best it can come up with."

She shoved herself away from the wall and reached over, taking my hand.

"Come on, Tabby," she said, leading me further down towards the lab, away from them. "Let's get out of here. Suddenly the air around here stinks."

❖

"Whoa." I looked back briefly to where Eden, Beth, and Gabby were still standing. "Remind me never to get on the wrong side of you."

"You see, beneath this demure exterior"—Libby looped her arm in mine—"lies the heart of a tiger. Mess with me or my friends, and hear me roar."

"Thank you for standing up for me." I pulled her closer. "I appreciate it."

"Any time, kid," Libby said, in the lousiest American accent

I've ever heard. We walked, arm in arm, into the lab and took up our usual bench at the back of the room. I unpacked my bag and watched, from the corner of my eye, as Gabby, Beth, and Eden trooped in. They took a bench over on the far side of the lab, despite there being a free one near me and Libby.

Was that deliberate?

"They don't even look ashamed of themselves." Libby's eyes bored into Gabby's back as she sat down. "The least they could do is look embarrassed for spouting such bile."

"I'm used to it," I said.

A whispered comment between Gabby and Beth.

A splinter of laughter, and a look my way.

I tried not to let the hurt show on my face. "I've had worse comments than that in the past." I glanced over to Eden. She was staring down at her books, her face white. Had she laughed, too? I couldn't be sure. "Shame Eden couldn't have backed me up, though." I looked away. The last thing I wanted was Gabby and Beth to see me staring at Eden.

"Why would she?" Libby said flippantly. "She's part of the witches' coven. Probably agrees with every word they—" She realized what she was saying.

"Do you think?" I asked, crestfallen. "She seemed unfazed about it when I first told her I was gay."

"I don't know," Libby replied. "All I know about Eden is, whatever Tweedledum and Tweedle-dumber do, Eden just goes along with it. Whether that's 'cos she wants to, or whether it's just 'cos she wants an easy life, I don't know."

"Neither do I," I said, flicking my eyes towards Eden again. "But I wish to God I did."

CHAPTER TWENTY-ONE

I woke up the next morning, Friday, to a text from Eden. My heart leapt at seeing her name on my phone. Was she going to tell me she'd been thinking about me since the clash outside the lab the day before?

She wasn't.

Hey Tabs! Just had email from Rob about fencing. Emergency meeting in the gym first thing. See you later xxx

That was it. I read it again, stupidly searching for the one word that wasn't there, as if I'd somehow missed it on its first reading.

Sorry.

All I could see, however, was a short, snappy note about bloody fencing. At least it was something. More importantly, it was more than I'd had from Amy after I'd told her what had happened. And Eden's three kisses were nice, I told myself as I rolled over onto my side and buried my head in my pillow, but they meant nothing, no matter how many times I stared at them.

I lay in bed a while longer, staring blankly at the wall. I knew I needed to get up within the next five minutes if I was to have any hope of catching my train to school. But still I lay there. I picked up my phone again and scrolled down to Amy's number, opening up a new message to her. Okay, she might not have contacted me, but I still had to tell her I wasn't coming to visit.

Hey you, I started to write. *Asked Dad about this weekend. He said no.* I deleted *He said no* and instead wrote, *He says I have to stay home and work...* I stared at it for a while, then wrote, *sorry,* thinking what an insipid word sorry can be at times, but not knowing what else to put. Then I wrote, *Love you, will call later,* put five kisses after it, and looked at it for a while before deleting it. How could I text her and tell her I wouldn't be coming? I knew Amy would be gutted that I wasn't visiting. The least she deserved was me telling her properly, rather than a hasty text sent at half past seven in the morning.

❖

"Are you heading to the gym?" Greg's voice sounded behind me as I entered the school's main entrance later that same morning. "I'll escort you."

He linked his arm in mine and fell into step with me. "Did you get my texts, by the way? You didn't answer."

"I didn't know they warranted an answer."

"Tetchy." Greg shot me a look.

"Sorry," I said. "I started to text Amy this morning to tell her I won't be coming up this weekend, but I bottled it." I leant against him. "I don't think she's going to be too happy with me."

"Shame. Why aren't you going?"

"My father," I said simply, "thinks I need to knuckle down to work rather than enjoying myself."

"And that makes you snappy?"

"The thing is, I wasn't all that bothered," I said. "I'm trying to be pissed off at him, but I'm failing miserably."

"What were you not bothered about?" Greg asked. "Him being tough? Or going up to see Amy?"

"Going up to see Amy." I went through a door and waited for Greg to follow. "Is that a bit shitty of me?"

"No, I don't think so," Greg said. "It sounds kinda normal to me." He stepped to one side to let a group of boys pass, then spoke again. "I think it's the natural progression of things, to be honest. I'd say it happens to a lot of people."

"What does?"

"That when someone moves to a new city, they don't know how they'll ever cope with being away from home, away from everything they've ever known," Greg said. "And then, over time, they meet new people, see new things, and realize moving away wasn't so bad, after all."

"Sounds about right," I said.

"Then the homesickness they thought they'd never get over eases, and they think about home less often 'cos they're so busy doing new things, and having this whole new life," he continued. "And then home gets forgotten—along with the people they left behind."

"I haven't forgotten home," I said. "And if my father had said I could go, then I suppose I would have gone."

"Even though you weren't that bothered?" Greg asked.

"Amy's my girlfriend." I shrugged. "I made promises to her. I'm not one for breaking them."

We rounded a corner, and I saw Eden some way in front of us, going in the same direction—to the gym for our meeting, I assumed. My eyes fixed on her as she ambled on ahead of us, unaware we were behind her. I gazed at her back, at the curve of her waist, her hair falling down around her shoulders.

"But now you have someone else to think about, don't you?" Greg said, following my gaze.

"I've tried so hard, you know?" I shook my head. "I've tried to ignore her, and avoid her, and not think about her." I stared at Eden's back. "For Amy's sake. I'm not being fair to her, I know."

"Love's shit sometimes, isn't it?" Greg said, putting his arm around me and giving me a squeeze. "But I guess this would explain why you're not gutted to not be going up North this weekend."

"I know I think about Amy less these days," I said truthfully. "Even though I know I shouldn't."

Greg pulled a face. "Seems to me, you're moving on from Amy faster than you realize."

"I think," I said, as Eden rounded a corner and disappeared from sight, "despite trying so hard not to...perhaps I've already moved on."

❖

The meeting in the gym was brief and to the point. The Queen Victoria Fencing Club had been entered into a national competition in Manchester, and much to my surprise, I was going to participate. I couldn't believe it. Me in a fencing championship? I could practically see the look of snobbish satisfaction on my father's face at that one: his daughter actually being good enough at something to be picked for a team.

My mind went into a tailspin. Okay, so it was only the qualifying rounds we'd been entered for, but what on earth made Rob think I was in any way good enough to take part in something like that? However, my brain was more in a muddle at the prospect of a whole day with Eden again, away from the confines of school, than at anything else.

I'd nearly reached my philosophy class after the meeting when I heard running footsteps coming up behind me. I'd been loping down the corridor, hands deep in my pockets, mind foggy with thoughts of fencing.

"Boy, you walk fast, don't you?" Eden's breathy voice sounded in my ear. "I've been practically chasing you all the way from the gym."

"I was miles away, sorry."

"So, what about Manchester, hey?" Eden said.

"I can't believe A, the organizers want Queen Vic to participate, and B, Rob thinks we're good enough," I said honestly.

"Have faith," Eden said as we entered the room. "He must think we're up to it, or he wouldn't suggest it, would he?"

She stood next to me at my table. "I'm glad I caught up with you, actually," she said. A swift look over the shoulder. No Gabby or Beth. "I didn't just want to talk about the fencing."

"Oh?" I asked, my heart beginning to thud in the side of my neck.

"I just wanted to say that…" Eden searched for the right words. "I thought what Beth and Gabby were saying yesterday was shitty."

So she had felt bad about it, after all?

I felt pathetically grateful.

"Understatement of the century." I stared rigidly down at my books.

"And that I've never mentioned to them that I already knew you were, you know, gay," she said, lowering her voice. "Which, considering the small-minded way they both reacted to it, was a pretty wise move on my behalf, I'd say."

"Small-minded I can cope with," I said. "I'm used to it. What I can't cope with is…" I looked at her.

"What?"

How could I explain to her that she'd hurt me by her silence? How could I tell her that all I'd wanted since I'd left school that day was a sign—anything—from her that showed me she felt bad about it?

"Nothing," I said. "Forget it."

She pulled her bag closer to her. Another brief look behind her.

"You're coming in to the extra fencing practice tomorrow, aren't you?" she asked.

"Sure," I said. "I'm gonna need as much preparation as possible if I'm not to look a complete idiot in Manchester."

"We could go together," Eden said breezily. "I could come by your house and pick you up, or you could come to me? We can Tube in together. It'll be fun."

"Awesome. I mean, yeah, if you want?" I stuttered. "Sure."

"Might even take you for a cappuccino in town afterwards if you're very good." Eden looked at me long enough to make the skin on my arms goosebump briefly. "Tomorrow's Saturday. It can't be all work and no play, can it?"

"Cappuccino. Perfect."

Inability to speak more than two words at a time. Not good.

"I'm so excited, aren't you?" Eden rubbed her hands together.

"Yeah, totally," I said.

And I was.

Excited and terrified at the same time.

CHAPTER TWENTY-TWO

Serendipity is a funny thing, isn't it?

I'd felt guilty about not going to see Amy. Or rather, I'd felt guilty about not being that bothered about not being able to see Amy. But now here was a twist of fortune, that meant at the very time I should have been going on a train to see Amy—if I'd been allowed—I'd be spending the entire day with Eden instead. And none of it was my fault, so I couldn't feel guilty.

Serendipity indeed.

All the previous angst I'd had over Eden not apologizing for Gabby and Beth's vitriol just floated away because she'd done one simple thing and had asked to come with me to fencing practice. All the hurt and anguish and torment that had been eating me up for nearly thirty-six hours after what Gabby and Beth had said to me just disappeared, as if by magic, purely because Eden Palmer wanted to travel to school with me.

Not with Greg or Rob, or anyone else.

Me.

And, despite my assurance to myself that I wouldn't let Amy down by text, I still ended up sending her the briefest of messages telling her I wasn't visiting, after all.

That, as you can imagine, went down like the proverbial lead balloon.

Strangely though, I managed to shake off the hurtful things she'd said to me in her reply. Eden was coming to my house, and right now, that was all I could think about.

She arrived just before ten the next morning. I'd already texted her directions from the nearest Tube station the previous night, telling her to look for the "ostentatious Georgian town house" down the road on the right-hand side with the equally pretentious BMW parked outside. Unsurprisingly, she found it straight away.

I'd already been up over an hour when she arrived. I'd showered, scrubbed, and buffed as if my life depended on it and had fretted for an age over a pile of clothes, dithering over which ones I thought I'd look best in.

Finally approaching satisfaction with my appearance, I gave my hair one last tweak, tugged at my top a bit, and went downstairs just in time to hear the doorbell ring. I jumped the last three steps as soon as I heard it, wanting to get the door before my mother—or worse, my father—got to it first, hoping to usher Eden back out before either one of them had the chance to talk to her.

I opened the door to see Eden standing, looking cutely flustered, on our doorstep. "Hi."

"Hi."

She looked amazing. She was wearing a khaki military-style coat, the kind which I would have loved myself, with the collar turned up, making her look even hotter than she normally did. Her hair was piled up on her head, just how I love it, and she'd darkened her eyes, so they appeared more vivid than normal. There was a hint of a new perfume, too. I had no idea what it was, but it smelled absolutely fabulous.

"Let's get out of here, shall we?" I said, grabbing my keys.

"What about your kit?" Eden asked, motioning towards my empty hands.

"Shit. Wait there." I entered the house again, muttering under my breath as I searched the hallway for my bag, which contained my fencing outfit.

"Are you off?" My mother's head appeared, as if by magic, in the lounge doorway.

"If I ever find my sodding bag, yes," I mumbled from deep inside the closet under the stairs.

"Has your friend arrived yet?" my mother asked.

"Yup. Where the hell is it?"

"Where is she?"

"Outside. Mum, have you seen my kit bag?"

"You left her on the doorstep?" My mother came out from the lounge. "For goodness' sake, Tabitha."

She put down the screwdriver that she'd been using to screw heaven only knows what in the lounge and opened the front door before I'd had a chance to free myself from inside the closet.

"Please excuse my daughter's manners," she said to a surprised-looking Eden, who was still standing on the doorstep. "Come in."

My mother opened the door wider for Eden to enter, then shot me a look of disdain as I fell out of the closet, kit bag clutched in my hand.

"I'm Tabitha's mum. Mrs. Morton. Annie." My mother extended her hand to Eden as my insides curled up at the politeness of it all.

"Eden," Eden said, sliding her eyes uncertainly towards me. "Uh, Palmer. Nice to meet you."

"Likewise." A saccharine smile that only my mother could do. "And you two go to Queen Victoria's together, do you?"

"Mm," Eden said. "We do, yes. And we do fencing together, too."

I thought that was as embarrassing as it would get, but no. Right on cue, after hearing our voices, my father decided to join in the stilted conversation, no doubt lured from his office upstairs by the sound of Eden's quiet, thoughtful, polite voice downstairs.

"I thought I heard voices," he said predictably, coming down the stairs, smiling broadly. "I'm Tabitha's father, David." Again, he extended his hand, while I died inside, just a little bit more. If that were even possible.

"Eden. Nice to meet you." Eden shook his hand.

"And you're off fencing this morning, then?" he asked, stating the obvious.

"Yup," I mumbled sullenly, just wanting to get the hell out of the house. "And we're late, so we better go."

"And what sort of fencer are you, Eden?" my father asked,

leaning against the banister, his hands in his trouser pockets, completely ignoring me. "Cautious? Do or die?"

"Well, a bit more cautious than Tabs." Eden laughed. "She's the do-or-die girl of the group." She looked over and caught my eye, making us both smile. "I take the more patient approach."

"So patient you busted my knee?" I teased.

We held eyes.

"You're just more scaredy than I am," Eden said.

"Scaredy, huh?"

"Yuh-huh. Scaredy."

"You're so going to regret saying that later."

"Yeah?"

"Yeah. You know it." I poked my tongue out at her.

We looked at each other awhile, Eden obviously staring me out. I caved first, grinning.

"Sounds like a challenge," my father finally said, looking slowly from me to Eden and back again.

"We better go," I said again, reaching down and picking up my kit bag. "Dunno what time I'll be back. Later this afternoon, I guess."

Finally we were outside, away from my parents and their stuffy greetings and extended hands.

"Well, that was my parents." I groaned as we walked away from the house and towards the Tube station. "Sorry about that."

"They seemed nice," Eden said, bumping my shoulder. "Stop stressing. You haven't met mine yet."

Yet?

"Does that mean I will some day?" I asked, suddenly feeling bold.

"Play your cards right, you will," Eden said, entering the station and pulling her Travelcard from her pocket. "Right," she said, "next train will get us to school for ten forty-five. And then, Tabby Morton, I'm going to take you straight to the gym and show you just who's the scaredy-cat around here."

Serendipity.

Hell, yes.

CHAPTER TWENTY-THREE

The Saturday of the fencing competition finally arrived with leaden skies full of rain. I lay sprawled in bed, in the early morning gloom of my room. Eyes closed, I listened to the wind howling outside, slamming the rain against my bedroom window, and felt proper, stomach-churning nerves for the first time since I found out about the competition.

The previous evening's practice had gone as well as—if not better than—all the others, and the sense of optimism I'd had after all the other training sessions was still with me, despite my nerves. It was going to be okay. I had faith in my admittedly limited abilities, but it was only the National Schools Championships, not the Olympics.

That's what I kept telling myself, anyway.

After listening to the rain for a bit longer, feeling strangely comforted by the sound of it outside, I showered and headed downstairs. I was greeted by the sight of Ed in his boxer shorts, sitting at the kitchen table. He was buttering a piece of toast with what looked like a pound of butter. I watched it ooze over the sides of the crusts and pool into a yellow gooey puddle on his plate. I immediately felt sick.

"You're up early," I said, my throat feeling tight at the sight of the melted butter. I turned away and busied myself with the kettle so I didn't have to see what he was shoving into his mouth.

"Away game today. Against Harewood United." Ed threw a

look towards his football boots, waiting for him by the kitchen door. He blew on his drink, making the steam mask his face for a second. "Your comp today, isn't it?"

"Yup."

"Nervous?"

"Bricking it."

"Good. No nerves means you don't care about winning."

"Thanks for the sports psychology."

"You're welcome." Ed looked at me over the top of his mug. "Mum and Dad are pleased you've found a hobby, you know."

I reached up and took a mug from the cupboard, then turned to face him.

"Are they?"

"Mm-hmm. I heard them talking the other night, just after you came home from one of your practice sessions," Ed said. "They said they thought your school could be the making of you, or words to that effect."

"Ha!" I snorted. "They're just pleased that all the money they're spending on sending me there seems to be rubbing off."

I spooned coffee granules into my mug and poured boiling water onto them.

"I told Dad I liked school the other day," I said, stirring my coffee and glancing over to Ed. "The look of relief on his face was so obvious, it was hilarious."

"They're relieved you're actually spending time at school rather than skipping classes all the time, like you used to," Ed said. He thought for a moment. "You do seem calmer, too. Since we moved, I mean. I thought you'd kick off big time and give them so much hell they'd put you on the first train back up North."

"Wanna hear a secret?" I sat down opposite him and sipped at my coffee. "That was my plan at first."

"Yours and Amy's plan, you mean?" Ed winked.

"You're not as daft as you look, are you?" I swivelled round in my chair as my phone buzzed and vibrated across the kitchen unit.

Eden? Please let it be Eden.

It was Amy.

Nervous? it said. There were five kisses after it.

I typed out a quick reply to her, something along the lines of, *Terrified. Can't eat breakfast,* and put a sad face plus five kisses back to her. I put my phone back on the table. Ed was watching me with amusement.

"Amy," I said, my face getting warm. I picked up my phone and waggled it at him.

"Sure," Ed said knowingly. "'Cos you always leap up like that for Amy's texts, don't you?" He got up from the table before I could answer. "Good luck later, yeah?" he said, ruffling my hair as he brushed past me and shuffled off into the hallway.

Busted.

To my surprise, I did manage to force down two pieces of toast for my breakfast. I made it to school twenty minutes before the minibus was due to leave, having finally shaken my parents off from their good wishes in the hallway, their calls of *Good luck!* following me down the road as I hastened to the Tube station.

Only Greg, Rob, and a year-eleven girl, Freya, were at school when I arrived. The rain hadn't stopped for the entire journey to school; the Tube had filled and emptied with people sporting dripping coats and umbrellas, their faces grey and washed out, fed up with the weather. My own coat was soaked from the ten-minute walk from Sloane Square station to Queen Victoria's, the part of my hair that had been exposed to the driving rain now splattered untidily across my forehead.

"There are things called umbrellas, you know," Greg called out as I rounded the corner of the school car park, and he caught sight of me.

"There are things called boots-up-arses, too," I muttered, coming to stand under the shelter of the school entrance. I pulled my hood down and ruffled up my hair with both hands, making it stick up in all directions.

"You're going to stink like a wet dog all the way up to Manchester on the minibus," Greg said. He sniffed and pulled a face.

"You do know how to make a girl feel good, don't you?" I

said, wiping the droplets of rain from my arms and flicking them at him. "Remind me why you don't have a girlfriend again."

I glanced up to see Eden hurrying across the car park, umbrella battling against the wind.

"See, Eden has an umbrella," Greg leant over and whispered in my ear. "You so need to have her as your girlfriend, let her show you how things are done."

"Shut it."

"Hi." Eden slowed as she approached us. She looked at me from under her umbrella. "Hey," she said softly, this time directly to me.

"Hey." We looked at each other for a while before Eden looked away again, smiling at the others.

"Bloody awful weather, huh?" Greg said as Eden came to stand under the shelter with us.

"At least we'll be indoors all day, though," Eden said, shaking her umbrella out.

I just smiled. What I really wanted to do was ask her if I could sit next to her on the minibus for the drive up North. But, thinking that would make me sound as if I was about five and we were going on a school trip to the zoo, I stayed quiet. Instead, I listened as Rob and Greg discussed some tactic that Rob had been working on all week and gazed out across the car park, willing the minibus to hurry up because I was cold.

"How're you?" Eden spoke next to me.

"Yeah, good," I said. "You?"

"Nervous," she said. "You?"

"Terrified," I admitted. "I don't know what I'm more nervous about—the competition, or having to wear those breeches."

Eden laughed. Her face lit up. "Ah, the lovely, lovely breeches. You've managed to get away without wearing them before now, haven't you?"

"Do you think they'll think less of us if we wear our sweats?"

"And let the whole school down?" Eden had a look of mock horror on her face. "Tabby Morton, how could you even think that?"

She turned to look as the minibus made its way into the car park and drove towards us, swinging around to come to a stop parallel to the shelter. Just in the nick of time, Liam, another boy from the team, arrived behind the minibus, cycling into the car park. He apologized to Rob as he slammed his bike into the nearest rack.

While Rob and Greg busied themselves loading kit bags and foils onto the minibus, I stood awkwardly with Eden and Freya, hoping and praying that Freya wouldn't do what I didn't have the nerve to do and ask Eden to sit next to her.

She didn't.

Instead, when she saw Liam return from locking his bike, her face lit up and she immediately left us, going straight over to him. I saw her say something to him and Liam nod in return before they both climbed up the steps into the minibus.

"I think Freya fancies him," Eden said, looking towards the minibus as the pair of them disappeared inside. "Probably been desperate to sit next to him."

"Mm," I said, staring down at my shoes and not wanting to catch Eden's eye. "Looks like you're stuck with me, then."

"I'll cope," Eden said, smiling.

The journey up to Manchester was long and tedious, thanks to a combination of driving rain, heavy traffic, and roadworks on the motorway. The only thing that made it bearable, of course, was having Eden to myself through it all. With everyone else paired off on the minibus, and each couple deep in conversation, I had the luxury of being just about a foot away from Eden for the whole journey up. It was heaven, just having her to myself again for a few wonderful hours.

"My parents, of course," she said as the minibus crawled along behind a line of traffic, "would rather I'd done something that involved a musical instrument." She grimaced. "My mother plays the cello," she added. "I think she would have liked me to have learned it, too, but it wasn't my thing."

"Well, my parents are stoked that I fence," I said, looking out of the window opposite me towards the traffic alongside us, then back to Eden. "Although when I first told my father what I was doing, he kindly advised me that *fencing requires skill and guile, of which you have neither, Tabitha*...or words to that effect."

"No way!"

"Yup. He's not one to mess about."

"But he feels differently now?" Eden asked.

"Apparently so, if his questioning me to death this morning about tactics was anything to go by." I raised my eyes to heaven.

We stayed silent for a bit after that, each of us either staring out of the window or fiddling with our phones. I sent a text to Libby while Eden had her head turned and was looking sideways out of the window, careful to shield the screen from her. I wrote: *Sitting next to Eden on the minibus. Result!* and grinned when a text from her came more or less straight back saying, *I know. Greg told me. Put your hand on her leg...you know you want to.*

I looked down at Eden's leg, just inches from mine. My hand itched to touch it. I tried to switch my thoughts off, thinking about anything other than Eden's thigh, then sat on my hands when my brain refused to cooperate.

Quit being an idiot, Tab.

"I thought your father was nice," Eden said, her mind presumably still on our previous conversation. "Very chatty."

"The one thing you should know about him," I said, "is that he's a crashing snob. I kinda think he was lured from his office by the sound of your nice accent the other day." I smiled tightly. "He probably thinks if I hang out with you long enough, it'll rub off on me."

"My accent?" Eden asked. "It's nondescript. I think your accent's lovely, though."

"For real?"

"Yeah. It's gentle, soft. Kinda mesmerizing. I often think you could lull me off to sleep with your accent." Eden shifted in her seat. "I mean, you know, 'cos it's so comforting." She realized what she'd said and immediately faced away from me to look out of the window.

I shuffled in my seat, too, still making sure my leg didn't touch hers. A slightly uneasy silence settled over us. I looked at her through the corner of my eye, trying to gauge her mood, but she just gazed out of the window. While I was still looking at her, she turned and faced me.

Matching self-conscious smiles tugged at the corners of our mouths.

"Maybe that sounded a bit weird," Eden faltered. Her eyes flashed over mine. "I mean…"

My phone rang, echoing intrusively around the quiet of the minibus. In a fluster I pulled it from my jeans pocket, nearly dropping it in my haste to make it shut up. "Amy, hi." Eden was still looking at me. Should I turn my shoulder from her? Too rude. I sat and stared straight ahead.

"I was just ringing to say good luck," Amy said. "Are you on your way?"

"Yeah." My voice sounded thin. I coughed. "We're about an hour away from the venue." Better.

"You're on the minibus? Cool," Amy said. "Are you with Greg?"

I threw a look to Eden.

"No, someone else."

"Who?"

"Eden."

"Eden again, hey?"

"Mm."

"Well, I'm sure you'll knock them all dead today," Amy said. "So to speak."

I laughed. "Hope not."

What was Eden doing? I flicked my eyes to her. She was texting. Good.

"I miss you," Amy said.

"Me, too."

"And I love you," Amy said. "I don't think I say it enough."

I moved in my seat. "Me, too."

"And I'm gonna come visit you at the weekend," Amy said. "I've decided."

"This weekend coming?" My stomach tightened. "Awesome."

"I figured your father's never going to back down and let you come up to me," Amy said. "Besides," she continued, "I think it'll be good for me to see you."

"Sounds great." I was being monosyllabic. I knew it, but there was something about having Eden sitting next to me, listening to every word, that made me hesitant.

Our brief conversation finished.

"Everything okay?" Eden turned in her seat to face me.

I'd sighed when I'd put my phone back in my pocket. She must have heard.

"Fine." I smiled.

Truth was, everything was far from fine.

Chapter Twenty-four

The fencing competition, when we finally got there, was awesome. Actually, it was beyond awesome. It was by far the best thing I'd ever taken part in, and I couldn't stop thinking about it, even for days afterwards.

When we arrived, we were ushered into changing rooms at the arena, more or less straight away; me, Eden, and Freya to one side, Greg, Tim, and Liam to the other. Each trio disappeared into their respective changing room, kit bags ready. There was much chattering and far too many nerves. This was a huge occasion for the school, Rob kept telling us. That didn't do anything to assuage my anxiety at representing my school for the first time in my life.

"At last we all get to see you in your breeches." Eden leant over and patted me on the back, looking over to Freya across the room. "Do you know this one has a breech-phobia, Freya?" she called out. I wanted to curl up in a ball.

"What could possibly be wrong with wearing them?" Freya called back. "I mean, look at me." She flapped her hands up and down her body. "You're not telling me these don't look the business?"

I looked at Freya's sparkling white breeches, cut just below the knee, and groaned.

"*You* look okay in yours," I said. "*You* have legs with shape, unlike my skinny, shapeless, puny things." I lifted one leg and waggled my foot.

"You forget—I've already seen your legs," Eden said, leaning over the bench next to me to rummage in her bag. "So quit being so coy about it and get changed."

She pulled out her breeches and shook them out, then held them to her chest and smoothed them down with her hands.

"When?" I asked, looking up at her. "When exactly have you seen my legs?"

"At the hospital that time," Eden replied, placing her breeches back on the bench and unbuttoning her jeans.

She remembered that? That means she must have remembered the *Simpsons* boy shorts, too.

Great.

I cringed. I also desperately tried to ignore the sight of Eden's legs as she wriggled her jeans down over her hips and down to her ankles. Not easy, bearing in mind she was bending over, just inches from me. She kicked her jeans off and bent over to retrieve them, revealing far more cleavage than I felt able to cope with minutes before a competition. Totally unfair. The wall to my left suddenly became very interesting as I steadfastly stared at it.

"Remember?" Eden asked.

By the time I turned back, Eden had pulled her breeches up and was buttoning them at the waist.

"Hmm?"

"You had to pull your trousers down in front of me at the hospital when you crocked your knee," Eden said matter-of-factly. "You were wearing *Simpsons* shorts, I remember."

Great. Fucking great.

"Anyone who can wear those in public has absolutely no right to be modest about either showing her legs or wearing breeches," she continued. "So get off your arse and get dressed." She whacked my arm playfully with the back of her hand.

"Ow."

"And quit with the *ow*s."

Sighing, I stood up. I took my breeches from my bag and, just as Eden had done before, shook them out and smoothed them down. I tugged my sweats down, after fumbling like an idiot at the waistband, aware of Eden standing insanely close to me. Thanking God and myself that I wasn't wearing any shorts with a cartoon character this time, I kicked my sweats off and yanked my breeches on before either she or Freya had a chance to see my skinny legs.

Grabbing my chest protector, underarm protector, and jacket, I turned away from both Freya and Eden, noticing that Eden had done the same. I pulled the stripy rugby shirt and T-shirt I was wearing underneath up over my head. The two body protectors swiftly followed, then the jacket. All done and dusted before Eden had even had the chance to turn round again.

"Looking the part now," Freya said, sitting next to us and pulling her white knee-high socks on, to complete the outfit. "I think we all look great."

"Well, even if we don't win, we'll still look good," Eden said, wriggling her feet into her shoes.

She might. I just looked like an idiot.

❖

We didn't win, as it happens. If I'm truthful, we had our arses whipped by teams that were far better than us. I didn't care. I'd had the best day ever with Eden, and now I had the prospect of having her all to myself for the return journey, too.

The coach back home was uncomfortably warm. I wriggled my top off from my shoulders, crumpling it up and putting it on my lap, stifling yawn after yawn. I was sure the warmth inside the bus, combined with the low murmuring voices of others around me and the monotonous drumming of the wheels on the road, would soon send me to sleep.

"Another three hours at least." Eden's voice wrenched me from my drowsiness.

I blinked, foggy brained. "Sorry?"

"Until we get back," Eden said. "At least another three hours."

"Oh. Yeah." I dug my knuckles into my eyes and stifled another yawn.

"Tired?" Eden asked.

"Knackered," I said. I dragged my hands through my hair and sat up straighter, trying to wake myself up. "You?"

"Shattered." She stretched. "I think the excitement of the day has caught up with me. I feel like I could sleep for a week right now."

Eden rolled her head across her headrest and looked out the window. She clenched her jaws, suppressing a yawn. We didn't speak again for a few minutes. I put my head back against my headrest and stared, heavy-eyed, up at the skylight of the minibus, idly watching the still grey sky scud past overhead. My mind had at last drained of thoughts.

"I'm so tired," Eden repeated.

I flicked a look her way, but didn't reply. She hesitated, then reached over and took my rugby shirt from my lap. She rolled it up and placed it on my shoulder. "Do you mind if I...?" Eden motioned her head towards it.

"I...guess not, no," I said, a bit taken aback. My muscles tensed as she adjusted my rolled-up shirt, then nestled her head between my shoulder and neck. She moved her head a little bit and wriggled until she was finally comfortable.

"Thank you," Eden murmured into my shirt. "I promise I won't fidget too much."

I gazed down at her hair, tumbling onto my T-shirt. A small part of me crumbled inside as she reached up and rubbed sleepily at her eye, then sighed with contentment. I tried to relax my muscles, sure that Eden would be able to feel that I was stiff with nerves and tension at having her so close to me. Everything inside me wanted to reach down and touch her skin, trace a finger along the outline of her cheek, which was so agonizingly close, it almost hurt to see it. I wanted Eden so badly at that moment. Agony and ecstasy, all rolled into one.

Soon, her breathing became deeper and slower. She was asleep. My shoulders finally relaxed, and I allowed myself the luxury of looking at her, safe in the knowledge that she couldn't see me doing it. My hand strayed towards her hands, lying limply in her lap, and

I let it hover over them, imagining how good they'd feel to hold and stroke. I don't know how long I sat there, just gazing at her, watching her breathe. All the time, I prayed my phone wouldn't ring or that no one would speak loudly and wake her up. I wanted us to sit like this for as long as we possibly could.

Finally, my own eyes became heavy with sleep again. With one last look at Eden, still fast asleep, I leant my head over and gently rested it on top of her hair. She stirred and shifted her position, sighing deeply as she did so. When she didn't wake, I closed my eyes and at last drifted off as well.

CHAPTER TWENTY-FIVE

Y ou two looked like you were made for each other." Greg came around the side of the minibus and put his arm across my shoulder. He whispered in my ear so that Eden, standing a few feet away, wouldn't hear. "I saw you. Don't think I didn't."

"So? She fell asleep on me," I whispered back, playfully shrugging his arm off. "What was I supposed to do?"

"In circumstances as lovely as that?" Greg put his arm back round me and walked with me away from the bus and towards the school entrance. "Nothing. I wouldn't have, either."

"Exactly."

It was now shortly before seven p.m., and we'd just arrived back in the school car park. Eden had slept on my shoulder for just about the whole journey home, only waking when the minibus exited the motorway and wound its way along the roads back to school.

I had slept only lightly—not the quiet, contented sleep that Eden had—and although I woke up way before she did, with a crick in my neck, I hadn't moved my head from hers for fear of waking her. I hadn't wanted to move it, either. Why would I? I'd loved the feeling of her resting on me. She'd slept peacefully, barely stirring. I'd wondered if she'd been dreaming, or whether she realized where she was, snuggled up cosily to me. I guessed she couldn't have had any sense of embarrassment at being so close to me, either. When she did finally wake, stretching so much that her whole body shook, she just unfurled herself from me, rubbed her face, and asked me where we were. Nothing more than that.

"You okay for getting home?" Eden's quiet voice behind me popped my daydream.

"Mm?" I spun round. Greg had left me and was standing by the school wall. I hadn't even noticed. "Yeah. Uh, well I'm just going to Tube it home. You?"

"Same."

She looked so tired and heart-wrenchingly lovely. I couldn't bear the thought that my day with her was about to end. "Look, it's getting late," I said, glancing at my watch. "Let's walk to Sloane Square together, and then I'll come with you up to your station and walk you home, yeah?"

Eden looked slightly taken aback. "You don't have to do that," she said. "You want to get home as well, don't you?"

"I'd be happier if we both caught the train together," I said, lifting my kit bag up. "It's dark, it's Saturday night, and you're going to have three connections home compared to my one, thanks to half the District Line being closed down tonight." A rush of protective feelings towards Eden swept over me as I spoke.

"And then once you've dropped me off, you'll have to travel back down the line alone," Eden argued, her face a picture of concern.

"*Pff!*" I waved my hand. "I'm a big girl. I can cope."

"But your parents..." Eden persisted. "They don't like you travelling alone after dark, do they?"

"Let me worry about my parents," I said, walking from the car park. "Come on."

I wanted to add that my parents worried unnecessarily. Both they and Eden should know that I was perfectly used to looking after myself, and that travelling on the Tube on my own didn't faze me at all. Years of fending off the narrow-minded comments people said to me, and how they looked at me, had hardened me more than most. A journey on the London Underground on a Saturday night would be a piece of cake. Okay, so my wanting to travel with her up to Kilburn was selfish, because I didn't want to leave her, but it was just as caring. Maybe I wanted to think that Eden was vulnerable because I wanted to protect her. Everything about her broke my heart, and I felt an overwhelming need to shield her from harm. Whether or not she needed me, I was damned if I was going to let her travel on her own after dark.

"Are you sure?" Eden asked, her eyes steady on mine.

"Absolutely."

We said our goodbyes to the others and headed off. The sky was pitch-black, the streetlights throwing out circles of yellow light, which rippled in the puddles across the pavement as we walked the short distance to the station.

"Have you been to Kilburn before?" Eden asked as we hopped on the first of the three trains that were needed to get us to Eden's station.

"Nope." I looked for a seat, but seeing none free, leant against a handrail. I moved so Eden could come and stand next to me as more people piled onto the train. "I've been to Maida Vale before, but not as far up as Kilburn."

"You'll have to come and visit sometime." Eden lurched and frowned as someone bumped into her from behind. "There are more Irish pubs there than you can shake a stick at."

The train juddered off, forcing Eden to stumble into me. Without thinking, I reached my hand out and grabbed her arm, holding on to it as the train rolled from side to side as it set off. Finally it calmed down. I dropped my hand and stared down at my feet. I was afraid to look at Eden in case she could read my emotions just from having touched her.

We got off at Victoria, pushing past the people getting on the train while we were still trying to get off, and joined the crowds milling around on the platform.

"We need the Victoria Line up to Green Park," Eden leant over and shouted in my ear above the hubbub around us. "Then Jubilee. That's it, then."

"Thank goodness." I shouldered my way through the crowds

and pushed my way along to the next platform, keeping my eye on Eden's back in case I lost her in the mayhem.

"Is it always this busy?" I asked when we eventually made it to our platform. I glanced up at the overhead display: five minutes until our train.

"Yup," Eden said, sitting down on one of the seats. "Saturday nights more so." She looked at me. "Are you feeling overwhelmed?" she asked, patting my leg.

"I've been living here for months now," I said, looking around the platform. "And I can't say I've done many Saturday nights out in the centre of town, 'cos that's not really my thing, but you'd think I'd be used to the chaos that is London by now, wouldn't you?"

"I don't think you ever truly get used to it," Eden said, leaning her head back and resting it on the wall behind her. "I think perhaps you just become immune to it." She pondered. "Does it make you homesick for Cragthorne?" she asked, turning her head towards me.

She remembered where I was from?

"No." I didn't miss a beat. "I don't think about Cragthorne so much these days."

"You don't miss your friends?" Eden asked.

"Truth is, I didn't have that many friends there," I said quietly. "Amy was my only friend, really. Sad, hey?"

"Not at all." Eden smiled. "You miss her though, right?"

"Of course."

Our eyes met.

"I kept myself to myself," I said. "The other girls at school were…judgemental. No point in hanging out with people like that, I say."

"You weren't out at home?"

I shook my head. "There were rumours about me," I said, "but it wasn't anyone's business."

"One of the great things about living in London," Eden said, looking away, "is that no one takes a scrap of notice of how you look, 'cos they've seen it all before, like, a thousand times."

"Gabby and Beth the exception to the rule, then?" I teased. "Their reaction to me is exactly what I was afraid of getting, back home."

"Gabby and Beth live in their own little world," Eden scoffed. "Heaven forbid anything that's not how they want it to be. Or anyone different, for that matter."

"I don't feel as self-conscious in London, that's for sure," I said, looking around me.

"You? Self-conscious?" Eden looked sceptical. "You always seem so confident to me."

Before I could answer, our train pulled into the station with a prolonged squeal of brakes, its doors opening the second it came to a halt. This train was quieter, allowing Eden and me to sit together for the one stop up to Green Park. We didn't speak, that human quirk of being reluctant to talk in silent atmospheres apparently rubbing off on us.

Finally we arrived at her station. I was cold by now, the stuffy heat of the Underground having been replaced by the chilly late-November air biting at my skin, now that we were outside and back up at street level. Pulling my rugby shirt over my head as I walked, I followed Eden down the street towards her house, noting how much smaller and less ostentatious the houses were compared to my street.

"Why did you say you were self-conscious before you moved to London?" Eden suddenly asked. "You always strike me as so confident."

"Impressions can be deceptive," I said. I hooked my thumbs into the straps of my bag. "I don't know," I continued, "small village, small minds, I guess."

"Cragthorne?"

"Mm." We strode on. "In London I'm just one of many people who are the same. Back home, if you were a bit different, people felt the need to comment. Probably because they didn't have anything better to do."

"There's nothing wrong with how you look," Eden said.

"Thanks." I stared down at the pavement as we walked on.

"I think your hair's nice," Eden said. "Suits your face well."

"It'd be better if it covered my face." I laughed. Seriously. When compliments come your way, the best thing to do is crack a joke, however lame.

"I mean it." Eden slowed down a little. "Not many people could have a haircut like that and get away with it, but with your cheekbones…" She whistled through her teeth. "Boy, what I'd give to have your cheekbones."

"Really?"

"Really. And your hair frames your face beautifully."

"I don't think *beautifully* is a word that's ever been associated with me." I laughed again, more out of self-consciousness this time. "If my father could only hear this conversation…"

"Then I'd tell him, too," Eden said, pointing at a house just in front of us. "This is me."

We walked to the front garden and stopped, standing awkwardly next to each other.

"Come in for a drink?" Eden asked. "It's the least I can offer, you having walked me to my door and everything."

I looked at my watch. "It's getting late," I said, reluctantly. "By the time I've gone back down through the Underground all the way to my station, it'll be knocking on nine."

Eden leant her head to one side and pulled a sad face.

I was crushed.

"But, you know what?" I said. "Hang it. I'd love to come in. Thanks."

I followed Eden into her house, down the hallway, then on through to her kitchen.

"Juice, Sprite, milk, fizzy water?" she asked, opening the refrigerator door. "Or something hot? Coffee? Tea?"

"Sprite's great. Thanks." I leant against the kitchen unit. Eden retrieved a small bottle from the inside shelf of the fridge and handed it to me.

"Eden?" A woman's voice called from the lounge.

"Yep." Eden opened her own bottle of Sprite and drank straight from the bottle. *Mother,* she mouthed as she pulled the bottle away from her mouth.

I heard a door open somewhere in the hall, followed by soft footsteps on the carpet. I hung back shyly as a face appeared in the kitchen doorway.

"So?" Eden's mother looked expectantly to Eden. "How'd it go?"

"Booted out, first round." Eden laughed. "This is Tabby, by the way." She rolled a hand in my direction.

"Megan," Eden's mum said, nodding at me. "Eden's mum."

"I think she already figured that out for herself," Eden said, taking another slurp from her bottle. She caught my eye, her eyes mischievous.

"So you haven't come home laden with medals and trophies?" Eden's mum leant against the door frame into the kitchen, her arms folded.

"Tabby won her bout," Eden said, smiling at me. "I got turned over practically before I even stepped into the arena."

"Have you been fencing long?" her mum asked me. I noticed her eyes slowly travelling the length of me, from my rugby shirt down to my battered Nikes, while she spoke.

"Just since the start of term," I said, my face growing warm.

"She's a natural," Eden said, catching my eye again.

"Do you live far from here?" Eden's mum pulled herself away from the doorway and took a glass from the cupboard. She took Eden's bottle of Sprite from her and poured a bit into the glass.

"Kinda," I said. I handed my bottle to Megan's proffered hand and waited as she repeated what she'd just done. "I live in Notting Hill."

"Tabby thought she'd walk me home. I fell asleep on the minibus on the way back, and she didn't trust me not to start sleepwalking halfway here," Eden said, picking up her glass.

"That was very nice of you." Her mother gathered the empty bottles and placed them in a plastic box by the sink. "But now that means you have to travel home alone. I can get Richard to run you back, if you like?"

"My dad," Eden added helpfully.

"It's cool," I said. "But thank you. I have a fencing foil in my bag if anyone gets funny with me." I drained my drink. "Actually, I ought to get going."

"Well, very nice to meet you." Eden's mother walked from the kitchen. "And thank you again for walking Eden home."

"Any time." I watched as she wandered back into the lounge, then turned and smiled at Eden. "I really should go," I said. "Parents stressing and all that." I placed my empty glass back on the unit and followed Eden to the front door, then waited behind her while she opened it for me.

She moved to one side to allow me to pass and watched me as I went down the first step, then turned to face her. We stood looking at one another briefly before Eden shifted her position, clearing her throat and staring out at an invisible point behind me. "Well, thanks again," she eventually said. "I really appreciate you going out of your way."

"No problem," I said, reluctantly turning away and moving down another step.

"Tabby?"

"Mm?" I turned back to face her.

"You know, you didn't look as bad as you say you did in your breeches today."

I laughed, remembering the fuss I'd kicked up about wearing them.

"Thanks." I looked down at my legs. "The sight of my chicken legs in the same arena as you didn't put you off your bouts, then?"

"Nah." Eden leant against the frame of her front door.

"My boyish, nondescript figure didn't make you think it was Justin Bieber himself fighting that large girl from St. Anne's?" I grinned.

"Boyish figure? You?"

"It has been called that, once or twice in my life."

"Tabby?"

"Yuh-huh?"

"Lemme tell you, your figure isn't boyish," Eden said softly.

"In fact"—she pushed herself away from the door frame and stepped back inside the house, placing a hand on the door—"I'd go so far as to say it looks pretty damned good from where I'm standing." Without another word, Eden started to close the door. "G'night, Tab." She smiled through the small gap in the door, finally closing it properly.

CHAPTER TWENTY-SIX

And those were her actual words?" Libby leaned closer. "*Looks pretty damned good from where I'm standing?*"

It was Monday morning, back at school. I'd been desperate to talk to Libby about what Eden had said to me, but my Sunday had been taken up with a long, lazy lunch out with my parents in the West End. It was, they told me, a celebration for the previous day, and I should have been happy to go out. I wasn't. Being out all day left me no time for any phone calls or, it seemed, for thinking about what Eden had said.

Of course, as well as happy, I should have been grateful that my parents had taken me out and were showing an interest in me for the first time in my life, but I wasn't. All I wanted to do, rather than sit in a restaurant in Covent Garden with them, eating an expensive and fancy Sunday roast, was to ring Libby and ask her exactly what she thought about what Eden had said. But it'd had to wait until Monday.

"Yup. Those were her actual words," I said, sitting with Libby at the first table we found in the canteen.

"And then she raised her eyebrow?"

"Yup."

"How?"

"How what?"

"Did she raise her eyebrow?"

"Well, like this." My eyebrows shot up. I shrugged.

"Did she shrug, too?"

"Be serious."

"And how was she looking when she did this?" Libby started to unscrew the lid from the drink she'd just bought, then waited for the fizz to die down before removing it completely.

"Apart from hot?"

"Apart from hot." Libby rolled her eyes.

"She looked normal, I guess."

"What's normal?"

"She just looked like Eden."

"That's helpful."

"That's all you're getting."

"Then maybe, I dunno, maybe you misinterpreted the situation?" Libby offered unhelpfully. "Maybe she wasn't waggling her eyebrows at you—maybe it was windy and she got some dust in her eye or something."

"It wasn't windy, Lib." I started fiddling with the leather bracelet around my wrist. "And I know what I heard."

"Hmm." Libby frowned. "So she gives you a comment like that, then shuts the door so you don't get the chance to answer," she said, still thinking. "But before that—and this is the most important bit—knowing you're looking at her, gives you a seductive wink?"

"It was raised eyebrows, Lib. I just said."

"Same thing."

"No, it isn't."

"It is. Don't quibble." Libby stroked her chin exaggeratedly. "Hmm. Interesting."

"And your psychological conclusion to all this behaviour, Dr. Libby?" I asked.

"She fancies you." Libby grinned, taking a long drink from her bottle.

"She does not," I said. "Stop torturing me. She's straight. She's dated guys all her life. She's being set up with Marcus from her French class, for God's sake."

"Is *being set up* with Marcus," Libby repeated. "Has she gone out with him yet?"

"Not that I know," I replied.

"So she's stalling," Libby said.

"Or maybe the time's not been right yet," I came straight back.

"And she told you that you have a good figure?"

"Mm-hmm."

"Okay, so it's the classic straight girl wants a bit of fun, then." Libby sat back in her chair and folded her arms, conclusion made. "She probably has every intention of dating Marcus, but in the meantime, she's having a bit of fun with you."

"Fun?" My heart sank.

"Fun," Libby stressed. "As in, straight girl meets gay girl who's confident in her gayness—as you are—and straight girl decides it'd be fun to flirt, knowing that nothing will ever come of it."

"Gee, thanks."

"You see it all the time," Libby said matter-of-factly.

"I never knew you were such an authority on lesbians," I said.

"I told you, my cousin's—"

"Dabbled," I interrupted. "I know."

"But you've got to admit, my theory does make sense, doesn't it?" Libby leant towards me again.

I stared down at my hands, defeated. "If she is flirting with me, then it's so not fair of her." I looked back up. "She knows I have a girlfriend."

Talk about having your bubble burst. Mine had totally ruptured.

"Why do I feel like I've stumbled across girl talk that's going to make me wish I hadn't?" Greg sat down beside us with a thump.

"Because you have?" Libby offered. "Well, actually, for girl talk, read girl trouble."

"Aren't they always?" Greg asked. He reached over and took Libby's bottle, then drank from it.

"Always what?" I asked.

"Trouble," Greg said, wiping his mouth with the back of his hand. He handed the bottle back to Libby.

"So it would seem," I said.

"Problems with the girlfriend?" Greg asked.

"If only it was that simple."

"Tabby has trouble with someone she wishes *was* her girlfriend," Libby chipped in.

"Eden, I presume?" Greg pulled a chocolate bar from his bag and started picking at the wrapper.

"Do you know anyone else in this school that makes her walk around with a face like that?" Libby gestured towards me.

"Thanks," I replied sarcastically.

"She's coming on to her," Libby said, lowering her voice. "Like, big time."

"I thought Eden was straight." Greg looked puzzled. He unfurled the foil wrapper from his chocolate bar, snapped off one block, then offered it to me and then Libby. I took my piece, thanking him, then put it in my mouth, loving the feeling of the chocolate melting on my tongue. "Although from the way she was acting towards you on Saturday, I'm starting to doubt that."

"That's what I just said!" Libby clapped her hands together, making both Greg and me jump. "I said, didn't I?" She looked wide-eyed at me.

"She was just being friendly on Saturday," I argued.

"Fell asleep on her shoulder on the way home," Greg said to Libby, making her eyes widen.

"She was tired," I said. "We all were."

"I didn't fall asleep on Tim though." Greg grinned and offered another piece of chocolate to Libby. When she shook her head, he ate it himself.

"Okay, so tell him what she said to you when you left her, then," Libby said, signalling towards Greg.

"We were talking about me on the way home," I began.

"Get to the crunch," Libby said, making a winding motion with her hand and earning another look from me.

"And we got to talking about the way I look, and my figure, and stuff—"

"Like you do," Libby offered helpfully.

"And I happened to say I thought it was too boyish—"

"And that's when she said—"

"*Looks pretty damned good from where I'm standing,*" I said before Libby could interrupt again. I shot a look at her, then back at Greg, his next piece of chocolate poised just in front of his mouth.

"Wow." A grin spread across his face. "I'd have paid good money to hear her say that."

"Now tell me she's not playing with her?" Libby said.

"Like a cat toying with a mouse, by the sounds of it," Greg said. "And boy what I wouldn't give to be that mouse."

"Stop being a twat, Greg." Libby rolled her eyes.

"Why? Eden's fit, we all know that." Greg looked hurt.

"Yes, and Tabby's crazy for her, so quit being such a bloke about it," Libby said. "Besides, she's already blown you out once, so don't even bother."

"She blew you out?" I looked at Greg, jealousy pricking at me. "I didn't know you'd asked her out."

"Yuh-huh," Greg said. "Beginning of term."

He offered me another block of chocolate, which I took.

"She said no when you asked her?" I asked, eating my chocolate.

"She did," Greg said. "Politely, but firmly. She was very sweet, actually. Worried in case she'd hurt my feelings, but she made it very clear she wasn't in the least bit interested in me."

A wave of relief washed over me.

"Have you ever considered," Greg said, leaning over towards me, "that she might—just might—like you?"

"As I've just been saying," Libby said.

"Hang on," I said to Libby. "One minute you're saying you think she's playing games with me, and the next you say she's genuinely interested?" I buried my head in my hands. "This is too fucked up."

"So she's bi-curious." Libby sat back triumphantly.

"Bi-curious?" I peered at her through my fingers.

"I've read about it," Libby said. "It happens."

I slid down further into my chair. This was all too much to get my head around.

"Whoever said being a teenager was easy?" Greg pulled my hands from my face. "And Amy? Where does she figure now?"

"The same," I said. "She's coming down on Saturday."

"Good timing."

"Isn't it just?" I replied. "Just how am I going to get myself out of all this mess?"

Greg spread his hands out. "I can see it now," he said. "The Tabby-Amy-Eden love triangle."

"You love rat." Libby caught Greg's eye and dissolved into laughter.

Their words rang in my ear.

Love triangle? Love rat?

That wasn't me. That wasn't what I was like. I was loyal. Devoted.

Just how the fuck had I managed to get myself into such an emotional mess?

Chapter Twenty-seven

You know we have to go to one of these lectures before Monday, don't you?" Eden said. "That means going to see it Saturday, writing it up on Sunday, then handing it in Monday."

"Lectures? Monday?" I sat at my desk staring dumbly at her.

"Earth to Tabby," Eden said patiently. "Mrs. Belling told us about it last week."

The week you told me I had a nice figure? You expect me to remember what Mrs. Belling said?

"We have to attend one of the four lectures on Freud at the museum for our psychoanalysis essay, which—"

"—has to be handed in Monday?"

"Now you're getting it."

"Shit. You're kidding me, right?" I stood up. How could it be the weekend already?

"So you want to come with me?" Eden asked.

"You'll be going to one with Gabby and Beth, won't you?" I said.

Eden held her arms out. "Do you even see them here today?" she asked. "They can't be bothered to come to today's lesson, so they're not going to worry about some old fart talking about Freud, are they?" She stood up, too. "Although I'm sure they'll be tapping me for some notes." Her face darkened. "So?" she asked.

"So...what?"

"Will you come with me to one of them?" she asked. "I thought perhaps the one thirty one?"

"Tomorrow?" I followed her from the room.

Amy.

Why did she have to come this weekend, of all weekends?

"Yes, tomorrow." Eden looked at me in amusement.

"I can't, I'm sorry." My mind was in turmoil. Could I bail on Amy so late?

Of course I couldn't.

"You've got other plans." Eden bounced her bag up onto her shoulder. "No worries."

"I'd love to, really, I would," I said, following her out across the quadrangle. "Amy's coming down, that's all. It's too late to ask her not to come. She's bought her train ticket now."

"I wouldn't expect you to cancel Amy," Eden said.

"It's an unscheduled visit," I said. "She seemed very keen to come down again." I fell into step with Eden. "I didn't think I'd see her again for weeks," I continued. "It'd be way too difficult to put her off."

I was rambling, I have no idea why. Just like I had no idea why I felt the need to justify Amy coming to visit me.

Eden stopped. She put her hand on my arm and smiled.

"I told you," she said, "it's cool. Quit stressing."

Couldn't Eden read me? Couldn't she see I was stressing because I would have given anything to go with her, rather than spend the day with Amy?

Eden started walking again. I followed her, wanting to say so much to her. The thought of Amy visiting deadened me every time I thought about it. That, plus the prospect of having to tell her I'd be dragging her off to a lecture across the other side of London.

That was going to go down like the proverbial lead balloon. I just knew it.

And it did.

❖

"A lecture?" Amy placed her hands on her hips. "Tell me you're kidding."

That irritated me. She'd barely been off the train an hour, as well.

"It's just half an hour, I promise." I looked at my watch, my insides squeezed tight with anxiety. I had ten minutes to get across to Hampstead before it started.

"And you tell me this now?" Amy persisted.

"I have to go to it, Ames." I started walking towards the Tube station. "How can I write an essay on psychoanalysis and hand it in on Monday if I don't?"

"Google it like the rest of us would?"

"Oh, sure. Like that's going to get me top marks."

Amy stopped dead. "Since when have you been so concerned with getting top marks?" she asked. She had a grouchy look on her face, but at least she'd started to follow me again.

"Since, like, now," I said, urging her to hurry up. "So, come on."

She dawdled. If I didn't know better, I could have sworn I heard her whine, like a spoilt child. I chose to ignore that.

"It's important to me," I said. "The lecture's going to give me so many things I can put into this essay."

"So you keep saying." Amy lagged behind. "And what about going to the Hard Rock Cafe?" she called out. "You said you'd take me."

I slowed my pace. "Which I will," I said, "once I've got this over and done with."

"Good." Amy was still a few paces behind me. "'Cos I told Sarah Mathers we were going."

Why wasn't she hurrying?

"You remember Sarah Mathers, don't you?" Amy called out again, to my retreating back. "Said I'd nick her a cup. Or a mug. She wasn't fussy."

"I remember Sarah," I called back to Amy. "And you can nick whatever you want, if you must. Just hurry, will you?"

I don't think my patience had ever been worn so thin.

❖

The museum was packed when we got there. Saturday tourists out in the foyer mingled with students, like me, rushing to get to the lecture before it started. Dropping my rucksack from my shoulders, I hurried to the entrance to the lecture hall and peered inside. There were still some seats left. I breathed out and turned to find Amy. She was lurking by the gift shop, a sullen look on her face.

"You coming?" I called out.

"And listen to some wacko talking about feelings?" Amy called back. "Nah. You're all right."

A surge of embarrassment washed over me as a few faces turned to look and see who'd shouted out across the foyer.

I strode over to her. "Freud's not a wacko, Amy. And psychoanalysis is—" I waved my hand. "Never mind." I looked around, aware we were being watched. "I'll be half an hour. No more, promise."

"Enjoy." Amy turned her back on me and ambled into the gift shop.

Mature. Real mature.

Shaking my head at her childishness, I returned to the lecture hall and took the first seat I could find, towards the back. I took a pen and notepad from my rucksack, all the while wondering what sort of mood Amy would be in by the time I returned. Why couldn't she see this was important to me? Why couldn't she understand, rather than making some puerile joke out there which other people were bound to have heard? Had she done it deliberately? To embarrass me? Well, she'd succeeded. Her petulance and infantile comments, bellowed out across the foyer, had done that, all right.

I scribbled on the notepad, pressing far harder than was necessary. All I'd asked for was half an hour to do something that was important to me. It wasn't like I asked much of her, was it? I texted her all the time. I Skyped her constantly, sometimes when I didn't feel like it. I sent her e-mails, telling her how much I missed her. Yet the one time I really need her to give something back to me, she...

"Of all the lecture halls in all the world."

I snapped my head up.

Eden.

"Where did you come from?" Such a dumb question.

"I just got here." Eden sat down next to me. "I looked for the first empty seat I could see, and what do you know? It's right here next to you."

"I thought you came to the earlier lecture." I stole a look past Eden, out to the foyer. Amy had disappeared. I slid down further in my seat. I'd no idea why.

"Nah," Eden said, reaching down to her bag, "By the time I got up and...well, you know." She followed my gaze. I must have been looking out to the foyer again. "No Amy?" she asked.

"She's out there," I said. "In the gift shop."

"Freud not her thing?"

"Hardly." I smiled weakly.

"I figured you'd have come to the five p.m. lecture." Eden looked at me. "I thought you'd want to spend most of the day hanging out with Amy."

"Mm." It was the best I could come up with.

"This is going to be the best ever," Eden said. "Don't you think?" Her face was animated. Alive. "It'll make everything Mrs. Belling has been saying in lessons so much clearer."

I thought back to Amy. Sullen, reluctant Amy hanging around the foyer telling me she thought the lecture was for wackos. She just didn't understand. Eden understood. Eden wanted to understand. Eden wanted to broaden her mind, whereas Amy was happy to tread water, never venturing into the unknown, never willing to open her mind or expand her knowledge. In life as well as anything else.

Light and dark. Positive and negative.

The lights dimmed. The hubbub in the hall quieted as a small man in a tweed jacket stepped up to the lectern. With one final look out to the foyer, and then a quick glance at Eden's profile, the lecture began.

CHAPTER TWENTY-EIGHT

"What did you think of his theories on the unconscious mind?" Eden hauled herself to her feet and waited for me to do the same.

"Interesting. Yeah." I sidestepped her and stood in the aisle. My eyes focused on the foyer outside, seeking Amy. I was torn. I knew Amy would be waiting for me, but I wanted to stay with Eden, even if just for a few minutes longer.

"And I wrote more than enough notes to nail this essay." Eden flicked her notepad.

"Me too." I turned to her. "I better go find Amy."

"Of course."

We stood and looked at one another a moment longer, neither of us willing or able to leave.

"You...uh...you want to talk stuff over later?" Eden asked.

"Stuff?"

"The lecture?" Eden asked. "I could ring you."

Yes, I want to talk to you. Of course I do.

"I'm not sure what time I'll be home tonight," I said.

"But if it's not too late, then you could ring—"

"—I could ring you?" We spoke at the same time. "Sorry." I stuffed my hands into my pockets and stared down at the floor, my face on fire.

"Are you analysed to death?" Amy's voice sounded beside me. I'd not even noticed her approaching.

"Hey." My head sprang up.

Act normal.

"Did you manage to fill your half hour okay?" I asked her.

"I bought a mug." Amy fished in a paper bag and brought out a yellow mug with a picture of Freud and the words *Freudian Sips* on it. "And a Freud rubber duck."

"As you do," I muttered.

I glanced at Eden. She was watching me.

"Amy, this is Eden from school." I opened my palm towards Eden. "Eden, this is Amy. From home." I wanted the ground to open up and swallow me.

Eden and Amy smiled at one another. They didn't speak. Instead, I was aware of each of them metaphorically sizing the other up. My two worlds colliding, right there in front of me, in a museum foyer.

Too weird. Way too weird.

Freud, I thought wryly, would be having a field day.

Finally Eden spoke. "Are you here just for the day, Amy?" she asked.

"I am, yes." I thought I detected Amy running her eyes up and down Eden when she replied. Again, imagination. "My train leaves at six."

"So we should go." I pressed my hand into the small of Amy's back and steered her away from Eden.

"It's only two o'clock." Amy frowned.

"Even so. Tubes, crowds." Babbling. Stomach-clenching. Babbling.

Did Amy really think I wanted to go? Nothing in me wanted to leave Eden at that moment. The thought of walking away from her and trying to act normally with Amy for the rest of the afternoon filled my heart with lead.

The stark contrast between Amy and Eden had never been as obvious as it was that afternoon. It was overpowering. Light versus dark. Now versus then. Eden versus Amy.

Polar opposites.

I shot a look at Amy. I tried to find a smidgen of what we used to have. God knows, I tried.

It wasn't there.

The thought scared me. I'd fought for so long, trying to quell my feelings for Eden. But there was no more fight left in me. The realization hit me harder than anything had ever done before: Eden was good for me. Amy was holding me back.

If I could have taken Eden's hand and run with her from the museum, I would have in an instant. Instead, I had to ignore my churning insides, paint a smile on my face, convince them both that everything was okay, and walk out of the museum. Away from Eden.

It was agony. With one final curt nod to Eden, totally stressing that she would think I was being rude, I ushered Amy away from her and out towards the exit. I felt like the biggest rat in the world, but my mind was clear. Possibly for the first time in months. No more playing around. I wanted Eden more than I wanted Amy. One hundred per cent certain.

But I couldn't have her.

That thought nearly killed me. And it didn't help that the last thing I saw as I left the building and glanced back over my shoulder was Eden.

She was still watching me, biting her lip.

Damn.

Chapter Twenty-nine

"She didn't have much to say for herself, did she?" Amy threw herself down onto a sofa at Starbucks. She stared out of the window, deep in thought.

"Who?"

Who! I knew full well whom she meant.

"That girl." Amy looked at me. "What was her name again?"

I swallowed. "Eden."

"I suppose she does philosophy, does she?"

"Mm-hmm."

"She looks the type." Amy stretched her legs out in front of her.

"She's not a type," I said defensively. "She happens to be very nice."

"Get you."

"Don't."

"Don't what?"

"Start." I sighed. The atmosphere, from the second Amy had stepped off her train a few hours before, had been strained, to say the least. It wasn't getting any better.

I thought about Eden, wondering where she was. Was she still at the museum, or had she gone home? I rubbed at my face as if to scrub her from my mind.

Eden refused to be erased.

You know how it is when you really don't want to be somewhere, but you don't have any choice but to stay? And it makes you so cranky you think you could scream? That's just how I felt at that moment. Waves of irritation washed over me. My cappuccino wasn't hot enough. The people on the next table were annoying me. The espresso machine behind the counter was too noisy.

And Eden wasn't with me.

This situation that I'd somehow managed to get myself tangled up in was overwhelming. I wanted Eden; I couldn't have her. I wanted to be loyal to Amy; I was struggling.

"What's with the face?" Amy asked.

I forced myself to relax. "Sorry, I was miles away." I sat back and crossed my legs. "How's your mocha?" I asked.

"Chocolatey," Amy said. "Want some?" She lifted her mug.

I shook my head.

"You like it here, don't you?" she suddenly asked.

"Starbucks? It's okay."

"London, you dummy."

Oh. "Yeah, I guess."

"More than you thought you would?" she asked.

"It's better than I was expecting, yeah." I studied her carefully.

"This from the girl who hates any kind of disruption in her life," Amy continued.

She wasn't wrong there.

"And you're happy here?" She blew on her drink. Studied me.

"Yes, but why?"

"Remember how we felt the night before you left?" Amy asked. She was smiling now, a soft look on her face.

"I was gutted at leaving you," I said.

"And all the promises we made to one another?" she said. "About how we'd be together again soon?"

"Amy, I…"

She waved away my protestations. "It's what you do when you're about to be dragged three hundred miles away from the first and only girl you've ever loved."

"I meant every word." I leant closer to her.

"I know you did," she said. "So did I."

Silence.

"Have you met someone else?" she finally asked. "Since you've been here?"

"No." My heart flailed in my chest.

Why would she ask that? Did she suspect something?

"Have you?" I asked.

Had she seen the way I looked at Eden earlier in the museum? Had she put two and two together?

"Yes."

I'd barely said two words to Eden while I was with Amy. That had been deliberate. How could she have—

"What did you say?" I snapped my head up.

"I said yes," Amy repeated.

"You've met someone else?"

Other voices in the room echoed around me.

"Who?"

"It's no one you know." My question was dismissed just like that.

"And all the stuff we said to one another?" I asked. "Before I left?"

"Like I just said. Knee-jerk promises of two people distraught at being torn apart," Amy said. She looked squarely at me. "I thought for a long time that you'd come back," she continued, "but as time's gone on..." She shrugged. "I can't cope with us being so far apart, never seeing each other. It used to be fun. Me and you skipping school, hanging out together. Living three hundred miles apart isn't fun."

School. Eden.

She was my first thought as Amy carried on talking.

I tried to look upset. I tried to look pissed off. God knows, I tried to look like I cared, but I couldn't. All I felt was pressure being released and an overwhelming sense of relief that I didn't have to go through the charade of pretending that I loved Amy any more.

"You changed." Her words jolted me back to her.

Focus.

"Why did you come down here if you knew you didn't want to be with me any more?" I asked.

"One last roll of the dice," Amy said. Short and to the point.

"Even though you were seeing someone else?" The words stuck.

"I wanted to see if we still had something," she said. "But the second I met you off the train, I knew we didn't."

As I looked at Amy, still talking, all I could think was she was totally right about me. I had changed. Amy had stayed the same wild, crazy girl I'd fallen in love with, and I was happy about that. I didn't want her to change. Why should she? No, this was all about me, and how different I was now. I knew I wasn't the girl who had left Cragthorne all those months ago. I'd moved on. And that was all down to one person.

Eden.

Thanks to Eden, I knew I was a better person than before. I was more mature and thoughtful. Nicer, even. She'd shown me, despite all my initial protestations and railing against moving away, that the move truly had been for the best. And as much as I hated to admit it, my father might have been right all along: moving to London could be the making of me.

Parting with Amy was so bittersweet. She was my final link with the northeast, and a small part of me would always love her because of that. But now London was my home. I was glad of that. I now knew that going back to Cragthorne would feel like a backward step.

I also knew that the one other change in my life I really wanted, I could never have. Despite that, all I wanted to do was run from the cafe and go find Eden.

CHAPTER THIRTY

"Tabitha?" My father's voice shouting up the stairs was an unwelcome distraction from my thoughts.

It was the next day. Sunday. I'd dropped Amy off at King's Cross the previous afternoon, both of us promising to text one another, both of us apparently relieved—each for our different reasons—that it was over. And that had been that. Two years together, and her face in her departing train's window was the last thing I saw of her. Or would ever see of her again, I supposed.

I'd spent the rest of that evening and a huge chunk of the next morning, too, figuring out what my next move would be. Would I tell Eden? Would it make a difference to her if I did?

"Tabitha? I know you're up there."

My father was many things. Patient wasn't one of them.

"Tabitha!"

Sighing, I swung my legs off my bed and stood up. I was exasperated that my daydreaming bubble had been popped by his persistence. I'd have to go right back to the beginning of my ruminations once I returned to my bedroom if I was to get my train of thought back on track again.

"Yes?" I leant over the banister and peered down towards my father.

"Why do you have to skulk up in your room all the time?" He was standing at the bottom of the stairs, one foot on the bottom step. I had half a mind to ask him why, if he was able to put one foot on the stairs, he couldn't have then carried on and put his feet on the other eighteen steps and come up to see me. Rather than me get off my bed to see him. But I didn't.

"I wasn't skulking," I said. "I was thinking."

"About?"

"Stuff."

"Fine." He gave me a look. "Right, well I just wanted to tell you that your mother and I have booked tickets for the theatre for Friday night," he said, still looking up at me. "So you'll have to fend for yourself, okay?"

"More freebies?" I grinned down.

"We paid for these," my father said impatiently.

"And you called me from my room to tell me that because…?"

"Because, while I'm perfectly happy to let you fend for yourself, your mother wants to know if there's anything you'd like her to get in for your dinner, because she'll be going out tomorrow and can get it then." He crossed his arms. "So?"

"Nah, I'm good." I leant further over the banister. "I'll get pizza in." I stopped, a thought coming into my head the second I mentioned pizza.

"Dad?"

"Mm?"

"Can I have a friend over on Friday night?"

"To come here?" My father looked taken aback.

"Yeah."

"Do you have homework this weekend?" he asked.

"It's just one night, Dad. Jeez."

"Fair enough." He turned to go. "Who's coming?"

"Eden," I said. "I thought I'd ask her if she'd like to come over for pizza and a DVD."

"Eden?" he asked, suddenly interested. "The girl I met before?"

"Mm. Her."

The change in my father's attitude at the mention of Eden was so split-second, it was all I could do not to laugh. His natural snobbery, having lain dormant for all of a few days now, surfaced with such speed, I was surprised he didn't choke.

"Of course you can," he said, smiling up the stairs to me. "Does she eat pizza?"

"Fuck's sake…" I muttered under my breath. "Yes," I snapped. "She eats pizza."

I stood up from leaning on the banister and made to go back to my room.

"Tabitha?" my father called up, still from the bottom of the stairs.

"Yup?"

"I think Eden's a very nice friend for you to have," he said. "I like her."

"Yes. You said before. When you met her that time." I poked my head back over the banister and grinned down to him, my grumpiness now well and truly gone. "But thanks. She's neat, yeah."

❖

"So, anyway, my parents are going out. Ed's already told me he won't be around, so that means I get the house to myself for the first time since we moved here." I watched as the others in the lab grabbed coats and bags and began filing out, our biology lesson over.

"So invite her over, then," Libby said, ripping a corner of paper from her pad and using it as a bookmark in one of her textbooks. "Tonight's homework," she explained. "Buggered if I'll remember the page number by the time I get home."

"You think she'll come?" I asked. "I've been dithering since Sunday about whether to ask her or not." I looked over to Eden.

Don't go.

"I nearly asked her at fencing last night," I continued, "but chickened out at the last minute."

"Do it." Libby stood, putting her coat on. "Invite her. You do want her over, don't you?"

"Yes and no," I said. "I'd give anything just to have her to myself for an evening, but..."

"But?"

"I'm scared," I said miserably.

"Scared of what?"

"Scared that the more time I spend with her, the more I'm going to fall for her," I said. "Especially now I'm not with Amy."

"I think you've fallen too far already to turn back." Libby put her hand on my arm. "So just enjoy being with her—as a friend if necessary. Surely being with her in any capacity has got to be better than nothing?"

"I guess," I said.

"Just ask her already." Libby picked up her bag. "Before she leaves the room. If you don't, I will."

"Don't you dare." I glared at Libby.

"Right, I'm done for the day." Libby pushed her chair back under the bench. "Text me tonight, yeah? You can tell me what she said when you ask her. Because you *will* ask her, won't you?"

"Sure." I pulled my chair forward so Libby could pass behind me. Gabby, then Beth, stood and made for the door, while Eden remained seated. She gathered her pens up and put them into her bag.

"I'll see you down there," I heard Eden say to Beth. She stood and closed her books.

"You not coming with us?" Beth hugged her textbooks to her chest.

"I'll catch up," Eden said. "Gimme two seconds."

I lingered at the back of the room, watching the pair of them, then packed my own bag, deliberately taking my time. Finally Beth left the room, and at last it was just me and Eden.

"How're you?" Eden sauntered towards the back of the room, her bag strung diagonally across her shoulders, her hands in her jeans pockets. She lowered her voice. "You were quiet at fencing last night. Everything all right?"

"Hey." I tried to look surprised and casual and nonchalant and calm all at the same time, even though my heart was racing. "I've had a lot on my mind this week," I lied. "Assignments and stuff, you know." I stood up.

We looked at one another, neither of us speaking.

Looks pretty damned good from where I'm standing...

Her voice flooded my head. That was what she'd said, wasn't it?

Why did you say that, Eden?

"And Amy finished with me." It was out before I realized it.

A shadow flickered over Eden's face. What was it? Surprise? Interest?

"I'm sorry," she said. She hesitated. "When?"

"Saturday."

"You didn't say anything last night." Concern this time.

"No." I hesitated. "I'm still getting used to the idea myself."

"Are you okay?" Eden asked.

"I'll live." I stared down at the floor.

She turned to leave. "Well, if you want to talk about stuff," she said, "you've got my number."

Courage swept through me. It was now or never. If I didn't ask her over on Friday then I'd regret it, I just knew. I liked Eden, I was free, and I wanted to hang out with her. Where was the harm in that?

"I'm glad I've seen you, actually," I said.

"Yeah?" She stood in front of me, hands still in her pockets.

"I was supposed to be having a DVD night with Ed on Friday, because my parents are going out to the theatre," I lied, my heart pounding. "But Ed being Ed, he got a better offer."

I shifted the weight from one foot to the other. "I asked Libby over," I said, "but she's busy. And Greg." I was shocked at how easily the lies left my mouth. "So I just wondered if you fancied coming over?" I asked. "I'll get pizza in." My cheeks flamed. "No worries if you can't, though."

"Am I fourth choice?" She was teasing. Nice.

"No, of course not." Why wouldn't my damn face cool down?

"Friday?" Eden asked.

"Mm."

"And pizza, you say?"

"Pepperoni, if you want."

"My favourite."

"I know." My eyes skimmed hers.

"Sounds awesome," Eden said. "I'd love to. Thanks."

"For real?" A twinge in the pit of my stomach. "Well, great. That's great."

"I'll bring some wine, if you like." Eden leant her hip against my bench, her hands still in her pockets. "You like wine, don't you?"

"Love it," I lied again. I was more a beer kind of girl.

"Any particular type?" Eden asked.

"Of wine?" I asked, immediately feeling stupid. Of course she meant wine.

"Mm." Eden's lips twitched in amusement.

"Red," I blurted. "Or white. I'm not fussy."

"Good," Eden said. "Let me know tomorrow what time I can come over, yeah?"

"Sure."

Eden opened her mouth to speak, but Gabby's voice behind her stopped her. She sprang back from me in an instant.

"There you are." Gabby leant her head in through the lab door. "What're you doing?"

Eden swung around. "I told Beth I'd only be a minute."

Gabby floated curious eyes from Eden to me, and back again.

"We're waiting for you," she said to Eden.

"I'm coming." Eden was immediately anxious. On edge. Without another word to me, she turned and zigzagged round the benches towards Gabby.

But if I thought I was already forgotten to her, I was wrong. Slinging a casual arm around Gabby as they both left the lab, Eden looked back over her shoulder at me, giving me one last fleeting smile before she disappeared from my view.

Chapter Thirty-one

A nd then she was all, *I'll bring the wine,* and it took every ounce of self-restraint not to leap across the bench and grab her," I said, smiling to myself at the memory.

"You like wine that much, do you?" Libby jabbed her straw into the top of her drink carton and sucked on it.

"You're hilarious, you know that?"

It was Thursday morning. Nineteen hours and fifteen sweet minutes since Eden had told me she'd be coming to my house to share pepperoni pizza and a DVD with me. Now I was in the canteen with Libby, still floating on an Eden-shaped cloud of happiness.

"So your hesitation in asking her over soon passed, then?" Libby looked at me in amusement.

"You told me to do it," I said, lowering my voice as two boys walked past our table.

"Only because I couldn't stand to see you pining away over her in front of my very eyes." Libby stirred her hot chocolate, then handed me her spoon so I could stir mine.

"Listen, don't expect too much, yeah?" she continued. "She doesn't know how psyched you are that she's coming over because she doesn't know that you're lusting after her like—"

"Like Pepé Le Pew? Please don't compare me to a French skunk again. You'll give me a complex." I stirred my drink, then tapped the spoon on the side of the mug. "I'm not expecting anything, Lib. I'm just stoked that she said yes, and I plan on having a great evening with her and enjoying her company."

"And her wine," Libby interrupted.

"And her wine," I repeated, "And to just...have fun hanging out with her."

The familiar grating, booming voice of Gabby rang out from across the canteen as she came in with Eden. Think buffalo in mineshaft. Only worse. And louder.

My eyes followed Eden. She wasn't looking my way.

"As a friend," Libby said.

"Huh?"

"Hanging out with her as a friend," Libby repeated. "You forgot that last bit."

"Yeah. Whatever." I looked over to see the two of them heading for their usual table over the other side of the canteen from us, my eyes following them as Gabby wrapped her arm around Eden. A sting of envy nipped at me. She said something to Eden, making her laugh out loud and jokingly throw Gabby's arm from her. Then they sat down, each one with a large polystyrene cup of some hot drink, and huddled towards one another, deep in conversation.

"Why do they irritate me so much?" Libby followed my gaze to the other side of the canteen.

"You still don't like Eden?" My heart fell. "After everything I've told you about her?"

"Jury's still out." Libby's face contorted as Gabby let out a shriek of laughter that echoed round the canteen. "Sorry." At least she did look apologetic.

"You should try and get to know her. Like I have," I said. "You'll see. She's so not like the other two."

"Maybe I'll get my chance right now." Libby lowered her voice. "She's coming over."

Blood rushed inside my ears at Libby's words, and I surreptitiously dragged my fingertips through my hair in an attempt to make it look tidier. Eden was making her way towards us, through the maze of tables and chairs. My heart jumped at the sincerity of her smile when we finally made eye contact.

"I'm glad I caught you." She stopped at the side of our table and stood, thumbs hitched into her jeans pockets. "Hey, Libby."

"All right?" Libby sat back in her chair, her arms folded across her chest.

"Can we take a rain check on tomorrow night?" Eden said, turning to face me. "I just realized I'm busy that night."

"Oh." I looked to Libby then back to Eden. "Okay."

"I already had something planned and I completely forgot about it," Eden said. "I'm so stupid sometimes. I'm really sorry."

Libby made a small, sniffing sound—discreet, but audible enough for both me and Eden to catch.

"No worries," I said, trying to ignore the acute disappointment stabbing at me. "Another time, yeah?"

"Sure," Eden said. "Another time." She stepped back from our table. "I better go. See you later maybe?"

She left before I'd answered, and headed back over to where Gabby was still sitting, now with Beth. I watched her walking from me, but seeing Gabby looking straight at me, I immediately looked away.

Was that it? No other explanation?

I was utterly deflated. All the happiness I'd felt over the last however many hours since Eden had told me she'd love to come over had just been sucked out of me. What was the point?

"That's a bummer." Libby dipped her head, trying to catch my eye.

"Understatement of the year," I said. "And, what? She just suddenly remembered that she had something else on?"

"Whatever it is, it must be important," Libby replied. Very diplomatic.

"Well I'm not asking her again, Lib," I said. "It took every ounce of courage to ask her in the first place, and now I feel like crap."

"I thought you said you had a sudden raging torrent of confidence yesterday when you asked her, and that nothing was going to stop you?" Libby asked.

"It didn't," I said. "But it just became a whimpering trickle, so I'm not asking her again." I gathered up my hot chocolate and cradled it in my hands. "I got pepperoni pizza in as well. Her favourite." I blew across the top of the mug. "Did I already tell you that?"

"Just a few times." Libby grinned. "You know I'd come over and hang out with you Friday if I didn't have the dreaded grandmother coming over, don't you?"

"Bring her over, too," I said gloomily. "Pizza feeds four, apparently." I sipped at my chocolate. "Do you think Eden knows I like her? Do you think they know?" I nodded over towards the three of them. "Is that why she cancelled on me? 'Cos she wants to keep her distance?"

"Dunno," Libby replied. Helpful.

"I don't know how she can't tell." I sighed. "I don't think I've been hiding it very well lately."

"Look," Libby said, "you're not gonna like this, okay? But I think you're reading way too much into why she's not coming over tomorrow."

"You think?"

"Yuh-huh." Libby nodded. "And I can totally understand why Eden wouldn't think twice about cancelling."

"Enlighten me."

"Because to her, you're her friend, right?" Libby offered.

"Guess so."

"A mate."

"Mm." That was more of a grunt than an answer from me.

"To Eden, you're just plain old Tabby who she does biology and philosophy with," Libby continued.

"Plain? Old?"

"Metaphorically." Libby put down her mug. "You're just the girl she fences with once a week who makes a nice change from Gobby One and Gobby Two. Someone else she can talk to. That's all. Nothing more."

"But her comment the other week?" I asked, frustrated. "People who just want to be friends don't say stuff like that."

"Just mucking about," Libby said bluntly.

"I feel like I can't breathe sometimes," I said. I pushed my mug away. Suddenly the thought of more chocolate made me queasy. "I thought it would be easier now that I'm not with Amy, but if anything, it's worse."

"So then you have to do like I've told you before," Libby said. "You obviously can't and won't avoid her. So you just have to try and ignore the fact that you fancy her and carry on hanging out with her as a friend—otherwise it's going to drive you mad."

"Like it already hasn't?" I slumped back into my chair.

"You're just complicating things," Libby said. "You need to keep everything much simpler."

"Nothing about my life is simple right now, Lib," I said. My heart sank, realization hitting me. "Absolutely nothing."

CHAPTER THIRTY-TWO

It was all such a mess.

I was miserable, totally unable to shake the negative feelings that had followed me round, hour by hour, since Eden had told me she was busy. When I should have been concentrating in my English lesson on act 3, scene 4 of *Titus Andronicus*, all I could do instead was go over and over all the interactions Eden and I had had over the last few weeks, trying to make sense of them all. I wanted to convince myself that Libby was right: the best thing for me—and my mental well-being—was to start treating Eden as the friend she was, and move on.

Sometimes, convincing yourself that something is right is the hardest thing in the world to do.

❖

"Didn't you know?" Gabby leant against the wall outside the classroom. "She has a hot date tonight."

Her words floated into my ears as I approached their queue outside the French room. I was with Libby on our way to our own class further up the corridor. Nothing that Gabby had just said registered in my mind. Until I heard the next part. That made me slow right down.

"Don't tell me Eden finally gave in?" Beth looked from Gabby to Eden then back to Gabby again. "And that all our nagging's paid off?"

"Yuh-huh." I saw Gabby put her arm around Eden. "And lemme tell you, Marcus is well up for it."

"Well, he's waited long enough, hasn't he?" Beth grinned. "You shouldn't have left him dangling so long, Eden. Poor guy's been going out of his mind."

"That's the point, dummy." Gabby pulled Eden in closer to her. "She was always going to go out with him, weren't you?" She looked at Eden. "But Marcus didn't need to know that."

I watched all this unfold from just down the corridor, near enough to hear, but far enough away that they couldn't see me. I watched as they all laughed at what Gabby had said.

"Ignore them." Libby pulled on my arm. "Just keep walking."

"Did I hear what I think I just heard?" I whispered to Libby. "Eden has a date tonight?"

"The Marcus, I presume?" Libby said.

"She said she was busy tonight," I muttered under my breath. "I never imagined it was because she was going out with Marcus."

"She is free to see who she wants," Libby said kindly. "You're not dating her. You can't dictate who she goes out with."

"I know that," I said. "Still hurts, though." I stopped walking, not wanting to have to pass them, and leant against the corridor wall. I felt sick. I plunged my hands into my hoodie pockets, clenching my fists inside them. Right then I really wanted to hit either Beth or Gabby, or better still, both of them.

"Treating him mean, huh?" Gabby's voice sounded again.

"Something like that, yeah." I heard Eden's voice for the first time.

Every word the three of them said about Marcus was like a hot knife being pushed, slowly, into my chest. Jealousy and hurt ate me up. I burned with loathing for Gabby and Beth, not only for setting up Eden in the first place, but for announcing it right now to just about the whole school. I never knew jealousy could hurt as much as it did. Listening to the three of them go on and on about how wonderful Marcus was was making me physically ill.

I detested Eden at that moment as well. I was furious with her on so many levels. For making suggestive comments to me.

For messing with my head—she slept on my shoulder, for fuck's sake!—when her intention all along had been to date Marcus. I'd chosen not to believe Libby; now the last little crumb of hope I'd had that Eden might actually like me had been blown away.

She was going on a date with Marcus.

"How can she do this to me?" I muttered to Libby as the door to Eden's classroom finally opened, and I saw them all file in.

Libby leant against the wall with me. "Some girls get off on being head-fucks. Eden's obviously one of them."

Sometimes the truth really hurts.

Libby looked at me. "I mean, your clue should've been in the kind of friends she has." She tossed her head towards Gabby and Beth as they both disappeared into the room. "Remember what I told you when you first asked me who they were? I told you they were a bunch of prima donnas who think the world revolves round them, and it's true."

I looked down at my feet. "But I thought Eden was different," I said. "She's the smartest, nicest person I've ever met."

We walked past Eden's room and my feet slowed. I leant just by the door frame and glanced in. She was sitting at her desk with Gabby and Beth. I looked over to where they were sitting, at the front of the room: all three were deep in conversation, laughing amongst themselves, giggling and whispering. My spine ran cold at the awful thought that Eden really was playing some fucked-up game with me, just for her own—and Gabby's and Beth's—amusement.

While I watched, my stomach filling with rocks at every laugh, Eden looked up at me. If she was feeling bad, her expression didn't show it. Instead, she studied me impassively for a few seconds, then looked away again.

"Smart and nice…and clever enough to reel you in," Libby said, pulling me from the doorway.

I was beaten. Defeated.

Eden and her games had won.

Chapter Thirty-three

"Right, no racking up any phone bills while we're out." My mother jiggled her coat on. She pouted at her reflection in the mirror, then fussed with her hair. "We're going to Garfunkel's for dinner afterwards, so don't expect us back much before midnight."

"Phone bills?" I sat on the bottom of the stairs, elbows resting on my knees, my face cupped in my hands. "When was the last time I used the house phone?"

I was in a foul temper. Watching my mother prancing about in front of the mirror and coming out with bullshit about phone bills was plunging me into an even worse mood.

"Just don't spend the whole night gossiping to whoever your latest mates are, that's all," my mother said, continuing to fiddle with her appearance even though it was perfect.

"Planet Earth to Mother," I muttered darkly. "I Skype, text, or use my minutes on my phone, remember? Have done so for the last hundred years."

"And you got yourself something in for dinner, didn't you?" she asked, completely oblivious to both my mood and my sarcasm. Much to my disappointment.

"Yup," I said, looking towards the kitchen. "Enough to feed a small platoon."

"I hope Eden has just as big an appetite as you do." My father appeared in the hall where we were talking, adjusting his tie as he did so. "Help you eat that monster pizza I've just seen in the fridge."

"She's not coming," I said. "She's busy."

"Shame." My mother grabbed her house keys from the hallway table.

"Mm." I stood up from the step, brushing past my father to get to the kitchen. Suddenly I needed a drink. I opened the fridge, ignoring the dumb pizza mocking me from the shelf, and took a bottle of beer from it.

"Are you okay?" my father asked from just behind me.

"Yup. Fine." I opened the beer and took a large gulp from it, coughing as the bubbles hit the back of my nose. "Gonna eat dinner, then find a DVD I haven't watched yet." I wiped my nose with the back of my hand. "Then go to bed."

"Not too many of those, please," my father said, nodding to my beer.

"Past caring, to be honest," I said. I turned to go.

"Tabitha." The usual warning voice.

"I'll stick to just this one, don't worry." I lifted the bottle and smiled sarcastically.

"You seem down," my father said, putting his hand on my arm and stopping me from moving. "And tetchy. You looked like you were flying high the other day, now you're prickly again."

"Goes like that," I retorted.

"You're very up and down lately," he said, his hand still on my arm. "I'm used to you being moody and sarcastic. Monosyllabic." He looked at me knowingly. "So it's been nice to see you so full of life these last few weeks. What's brought you down again?"

"I'm not down," I lied. "I'm fine."

My father looked at me, longer than I felt relaxed with. "If there's something bothering you, you can tell me or your mother, you know that?"

"Yup."

"Is there anything you want to tell us?" He rubbed his hand on my arm.

Yeah right. Like I was going to tell him about stuff? Like he'd understand?

"Nope."

"Are you in trouble at school?"

"Why do you always think I'm in trouble at school?" I slammed my bottle down on the kitchen unit.

My father dropped his hand from my arm. "Habit," he said. "The fact you were always skipping school in Cragthorne is a start."

I looked down at the small pool of beer that had jumped out of the bottle and spilled onto the kitchen unit when I'd slammed it down, the small bubbles in it popping and chasing after one another.

"Or perhaps because of all the phone calls we used to get, thanks to you always being in trouble or mixed up in something that didn't concern you," my father continued. "Want me to go on?"

"That was then," I said. "I'm different now."

"I'll take some convincing on that one, I think." My father stood, hands in his pockets.

"Seriously, Dad," I said. I didn't want to have this conversation one little bit. Not tonight. "School's fine. I'm not in any trouble, everything's just hunky-dory, I swear."

"Well, if you're sure…" He looked away as my mother called to him from the front door.

"I'm sure," I said, wandering into the front room and swigging from my bottle. "Never been surer."

❖

The house was eerily quiet after my parents went out. Once they'd finally closed the door behind them, my mother giving me one last lecture about switching ovens and lights off, I was alone.

And it was always when I was alone that I did the worst of my thinking.

I don't know how long I sat in the front room after they'd gone. I stared moodily at the swirling pattern on the rug at my feet, empty beer bottle in my hands, imagining Eden out on her date with Marcus.

She was with him now. Laughing, hanging on his every word just like I hung on every word of hers. He had his arm around her.

She liked it. They had an instant attraction, and now Eden was wondering why she'd waited so long to date him. He was everything she was looking for in a guy: funny, attentive, good looking.

Would she tell me all about it at school on Monday? I knew I wouldn't be able to cope with that. Would I make a show of myself?

Two hours passed.

Eden and Marcus barely left my thoughts.

By the time I'd mentally dragged myself back to the here and now, it was pitch-black outside. I was aware of a strange white light pooling in front of me, coming from the moon, and realized with a jolt I'd been sitting in total darkness for goodness knows how long. I stood up, jarring myself back to reality, and immediately felt freaked at being in the dark on my own. Imaginary creepy shadows danced in the corners of the room. I began switching lights on, gaining comfort from the soft lighting being thrown out around me, illuminating corners that just seconds before had totally weirded me out.

I grabbed another beer from the fridge, ignoring the uneaten pizza, and went to my room. Knowing the only person who could make me feel better would, in all probability, be on Skype, I picked up my iPad.

She'd make it all okay. Libby would tell me the things I really needed to hear right now.

She answered after around a dozen or so rings, just at the point where I was going to give up. Relief spread over me as I saw her friendly face flicker into life on the screen, quickly followed by a wave of nausea as I saw she was eating a tub of ice cream.

"Is that all you do? Eat?" I shuffled myself back on my bed and balanced my iPad on my knees.

"It's Friday," Libby said through mouthfuls. "So that means just one thing. Ben & Jerry's." She lifted the tub up and peered at it. "Caramel Chew Chew, to be precise."

"Nice."

"And I've escaped The Grandmother for five minutes, so I

can chill out up here without being asked every five minutes about school and boys. In that order." Libby licked her spoon. "So you okay?"

"Not really," I replied. "Thinking about stuff too much." I lifted my beer. "This is helping though."

"Eden?"

"Who else?" I put my beer down then started picking at a loose bit of thread on the seam of my jeans. "She's out with Marcus and it's all I can think about. Her with him, probably making out somewhere while I'm sitting here with knots in my stomach 'cos I'm so eaten up with jealousy." I looked at Libby, still vigorously spooning ice cream into her mouth. "I hate it, Lib. Just hate it."

"I wish there was something I could say that would make it better," she said, scraping her spoon round the side of the tub. "But there isn't."

"Why do I always fall for the straight girl?" I pulled at the thread on my jeans until it came away in my fingers.

"You fell for Amy," Libby offered helpfully. "She wasn't straight."

"You know what I mean."

"London's full of lesbians," Libby said. She gave her spoon one final lick, then tossed it back into the empty tub. "Find someone else. Go to a club, meet someone. Forget about Eden."

"I think I've proper fallen in love with her, though." I picked up my beer again. Stared miserably at the label. "I can't just switch that off and pretend it doesn't exist."

"You love her?"

"Reckon so," I said. "How is it, though, that love can be so fab and so shit at the same time?"

"If I knew the answer to that, then I'd be…" Libby opened her mouth to speak, then closed it again. "Well, I don't know what I'd be, but you know what I mean."

"Thanks for always listening to me," I said. "I mean, for listening to me banging on about Eden all the time."

"S'okay." Libby grinned. "It's what friends are for, isn't it?"

"But I appreciate it," I said truthfully. "If I didn't have you to talk to, then I think I'd go nuts."

"Your parents left already?" Libby asked.

"Yeah, theatre." I waved my hand over my mouth, mock-yawning.

My phone vibrated across my desk on the other side of my room, lighting up the ceiling above it.

"Phone's ringing," I said. I swung my legs off the bed. "Wait a sec."

I put my iPad and beer down and went to my phone.

Icicles cascaded down my neck when I saw who it was. I stared at it, not daring to believe it was true, then went back over to my bed and spoke to Libby again.

"It's Eden," I said.

Chapter Thirty-four

W hat does she want?" I looked at Eden's name, flashing on and off.

"Well, answer it, dummy," Libby said. "And then you'll find out. Quick, before she rings off."

"Okay, wait." I put my iPad to one side.

"Hi, Eden." My voice was wobbling. "How're you?"

"Can I come over?" Eden sounded quiet.

"What? Now?" I looked at my watch. Nine thirty p.m.

"Yeah."

"Sure, if you want."

"I do want, yeah," Eden said. "I'll catch the next train over. Be with you in about half an hour, okay?"

"Sure. Where are you at the moment, then?" I asked, puzzled. "Aren't you still out with Marcus?"

"I'm…just out," Eden said. "No, I'm not with Marcus."

"Right," I said uncertainly. "Well, I guess I'll see you in a bit, then."

Eden didn't say goodbye; instead she just finished our call without another word.

I put my phone down and picked up the iPad. "Did you hear all that?" I asked Libby.

"I only heard you," Libby said, "not her. Is she coming over?"

"Seems like it," I said.

"What are you going to say to her?" Libby asked.

"Dunno." I shrugged. "It's kinda hard to stay pissed off with Eden when she's standing in front of me looking so damned hot."

"TMI, thanks." Libby grinned.

"Look, I'm gonna go," I said. "She'll be here in half an hour. Just enough time to make myself look a bit more presentable."

"Okay," Libby said. "Text me later, yeah?"

"No worries." I shut down Skype and looked at myself in the mirror. Pulled my top off and replaced it with the rugby shirt I knew Eden liked. It was creased. Would she notice? At least it was clean, unlike my jeans. A hasty change of trousers, a good clean of my teeth, and a squirt of something smelly that I found lurking on my table five minutes later, and I was good to go.

Then I waited. The house fell deafeningly quiet again as I paced around, waiting for Eden to arrive. I sat in the lounge, flicking through a magazine my mother had left lying on the coffee table. I ambled into the kitchen and stared blankly out of the window for a while. I returned to the lounge once more, picking up the magazine again and reading the exact same page I'd just been looking at, moments before.

Time, it appeared, refused to march on.

Finally, the doorbell rang and Eden was at my house. I opened the door, suddenly half-expecting to see her with Marcus after all. She was alone. She looked shy. Nervous, even. Adorable.

How could I have ever been angry with her?

"Sorry, come in," I said. I was just staring at her. She stepped up into the hall, and I caught the usual brief but lovely smell of her perfume as she came past me.

"Wanna come up to my room or stay down here?" I asked. I motioned towards the lounge door.

"Are your parents in?" Eden asked. "I thought you said…"

"Relax, they're still out," I said. "They've gone to the theatre, with dinner afterwards. They'll be gone for hours yet."

"And your brother's out, too?" Eden looked to the lounge door.

"Yup," I said. "God knows where, but knowing Ed, we won't be seeing him till the early hours either." I saw her relax a little. "Want a drink?"

Eden shook her head. "Can we go upstairs?" she asked.

"Sure." I stepped up onto the first stair and looked back at her. "Are you okay?"

"I'm fine." She smiled uncertainly.

We climbed the stairs in silence and entered my room, Eden looking around as she came in.

"Nice room," she said. "Big."

"It's all right, yeah," I said, sitting on my bed. "Nice view of the park out front in the daytime." I jabbed my thumb towards the window.

She stood, shyly, I thought, in the middle of my room.

"Sit here?" I patted the bed next to me. "Or there's a chair behind you."

Eden turned round, looked at the chair, then back to face me. "I'm okay," she said. "You've been having a good evening, by the look of it." She lifted her chin towards my half-empty bottle of beer, still on my bedside cabinet where I'd left it.

"I don't usually…"

"Can I?" Eden walked over and picked the bottle up. She drank from it, and shivers tingled down my spine at seeing her drink from the same bottle I'd just drunk from, her lips touching the same glass my lips had.

"So how was your date tonight?" I spoke, just to break the silence.

"It was all right."

"Just all right?" She was looking down at the floor, so I lowered my head to try and make eye contact. "And Marcus?"

"Fine." Finally she lifted her head and looked at me. "I left early, actually."

"Oh?" My heart gave a small leap. "Why?"

"I didn't want to be there any more."

"I see."

"I like your picture." She wandered away from me and over to the wall opposite my bed. She swung the beer bottle idly and looked up at an old black-and-white poster I had of the Eiffel Tower, in various stages of construction.

"Amy bought it for me," I said. "Christmas before last."

"It's nice."

"Thank you." I took a deep breath. "Why did you leave your date with Marcus early? Didn't you hit it off?"

"I told you," she replied. She drank from my bottle again but didn't turn to face me. "I didn't want to be there."

"So..." I said. "You came here instead?"

"Looks like it." She was still looking at my poster. "I love the way the shadows bounce off the side of the tower here, don't you?"

"Why are you here, Eden?"

She didn't answer. Instead, she just stared at the wall in front of her, biting at her lip, deep in thought.

"I don't want to be your friend any more, Tabby," she finally said.

The skin on the back of my neck prickled. Cold and piercing, like Eden herself had stabbed me with a million pins.

"What?"

"I don't want to hang out with you as your friend any more," Eden repeated, still staring at the wall. "I don't wanna have coffee with you as a friend, or go eat tapas as a friend, or come around here as a friend." At last she turned and faced me. "Our friendship—it's over."

Chapter Thirty-five

Have I done something wrong?" I stared open-mouthed at her. "I mean, I know I was out of order being annoyed with you for going out tonight, but that's only 'cos I'd got pizza in and I'd kinda thought you wanted to hang out with me and I was pissed 'cos you didn't." I was burbling. I couldn't help it.

"You were pissed off with me for going out with Marcus tonight?" Eden asked.

I didn't answer. Instead I said, "Don't you like me?" My voice was strained. "I kinda thought we got on okay, you know?"

"We do." She stared down at the bottle in her hands. "I had this all sorted in my head on the way over here," she said. "Exactly what I wanted to say to you, how I was gonna say it." She gave a small laugh. "Now I'm here, all I can talk about is your bloody poster."

She breathed out slowly, then swallowed hard. "I don't want to be your friend any more. I want to be your girlfriend. I want to hang out with you as your girlfriend. I want us to have Saturday morning coffee dates as girlfriends. I want you to come drink beer with me as my girlfriend." She drank back some beer, as if for moral support.

I stared at her, my pulse thudding in my temple.

"I only want to be your friend at school," she continued. "Outside school I want us to be more." She looked at me, her face a mixture of worry and dread.

I couldn't speak, too shocked by what she'd just said.

"Please say something." Eden stood awkwardly in front of

me in the middle of my room. "I really like you, Tabby, and if I'm right—and I think I am right—you like me, too."

I nodded, very slowly. "Very good," I said. "Very convincing."

"I'm sorry?" Eden's face fell.

"I know what you're doing," I said, leaning back on my elbows. "The game you're playing."

"Game? This isn't a game, Tabby." Eden's voice caught in her throat. "This is about as far from being a game as you could imagine."

"And you expect me to believe that?"

"What?" Eden said, suddenly angry. She put the bottle down on my desk. "I've been petrified about telling you that I like you, and you think it's all a joke?"

"I do," I said. "And I think Gabby and Beth have put you up to it."

"I'm standing here, pouring my heart out to you, feeling like I'm going to faint at any moment 'cos I'm so fucking nervous, and you think I'm doing it to be funny? To have a laugh at your expense?" Her face crumpled. "Well, thanks. Thanks for nothing." She stalked to the door.

I got up from my bed and moved towards her.

Don't let her leave.

"So, what about the date with Marcus tonight?" I asked.

"I was pushed into seeing him by Beth and Gabby," Eden replied. She leant against the wall next to my door, looking completely beaten. "They just went on and on about it—drip, drip, drip—until I thought I was going to scream. All the comments, the innuendo, all the little digs. So I agreed to meet him just to shut them both up."

"You looked like you were up for it when I saw you at school," I said. The words hurt.

"You have no idea how I felt!" Eden responded fiercely. "There wasn't any part of me that wanted to go out with him."

"Seriously?"

"I swear."

"And they didn't put you up to this? For a joke?" I asked. "Come on to stupid, small-town, gay Tabby? See if you can make her fall for you, and then have a good laugh about it?"

"For shit's sake, Tabby!" Eden looked exasperated. "Do you think I'm chained to those two? Do you think my whole life revolves around them?" She stared at me, furious. "More importantly, do you really think I'm that much of a bitch? That I could ever do something like that?"

I stared at her.

Answer her, Tab.

I couldn't.

"That's not me," she said. "That's not who I am. And if you think I could ever do something as nasty as that—and to you, of all people—then you so don't know me." She pushed away from the wall. "And that really fucking hurts, 'cos I think you're awesome."

"I thought…"

She glared at me. "I'm seventeen, Tabby. And yeah, I'm confused, but I'm old enough to know I don't play games with people." She yanked the door open. "Just forget I ever said anything."

"Eden, wait!" I went to her and put my hand over hers, stopping her from going any further. "I'm sorry."

I pushed the door shut again and put myself between it and her, worried she'd try to leave again.

"You really like me?" I asked.

"I do," Eden said. "I spent the whole time I was with Marcus tonight just thinking about you." She lowered her eyes. "The only good thing about going out with him tonight was it gave me the kick up the arse I needed. I sat looking at him, just wishing I was with you instead."

"For real?"

"For real." Eden swallowed. "He wanted to kiss me, but I knew I didn't want to kiss him because…" Her voice went quiet. "Anyway, I bailed on him. Told him I had a headache."

"Poor guy."

Yeah, right.

"This is so weird, telling another girl I like her," Eden said. "But I do like you. A lot. And the more time I've spent with you, the more I've realized that."

"Really?" A feeling in my stomach. Nice.

"Really, truly, honestly. Even though I've never fancied another girl before," Eden said. "So I don't know why I've got so drawn to you. But I have." She looked at me. "Something about you stood out the first time I met you, then stayed. I tried to shake it off, but it kept coming back." She looked like she might cry.

She didn't, though.

Instead, she gazed up towards the ceiling, breathing hard. "I can't stay away from you," she eventually said, lowering her head and looking straight at me. "I don't want to stay away from you. You make my heart do this crazy-stupid thumping whenever I see you, and I've never had that with anyone before." The words tumbled out one after the other. "All I know is lately you're all I think about. It scares and excites me and confuses me that you're on my mind all the time, but I like thinking about you, and there doesn't seem to be a thing I can do about it. You have to believe me when I tell you I'm not playing games with you," she said. "This is me telling you I like you, and I want you, and…and I wish you'd bloody well say something!" she said, laughing shyly. "Please tell me I've said all the right things." She looked away, unable to meet my eyes any longer.

I shouldered away from the door, my legs feeling curiously unstable. This wasn't happening, was it? This was just my imagination running riot yet again. I reached over and took her hands, waiting for her eyes to return to mine. I ran my thumbs over her skin; they felt real, warm, and soft.

No, it was happening, all right. She was really here, saying all the things I'd been wanting to say to her for so long but hadn't dared to.

"You're shaking," I said.

"I'm terrified."

I took a deep breath and looked down at our entwined fingers.

"The first time I saw you," I eventually said, "that was it. I just knew I wanted to get to know you better."

"I don't remember..."

"Why would you?" I said. "But I noticed you. So, firstly, in answer to your question of whether or not I like you, then yes. I do. A lot."

Eden's face flushed endearingly.

"Secondly, I think you're the most awesome, beautiful, funny, clever, and the nicest person I've ever met, and I thank God that my parents dragged me down to London, or else I'd have never met you," I said. "And that would be unthinkable."

"Beautiful and funny, huh?"

"Yup." I squeezed her hands. "And I'm sorry I thought you were doing this as a joke, to wind me up, or that Gobby and Beth were involved somehow. I just couldn't ever imagine that you would feel the same way about me."

"They're my oldest friends," Eden said. "We've known each other since we were thirteen. But that's not to say they know every tiny detail about me." She gazed at me. "My life doesn't begin and end with those two, Tabby."

"But I thought—"

"Maybe once," Eden said. "But we're older now. I keep more to myself just lately."

"Like the fencing?"

"There's loads they don't know about me," Eden said, "and I want it to stay that way." She stepped closer. "They're not the most important things in my life any more. You are," she continued. "You do believe me, don't you?"

"I do, yes," I said. "Okay, maybe not to begin with, but I do now."

"Good," Eden said. "It's important you trust me."

"So where do we go from here?"

"You can kiss me," she said. "If you want to, that is."

"Are you sure?" I asked hesitantly.

Eden didn't reply. Instead, she slowly released my hands and put her arms around my waist, pulling me closer to her. "I'm nervous," she said, gazing at me with a look so melting, it was all I could do not to kiss her, there and then.

"Never kissed a girl before, hey?" I brushed her hair from her face.

"No, just never kissed someone I fancied so much before." Eden lowered her eyes.

Okay, that worked for me.

Without another word, I took her face in my hands and leant my head forward. I pressed my lips to hers, feeling them part slightly as I did. They felt warm and soft against mine, with a faintly sweet taste that made my senses explode like fireworks. I kissed her tentatively to begin with, worried she'd change her mind mid-kiss and back off. She responded just as I hoped she would. She kissed me back confidently, wrapping her arms tighter round me and moving her hips against mine, forcing me back against the wall.

"Wow," I said as we broke away. "For someone so nervous, you sure kiss well."

"You're not so bad yourself," Eden said. She rested her head on my shoulder and sighed.

"You okay?" I pulled my head back and looked down at her, worried by her sigh. "Didn't you like it?"

"It was perfect." Eden lifted her head. "It was nice. Just like I imagined it would be."

"You've imagined this?" I asked.

"Lots of times."

Hell, yeah.

"Want to do it again?" I asked. My insides flipped over when Eden nodded.

We locked eyes, both gazing tenderly and shyly at one another again. Slowly, Eden bent her head and brushed her lips lightly against mine, then more forcefully, just like before. Her tongue grazed against mine, making me kiss her back more hungrily, my fingers running up and down her back, pulling her tight against me.

Our foreheads met, both of us with our eyes closed. She was real. She was here, and she was in my arms, exactly where I wanted her to be. And she liked me! How awesome was that? Those agonizing months and weeks and days and nights just thinking about her, wanting her, all melted away as we held one another, heads still touching.

"Is this real?" I said, thinking aloud. "Did you really just tell me you liked me?"

"Mm-hmm," Eden said. She unlinked her arms from my waist and led me by the hand to my bed.

She sat down, and I followed.

"I can't believe I had the guts to say anything to you," she said. "I'm glad I did, though. I've been so worried about telling you, wondering what you'd say. But I knew if I didn't tell you how I felt, I'd regret it."

She wriggled herself backwards and leant against my wall, her long legs kicked out in front of her. I mirrored her action, propping myself against the wall to sit next to her, and put my hand on her leg.

"I think you telling me you'd split up with Amy gave me the nerve to do something," she said, watching my fingers trace up and down her leg. "I suppose all the while you were with her, I knew you wouldn't look twice at me. So I ignored what I was feeling for you."

"If you knew you liked me, why did you go out with Marcus tonight?" I asked, playfully digging my fingers into her skin and making her squeal. "I know you felt pressured into it by Gobby and Beth, but did you really have to go?"

"I didn't have to go, no," Eden said. "But apart from getting them off my back, I guess I also thought if I did go out with him, it might help me forget about you, and my feelings for you." She stopped. "Perhaps I thought I might fancy him after a night out with him. Stupid, really."

"Maybe," I said. "Was it awful?"

"I was miserable because I was missing you," Eden said. "I felt absolutely nothing, even though Marcus is a lovely guy, and he'll make someone an amazing boyfriend." She looked at me. "But he's not you, is he?"

"Guess not." I traced my hand up and down her leg again.

"I'll have fun explaining why I stood him up to Gabby and Beth, though." She pulled a face. "Sometimes I wish they'd just keep the fuck out of my life."

"Well, in fairness—and I'm not backing them up here, 'cos I can't stand the pair of them—they don't know you like girls, do they?" I said.

"Girl, singular," Eden corrected. "Not girls, plural."

"Never even a hint of it before?" I teased. "Not even the teensiest attraction to another girl?"

Eden thought for a moment. "Maybe I've been curious before," she admitted. "But never curious enough to do anything about it." She looked at me. "Until you."

"And William?"

"What about him?"

"No attraction there either?" I asked.

"Nah." She laughed. "Sometimes I even thought I was missing some sort of sexuality gene, you know? Up here." She tapped at the side of her head. "I felt numb with William, like something was missing. I thought it was just that he wasn't The One, but then I felt numb with Marcus tonight as well." She took my hand. "You're the only one who's ever made me feel anything," she said. "I've seen other girls before and thought they were nice, but I've never wanted to find out if that meant I was attracted to them. Does that make sense?"

"I think so."

"But with you, it's different." Eden caught my eye. "And being around you, seeing you most days, hanging out with you, made me realize I wasn't missing any stupid gene. I just needed to have a Tabby Morton in my life."

"That's cute." I reached over and squeezed her hand.

"It's true," she said, squeezing it back.

"C'mere." I reached my arm up and put it around her neck, pulling her to me so her head was resting in the crook of my neck.

"I feel a bit scared, though," Eden mumbled into my neck. "Scared of being with a girl, I mean."

"Then don't think of it as being with another girl," I said. I kissed the top of her head. "Just think of it as being with me. We can hang out like we did before, we can do all the things we did before, and no one else needs to know a thing. The only difference is we'll both know—and that's all that matters." I pulled her closer to me. "We can take this as slowly as you like, Eden. I'll never make you feel awkward, okay? I've waited long enough for you, so I'm not going to rush anything or make you do anything you don't want to do."

I waited for her to answer, but she didn't.

"Okay?" I repeated, smiling as I finally felt her nod her head against me.

Chapter Thirty-six

L ove.

What an awesome feeling it is. What other emotion can make you feel like you're ten feet tall and your heart might burst, but simultaneously make you lose all rational thought because you're so happy, it's all you can do to put one foot in front of the other and walk in a straight line?

When Eden left me that night, I had to stop myself from flinging every window in the house open and shouting out across the rooftops with happiness. That's what finally getting together with Eden meant to me.

Sleep was impossible, as I knew it would be. Eden and I texted one another constantly after her dad had collected her and taken her home, right up until I heard my parents' key in the door, and I figured it had to be sometime past midnight. She'd said all the right things in her texts: she liked me, she couldn't stop thinking about me, she was relieved she'd found the courage to tell me how she felt before it was too late.

It was beautiful.

It was everything I felt like I'd waited a lifetime to hear.

❖

"Tabby, do you have any idea what time it is?" Libby croaked down the phone at me.

"It's seven forty-five a.m., Saturday the twenty-ninth," I said.

I turned onto my side and burrowed my head into my pillow. "I couldn't sleep."

"No shit."

"Anyway, if you don't want to be woken up by people ringing you, then you should switch your phone off, shouldn't you?" I imagined the look Libby was giving me. I didn't care. I was too damned happy.

"I keep it on for emergencies," Libby said sleepily.

"Well, this is an emergency."

"Let me guess?" Libby said with a groan. "Eden?"

"Yeah, but not how you think." Heat spread over me. An image came flooding back to me: Eden, standing in the middle of my room, her hands in her pockets. I grinned into my pillow.

"She explained about Marcus, then?" Libby asked.

"Mm-hmm," I replied. "Big time."

"And he wasn't the stud Gobby and Beth made him out to be?" I heard Libby yawn.

"Nuh-uh," I said.

"She told you that?"

"She did." I bent my knees up under my duvet. "She told me something else, too."

"Hit me."

"She likes me." I bit at my lip. "She told me last night that she likes me."

"As in—?"

"Yup."

"Are you sure?"

"Well, we made out, so yeah, I'm sure." I lowered my voice. Parents have ears.

"You kissed?"

"Mm-hmm. For ages."

"Ages? Now who's the stud?" Libby laughed.

"Yep." I sighed contentedly. "And it was amazing."

"Who kissed who first?" I could hear Libby shuffling around, presumably pulling herself up straighter now I'd got her interest.

"I kissed her, 'cos I could sense she was nervous, and she kissed me back for our second one." Every moment was still clear in my mind. "Then let's just say she wasn't nervous after that."

"So what else did she say?" Libby asked. Her voice was animated, attention well and truly gained.

"Just that she walked out on Marcus and came straight over to me."

"Is that what she did?" I heard Libby give a victorious laugh.

"Yuh-huh," I replied.

"And Dumb and Dumber didn't put her up to it?" Libby asked slowly.

I shook my head. "Nope. Even though I thought she was messing with me when she first told me."

"How do you feel about it?" Libby asked.

"How do I feel?" I sat up, pulled the duvet back, then swung my legs over the side of the bed. "I feel happier than I've ever felt in my life." I heard my stomach rumble. "And I also feel absolutely starving, even though Eden and I managed to polish off that pizza between us last night."

"I thought love was supposed to make you go off your food." Libby laughed.

"Yeah, right." I stood up, ruffling my hair with my hand. "I'll catch you later, yeah?"

Libby paused. "Tabby?"

"Mm?"

"I'm pleased for you," she said, sincerity in her voice.

"Thank you," I said. "That means a lot."

A silence settled between us. Friendly, not awkward though.

"I wanted you to be the first to know," I eventually said. "I'm gonna text Greg and tell him, too."

"You're going public?" I heard Libby stifle a laugh. "Gobby and Beth are going to freak."

"No." I stopped her. "Definitely no going public. Eden's adamant."

"Understandable."

"Now I really need to go eat." My stomach complained again. We finished our call. I wandered down to the kitchen, stopping in the doorway when I saw both my parents sitting at the table, eating breakfast. I had this sudden, irrational notion that the pair of them would be able to tell what had happened the night before, just by the look on my face. Instead, they barely acknowledged my presence as I walked in and went straight to the fridge.

"Good night?" At last my mother looked up from her paper as I took a carton of milk from the fridge and set it down on the unit.

"What?"

"Don't say *what*, say *pardon*." My mother looked back down at her paper, idly turning the page. "Did you have a good night last night?"

"It was all right, yeah," I said, pouring myself a glass of milk. "You?"

"Very nice, thanks," my mother said, not looking up from her paper. "One day I might convince you that Anton Chekhov is more than *some bloke who wrote a play about seagulls*, as you once told me."

"Doubt that." I leant against the kitchen unit and drank back my milk.

"And this from the girl who's doing English literature at school." My mother dripped with sarcasm. She glanced up at me again. "Please don't tell me you ate that entire pizza on your own last night, Tabby," she said. "Stuff like that's not good for you."

"Like Chekhov," I muttered, pouring myself another glass of milk.

"Did another friend come around in the end?" My father finally dragged his attention away from the *Financial Times*. "Or did you spend the evening slumped in front of the TV with a supersize pizza on your own?"

"Yeah, Eden came around," I said, my face burning at the mention of her name. I hastily sipped at my milk, hoping neither of them had noticed.

"Oh?" My father leant back in his chair. "Not too busy after all?"

"Nope," I said, wanting to add *not that it's any of your business*. "She was, then she wasn't. So she came around."

"Did you have a nice time?" my mother asked.

Yeah, we made out in my bedroom.

"It was fine, thanks," I replied. I chewed at my bottom lip. That indicated nervousness. I stopped.

"And she got home okay?" My father was persistent.

"Yes, of course," I said. "Her dad came and collected her just after eleven."

"Good." My father returned to his paper, satisfied.

"I'm gonna hang out with her in town today, actually." I looked at the clock on the wall. "So I better go take a shower."

I drank back the rest of my milk, grabbing a handful of biscuits from the jar on my way out of the kitchen before they could ask me any more questions about Eden. I went back to my room, taking the stairs two at a time because…well, just because I wanted to. That was what being in love with Eden did to me.

My phone was still on my bed from when I'd just been speaking to Libby. On impulse, I picked it up, sending a text to Eden that just said, *Any regrets?* then went to shower, knowing that if I didn't, I'd just sit on my bed waiting for her to reply, getting more and more anxious the longer she took to answer.

By the time I'd showered and dressed, Eden had replied. Her text just said, *Woke up with a huge, soppy grin on my face, so what do you think? Can't wait to see you later xxx*

I sat down on the edge of my bed, reading her text three times, smiling more each time. She couldn't wait to see me, and I was dying to see her again, even though we'd only said goodbye less than twelve hours earlier.

Love. What an awesome emotion.

Chapter Thirty-seven

Eden was waiting for me at Covent Garden as we'd arranged. I felt absurdly nervous at the prospect of seeing her and had changed four times before I'd left the house. I'd spent ages messing around with my hair, too, pulling it first one way then the other until it looked like it wasn't going to stick up in all directions. I wasn't overly happy with how it looked, but I figured if I didn't get out of the house and down to the station within the next five minutes, I'd be late.

And I never, ever wanted to be late for Eden.

I needn't have worried about my clothes or my hair, though. When I first caught sight of her as I came up the escalator from inside the station, the look on her face made it clear I'd definitely made the right choice. She hastened to me once she'd seen me and pulled me straight into a bear hug. I savoured every second of it.

"I missed you," she whispered into my ear as she held me, pulling away before I'd had the chance to tell her I'd missed her, too. "You look nice." Her eyes scanned me.

"Have you been here long?" I asked. The shyness remained, despite everything.

"No." She squeezed my hand, then let it drop. "But long enough without you."

We left the station in silence and went out into the diluted winter sunshine. The cold hit me, and I wished I'd gone for warmth rather than looking good in a thin jacket. I strolled alongside her, my hands dug deep into my pockets, my jacket buttoned up tight around me.

I was freezing, but I didn't really care. I was here. I was with Eden, and I loved being with her, knowing what I now knew: she liked me as much as I liked her.

The cold weather meant nothing to me as long as I had that thought in my head.

"What do you want to do?" Eden eventually spoke. "Maybe we could walk down by the river? It's nice there."

"Anything you want." I smiled. "I don't care as long as I'm with you."

We headed down to the Thames, slowing our pace as we reached it, and began strolling along the pavement that ran adjacent to it. As we walked, I kept glancing across at her, wanting to pinch myself to reassure myself that this really was happening. She had her hands in her jacket pockets. I so wanted to link arms with her, or take her hand. But I was scared. So, instead, I took my cue from her and kept both my hands resolutely in my pockets, too. It didn't matter. I was with her, walking along beside her, listening to her talking about some Australian band who were playing in London. That's all I cared about—just being with her.

"So are you up for it, then?" she asked.

"Up for what?"

"Going to see this band next year? Vendetta Wire? I thought we could go see them together."

"Together?" I slowed down.

"Yes, silly." Eden laughed. "Me and you. Together."

"Awesome." Excitement in the pit of my stomach. "I'd love to."

"I'll check out tickets then, shall I?" Eden asked. "Neither Gabby or Beth can stand Vendetta Wire, but I think they're amazing."

I stopped walking. "So you're asking me only 'cos you know Gobby and Beth won't go with you?"

Eden slowed, too.

"No," she said. She lowered her voice. Glanced around. "I'm asking you because I want to go with you. As your girlfriend. I shouldn't have mentioned their names. That wasn't what I meant."

"As my girlfriend?" I looked across at her. "Does that mean we're dating now?"

"Didn't I make it obvious that's what I wanted last night?" Eden said. "Or in my text this morning?"

"I guess maybe I didn't know if you wanted to be with me like that," I said, "or whether you just wanted to make out with me. See how it was."

Eden steered us over to a bench overlooking the river and sat down, pulling me with her.

"I haven't changed my mind," she said. "I can tell you one hundred per cent, nothing's changed since last night."

"Good."

I so needed to hear that.

"When I got home last night, all I wanted to do was ring you and hear your voice again," Eden said. She turned slightly on the bench so she was facing me more. "When you told me you felt the same, it was like I'd waited my whole life to hear that," she said.

Her eyes wavered from mine as she gazed down the road that ran alongside the river. I sensed her stiffen. She moved away from me on the bench and looked back down the road again, focusing intently on a point further down the riverside.

"Shall we go?" Eden stood before I could answer.

Mystified by her abruptness, I did as she wanted and stood. Eden strode out, just in front of me, back in the direction we'd just come. I quickened my pace, running the last two steps to catch up with her.

"Where are we heading now?" I asked.

"Just this way." She glanced back. Her face darkened.

I hurried behind Eden as she crossed the road and ducked down a deserted street. Her mood, so buoyant just before, was now black.

I joined her down the side street and stood, expressionless, in front of her.

"It's them." She pressed her back against the wall.

"Who?"

"Gabby and Beth."

"So what?" I went to the end of the street and peered round the corner. Sure enough, the pair of them were walking down the street. But way further back. They'd never have seen us, I was sure of it.

I came back to Eden.

This was stupid. Hiding down a side street in case Gabby and Beth spotted us? We were just sitting on a bench! Not making out or holding hands. I was cold. I was hungry. I didn't give a flying fuck about whether those two idiots saw us or not.

But Eden clearly did.

"It's not the end of the world if they see us," I said.

"I still haven't explained about Marcus," Eden replied.

"Explained? Eden, you don't have to explain yourself to anyone," I said. I tossed a look back down the street. "Especially not to them."

"Even so."

"Are you scared of them?" I asked. "Is that what it is?"

"No." She flashed me a look.

"Don't you think they'll think it strange if they find us both hiding down here?"

"Who's hiding?"

"You are. We are."

"I'm sorry."

"Do you think they even saw us?" I asked. "I didn't see them. How could they have spotted us?"

"I'm sorry," she repeated. Her face was pale.

"Wait here." I returned to the end of the street and looked round it again, just in time to see them both disappear down the steps of an Underground station.

"They've gone." I went back to Eden and stood with her, my back against the wall, too.

"I'm sorry," Eden said again. "I'm being stupid." With a final quick look round, she slipped her hand into my pocket, taking my hand in hers. "Your hands are freezing!" She wrapped her fingers tight around mine, immediately warming my cold skin. "Are you cold?"

"Frozen." I shivered, like you do when someone asks you

if you're cold. "But it'll teach me for wearing useless clothes in winter."

"Useless, but cute." Eden squeezed my fingers, then removed her hand from my pocket. "C'mon." She beckoned me to follow her.

"Where are we going?" I pushed away from the wall.

"Cafe and then the movies," Eden said, taking my hand. "There'll be shit-all on probably, but I can't bear to see you shivering like a whippet for the rest of the day."

She started to walk away, reaching out and pulling me along with her. "Besides," she added, "Beth and Gabby hate the movies."

❖

I was complete. I'd always thought my life, before I moved to London, was doing okay. Then, quite without warning, this amazing girl came into it and made me realize my life had been pretty much a big black hole of nothingness without her.

Okay, so I was lame letting Eden practically throw me down a side street without a thought for my feelings the day before. I was also so wrapped up in her, I'd have done anything for her.

That's what love does to a person.

I loved Amy. Don't get me wrong. I loved her unconditionally, madly, spine-tinglingly. Totally. She was my world for two years, and I thought we'd be together forever. I thought we'd go through university with one another, live together, and then I thought we'd end up marrying.

She was everything to me.

Until I met Eden.

Amy was a livewire: argumentative, frequently critical of me, and sometimes extremely intolerant. Life with Amy was like walking on a tightrope without a safety net. I was crazy about her... or at least I thought I was. As far as I was concerned, that's what being with someone was supposed to be like—an unpredictable and fiery roller coaster of a ride.

Meeting Eden changed all that.

Eden made me realize that in order to be on a level playing field with someone, you have to treat them with kindness, respect, and empathy. You have to value them as much as you'd want them to value you. The Saturday I'd just spent with her was possibly the best day of my life—better than the day we spent together on the Eye, and better than the fencing trip to Manchester.

Because she wanted me.

She wanted me as much as I did her, and after the hiccup with Gabby and Beth, she treated me with so much affection and tenderness that my time with Amy seemed like it had never happened. She made me complete. I was living in a huge Eden-shaped bubble, and I never wanted it to burst.

Chapter Thirty-eight

S omeone's happy."
    I'd been whistling and I hadn't even realized it. I never whistled. My father knocked on my door, then poked his head round before I'd even had the chance to tell him it was okay to come in.
    "Is the sun shining? Is it half-term?" he asked. "Because when I last looked, it was raining outside and you still had three weeks of school left before the holidays."
    Staring out of the window at a pair of blackbirds chasing each other around in the sky, I wondered what Eden was doing at that precise moment. Was she thinking about me? Was she whistling, as I apparently was? Could she even whistle?
    "Hello?" My father's voice seeped into my consciousness. "Earth to Tabby?"
    "Mm?"
    It was now over a week since Eden had left her date with Marcus to come and tell me she liked me. In that time, there'd hardly been a minute when we'd not been in contact. School carried on as normal. I continued to hang out with Greg and Libby, while Eden hung out with Beth and Gabby—that didn't change. Looks between me and Eden were exchanged in class, although they must have been totally undetectable to anyone but me because nobody picked up on them. It wasn't ideal, but I didn't care. I knew everything would change once the school day was over and Gabby and Beth were no longer around.
    Then Eden was all mine.
    "You were miles away." My father again.

Was he still here?

I blinked.

"It's Sunday, I'm not at school, and I don't have any homework to do for a change." I so could do without a lecture right now. "That'll do for me."

"So you'd rather sit up here and daydream, huh?" He came further into my room.

"Don't start."

"I wasn't about to," he said. "Can I?" He gestured towards my bed, indicating that he wanted to sit down.

"Go for it." I immediately felt bad for thinking he'd come in to have a go at me. "Sorry."

"What for?" My father sat on the edge of my bed, his hands tucked under his legs.

"For thinking you were going to have a go," I said.

"An apology"—his expression was dubious—"from the girl who never says sorry about anything." He avoided my eyes. "That was a joke, before you get uppity about it."

"And not a very good joke at that," I muttered.

"You're happier again," my father continued. "This last week, I mean. Got a bit of spark back in you."

"Have I?"

"It's good to see." He stared down at his legs. "I know you hated me for bringing you down here, but as the months have gone on, I'm becoming more and more certain it was absolutely the right thing to do." He hesitated. "I think you're happy here. Am I right?"

"I am happy, yes," I said, a smile spreading across my face. "Very. I love it here. I never thought I would, but I do. I can't imagine being anywhere else now."

Or being with anyone else.

"One time we spoke about London, you told me you thought it *sucked*." He did that irritating quotation thing with his fingers. "You're saying it doesn't any more?"

"I guess not," I said. "Maybe London's changed."

"No, not London. You've changed," he said, adding, "for the better, I mean."

"Thank you." I reflected. "I'm certainly happier than I was when we first moved here."

My father cleared his throat and shifted his position on my bed. His brow creased in thought.

"Is it Eden?" he finally asked.

An icicle slithered down my back.

"I'm sorry?" I asked.

"Is it Eden who's made you happier?" He scrutinized me.

I swallowed in an attempt to clear my dry throat. "I don't know what you mean," I said, my voice reedy.

"Since Eden came into your life, I've noticed a change in you," my father said. "Can I assume it's her to thank for turning your mood around?"

"Eden, Libby, Greg, fencing, school," I said. "School definitely makes me happy."

"Because Eden's there?"

"Because Eden's there." Barely a whisper.

"And you like Eden." It wasn't a question.

"Yeah, she's cool," I said.

"No, Tabitha, I mean you *like* like Eden?"

I nodded, not sure how to answer.

"And she likes you just as much?"

"She does," I replied after a pause.

"Okay." He drew the word out.

"Okay?" I asked.

"Okay." Better.

"But don't start telling me it's wrong," I said, "or that you're disgusted. Because if you do, I'm walking out of this room right now."

My father breathed out slowly, thinking. "Tabitha, I'm not going to tell you anything like that." He sat up straighter. "But I'm not going to tell you I completely understand, either."

"There's nothing to understand," I said. "She makes me happy, I make her happy. End of."

"I've had an inkling for years that you might be..." He spun his hand. "More so just recently, though."

"Might be…?" I spun my hand, too.

"What do you want me to call it?" he asked, an exasperated look on his face.

"Gay, Dad," I said. "You can say the word. It's not going to bite you."

"Okay, so I've had an inkling for years that you might be gay," he said. "Better?"

"So why didn't you ever ask me?" I asked.

"Would you have wanted me to?"

"No."

"I thought not." He reflected. "And Amy?"

"What about her?"

"Was she your…"

"Girlfriend?"

"Ah, yes. Before?" Apparently he had trouble with that word, too.

"She was."

"And how many others have there been?" he asked.

"Please! Just because I'm gay doesn't mean I'm some serial Romeo, you know."

Unbelievable.

"Juliet," my father corrected. Such a pedant.

"Juliet, then," I said. "There's only been Amy and now Eden."

"And any ideas what turned you gay?" he asked.

"Turned me?" My voice rose a touch. "Nothing turned me. I wasn't out walking in the woods one day and got bitten by a huge gay monster who, with one chomp, sucked me into a vortex of gayness." I scrambled my legs off the bed and got up to leave. "This is pointless."

"I'm sorry." He put his hand towards me, beckoning me to take it. "Do you want to know what I think? Are you interested?"

I took his hand. It felt strange being there. Primarily because I could count the number of times I'd ever held my father's hand on, well, on one hand.

"I want to know what you think, but I don't want a lecture," I said. "You can't tell me to change."

My father shushed me. "I'm not going to tell you to change." He looked at me. "The way I see it, Eden has been something of a godsend for you."

"You think?"

"I do." A definite answer.

"How?"

"Before we moved to London, you were an immature, stroppy, moody teenager," he said.

"Thanks."

"But since meeting Eden, you've grown up," he said. "You're less argumentative—even your mother's noticed that."

"You've talked with her about stuff?" I asked.

"Of course," he replied. "You seem to be doing well at school, too. That's a first." He smiled. "And you're obviously doing really well with fencing, and we can see how dedicated you are to it. That's the first time you've stuck at something. We're proud of you for doing that."

Compliments. I could get used to this.

My father thought for a moment. "And Eden," he eventually said.

"What about her?"

"Your face lights up when you talk about her. You're animated, alive, vibrant when you're around her." He squeezed my hand. "You think I don't notice these things, don't you? You think I'm so wrapped up in my work that I don't notice when my kids smile when their phone beeps and they think no one's seen."

"I…"

He quieted me again.

"You think I'm such a bad father that I couldn't see how you looked at her that day she came here just before you both went to Manchester," he continued, "and you think I'm so selfish and concerned with making money that I can't see when my own daughter's so happy she's practically radiant?"

I stared at him, too dumbfounded to speak.

"Well, I'm not," he said. "And if it's Eden that's making you like this, and if it's her I have to thank for changing you, then who am I to tell you that what you're doing is wrong, or that you can't see her? What kind of parent would that make me?"

"Thank you," I mumbled, my face hot with embarrassment.

"I can see how much Eden means to you, Tabitha." He patted my hand. "Since you met her, you're calmer. Nicer to know. I used to worry about you, but I think you're going to do just fine, and I think you're going to turn into a very nice young woman."

I looked at him from the corner of my eye. "A nice young woman?"

"A very nice one."

"Just don't expect me to suddenly stop wearing jeans and start wearing dresses, okay?" I glowered. "I don't do dresses."

"I wouldn't dream of it."

"What about Mum?"

"I don't think she'll expect you to start wearing dresses, either."

"You know what I mean."

My father took a deep breath. "You leave your mother to me," he said. "She'll be fine."

CHAPTER THIRTY-NINE

B ut she wasn't," I said to Libby the next day at school. "Fine, I
mean."

"Awkward." Libby leant against the wall outside the Science
block. "And after your dad had been so awesome about it?"

"I know." I scuffed my foot in the ground. "I was summoned
to the dining room yesterday afternoon, like a condemned prisoner
going to the gallows."

"And then?"

"My dad had obviously only just told her, by the look on her
face." I put my hands in my pockets and leant against the wall next
to Libby and Greg. "I think she took it worse than he had."

"Did she go mental at you?" Greg asked.

"Not at first," I said. "That happened later, when she'd had time
to think about it."

"What the?" Libby flashed a look at Greg.

"I know, right?" I studied the tarmac on the ground,
remembering.

Arguments. Shouting. Crying. Appeasement from my father.

She'd even mentioned my grandmother. I've no idea why, she's
been dead for three years. And it's not like Mum ever got on with
her, anyway. "I'd been so stoked that my dad had been so brilliant
about it. I thought, of the two of them, he'd be the one who freaked,
not her."

"Well I think you're amazing for coming out to your parents."
Greg suddenly leant over and grabbed me into a hug, nearly
knocking me off my feet. "Seriously."

"Thank you," I wheezed into his jacket. "And I think you've been awesome since the day I met you," I said, releasing myself from his grip. "In fact, you both have, right through all this."

"I don't think I'd ever have the nerve to tell my parents I was gay, though," Greg said, leaning back against the wall. "I think it was very brave of you to do it."

"Good job you're not gay then, hey?" I reached over and playfully punched him on the arm.

"Very good job, I'd say," Libby said to Greg.

"Would you now?" Greg returned her gaze while I stood watching the pair of them. The penny, while not completely dropping just yet, was well on its way.

"Am I missing something?" I asked.

"We, uh…" Greg began.

"Are sort of dating," Libby finished.

"For real?" A grin spread across my face. "Since when?"

Libby flashed Greg a look. "Since the day you went to Manchester for the fencing thing."

"We texted each other all day and it kinda spiralled from there," Greg said.

My brow creased. "But that was ages ago."

"We know," Libby said. "But we thought, with everything going on, all the shit you'd been going through, it would be the last thing you'd want to hear."

"Your two best mates getting it on," Greg added.

"Well, I think it's fabulous," I said. I meant it, too. "And I think you two are made for each other."

"Like you and Eden?" Libby nudged my arm. "Hey, maybe we can start going out on foursomes?"

"You're funny." I rolled my eyes.

"So do you think your mum's gonna be okay with everything?" Greg asked.

"She'll have to be okay with it," I said. "Anyway, I've got my dad and Ed on my side, so at least two of them are with me."

"You've never called him your dad before, you know," Libby said.

"Haven't I?"

"Nuh-uh." Libby shook her head. "Always your father, never your dad."

I looked down and exhaled. "I guess he never felt much like a dad before. A father, yes. But not an actual dad. Does that make sense?"

"Perfect sense."

"And Eden knows?" Greg lifted his chin in the direction of Eden as she rounded the corner and approached us.

"She does." I kept my eyes on hers the whole time she came closer, my pulse quickening with nerves and excitement with every step she took towards me.

"You okay after yesterday?" She glanced around her. Coast clear.

"Coming out to both parents in one afternoon is gonna test anyone really, isn't it?" Libby said, a bit too sarcastically for my liking.

"I think she's very brave, yeah." Eden faced me. "So, are you? All right?"

"I'll live," I said. "The last thing my mother told me last night was that I had to give her time to come to terms with things."

"That was big of her," Greg muttered.

"Understandable, I guess," I said. "It's not every day your daughter tells you she's gay, is it?"

"But your dad was a hero," Eden said. She leant against the wall with me, so that now all four of us were lined up against it in a row.

"Total hero." I twisted round to face Eden, one shoulder leaning against the wall. "And now it means I don't have to play this stupid game of pretending you're just my friend," I said. "It means you can come around whenever you want, as my girlfriend. We don't have to creep around, being quiet, locking the door every time we want to make out in my room."

Eden didn't reply.

I ploughed on. "You've no idea how awesome the thought of that is," I said, "after years of sneaking around with Amy."

Eden nodded, then looked at her watch.

Lame reaction. Totally not what I was expecting.

"I have to go," she said. "Meeting Gabby and Beth in the library." She made to leave. "I'm glad your parents know," she said, smiling. "It must have been tough, keeping it quiet for so long."

"Will I see you later?" I asked. She'd only just got here. Why did she have to go already?

"Sure." She nudged my arm. So damned platonic. Then she turned and walked back across the yard from the same direction she'd just come.

"I think," Libby said, pulling herself away from the wall, "that Eden is going to find being gay even harder than your mother does."

"Tabby's mother isn't gay, Lib," Greg noted.

"Arsehole." Libby spun round and flitted a hand at him. "I think she might need time to get her head around everything, wouldn't you say?"

"I know," I said, my heart sinking as Eden turned the corner and disappeared from sight once more.

❖

I didn't see Eden alone again for two days after that. Sure, we Skyped at night, but for actual physical contact, for the one thing that I really craved? Nothing.

Our fencing classes had now finished because of the Christmas holidays, which were just weeks away, so it wasn't even as if I could be alone with her in the gym. So frustrating. The only time I did see her in school was during our biology and philosophy lessons, when the chance to have even just five minutes alone with her was impossible. After each lesson, the most I could hope for was a glance my way and a texted promise—presumably when Gabby and Beth weren't near enough to see her use her phone—to try and meet me down in the canteen later.

But they were promises that never materialized.

Eden's canteen time was repeatedly hijacked by either Gabby

or Beth, or more often than not, both of them. Exasperating, sure, but my poor, loved-up brain kept telling me that our fleeting encounters were better than nothing. The knowing looks passed between us had to be enough to keep me going until the next time we could be alone.

That finally happened a few days later. A text from her telling me she was on her way to the canteen—alone—and wanted to buy me a coffee was enough to make me leave the library in a clatter of pens and hastily shut books. That, plus a burbled apology to Libby, who shrugged in understanding, telling me to "get my arse down there before the two wicked witches turn up and whisk her off."

Everyone should have a Libby in her life.

Eden was waiting for me by the time I made it down there. She was sitting in the middle of the canteen, away from her usual spot by the window. Her eyes frequently swept towards the door, her fingers fiddling idly with what looked like a plastic spoon. The captivating smile on her face when she, at last, saw me as I picked my way around the tables towards her was worth all the two-word texts and brief glances I'd had to endure over the past few days.

Her eyes never left me as I sat down opposite her, drawing me in to her, like they always did. "I got you coffee already," she said. "I hope that was okay?"

"Perfect." I was still enveloped by her eyes.

"I hope I didn't haul you away from something important." She tore her gaze from mine and looked down at the plastic spoon, still in her hands. "I just wanted to see you."

"Nothing would have stopped me." I poured a packet of sugar into my coffee and stirred it, then looked around me. "Where are the Terrible Twins?"

"Beth has a rehearsal for the school musical," Eden said. "Gabby went along to tell her how good she is."

"You didn't feel like going, too?" I asked.

Eden shook her head. "They asked me, but I figured it would be the perfect chance to have you all to myself for a bit."

"Smooth." I caught her eye again, making her blush adorably.

"I was thinking," I said, picking up my coffee cup. "Fancy coming over to mine tomorrow night?"

"Will it be a Meet The Parents Officially Now That You Are Out evening?" Eden asked. Her face clouded with anxiety.

"Relax." I sipped at my coffee. "My parents are never in these days. Civic bash in Kensington tonight, Black tie do up in north London tomorrow, and dinner with some MP on Saturday," I said. "This is what happens when you're a bigwig in the City. You have to network." My eyes went heavenwards. "So I was thinking DVD, takeout, and then, uh, make out." I looked at her over the rim of my mug, one eyebrow arched impishly.

"Now, that sounds like a plan," Eden said, draining the rest of her coffee. She glanced around her. "My parents are springing a surprise party for my eighteenth next Saturday," she eventually said. "Did I already tell you?"

"Hardly a surprise if you know about it now, is it?" I leant my head to one side.

Eden grinned. "You know what I mean." She licked her spoon. "It's not really my thing, but, well, I don't want to disappoint them." She looked across to me. "Will you come? You can bring Libby if you want?"

"And Greg?" I asked. "Gabby and Beth will love that. All three of us there to wind them up."

"The more the better," Eden said. "Then they won't ask me why I've invited you." She stopped herself. "I mean—"

"I know what you mean."

I smiled.

It was forced.

"I'm sorry."

"Does this mean I have to buy you a present now?" Change the subject. "Even though your birthday's not for another nine days?"

"Of course!" Eden leant back in her chair, her eyes playful. Grateful I wasn't dwelling on her last comment, I guessed. "The bigger the better."

"So, how about I take you into town after school tomorrow?" I said, dipping my head to catch her eye. "And we go present shopping, then pick up something to eat back at my place?"

"Sounds perfect," Eden said.

"Like you," I said.

She saw me still looking at her. "What?" she laughed.

"Nothing," I said. "Just that I think you're awesome."

"I think you're awesome, too," she said, her hand straying towards mine before she checked herself and drew it back.

"I want to tell you something, but promise you won't run a mile, okay?" I said.

"Okay," she said. There was uncertainty in her voice.

I hurtled on anyway.

"You promise?" I asked.

"I can't promise if I don't know what it is."

"Then I shan't tell you," I said, drinking my coffee.

"All right already," Eden said with mock exasperation. "I promise."

"I think…"

"That?"

"That having to make do with chance meetings in the corridor, and not knowing when or if I'm going to see you on your own from one day to the next," I said, "makes me want you all the more." Too much dithering. There was more I wanted to say, but I just couldn't bring myself to say it.

"I want you, too." She leant back. "You know that."

Ah well. What the fuck.

"And," I began.

Just do it.

"I think," I continued, "that I might…possibly be in love with you." I rattled it out before I had the chance to change my mind.

Eden didn't speak. Instead she dropped her plastic spoon into her empty coffee mug and shuffled in her chair. She didn't say anything.

Ever wanted to press Ctrl+Z in real life?

I so wanted to undo what I'd just said.

"I also think," I said, pushing my now-empty coffee mug away from me, "I just said the wrong thing."

Eden shook her head. "You didn't."

My heart started beating faster. "Do you love me?" I looked at her hopefully.

Eden thought for a moment. Opened her mouth to speak, then closed it again. "What I feel for you can't be labelled with just one word," she finally said.

Ouch.

"It might be one word, but it's a nice word," I said, hurt. "People like to hear it. I like to hear it."

The fire door to the patio outside suddenly swung open, bringing with it a blast of cold winter air. Eden shivered, running her hands up and down her arms.

Talk about timing.

"Are you cold?" I asked, worried.

"Frozen," she replied. "Have been all day." She looked down at her thin long-sleeved top and pulled a face.

"Here." I unzipped my hoodie and handed it to her across the table.

"Now you'll be cold," Eden said, taking it from me.

"I'll live," I said. "Keep it until tomorrow if you want."

"Thanks." She put my hoodie on, zipped it up, and tucked her hands deep into the pockets in an attempt to warm up.

She looked lovely wearing my top. Just seeing her sitting huddled in it, her hands in my pockets, made me love her more. If that were even possible. I knew by the time she gave it back to me, it would smell of her and of her perfume—a reminder of her whenever I wore it again.

Our awkward conversation about love appeared to be over, thanks to the unwanted interruption. To be honest, I was grateful for the distraction. I didn't want to think too hard about her inability to reciprocate after I'd told her I loved her.

"Want another?" I gestured towards her empty mug when it was clear she wasn't going to say anything more about the inadequacy of the word *love*. I held out my hand. "Back in a minute." I got up and left her and joined the short queue of people already waiting.

I ordered us another coffee each, picking up a chocolate bar that I knew Eden liked. Using my last five-pound note, I paid for them, groaning to myself because I knew I'd have to tap Dad for some more money when he'd already given me my week's allowance. That would take some explaining. Then, of course, I'd get the usual lecture about *must try harder to spin your money out, Tabitha,* which I'd ignore but point out that he and my mother liked to buy at least three bottles of wine a week. And not the cheap plonk, either.

I made my way back over to our table, swerving my hips around a table full of giggling girls. They were busy poring over a magazine cover showing some guy with his top off, and fussing like a bunch of ten-year-olds.

When I got back to the table, Eden's chair was empty. My hoodie was hanging untidily over the back of it, so I figured she'd gone to the loo while I was in the queue, and I just hadn't seen her. I placed her coffee and chocolate bar over on her side of the table, opened a packet of sugar for mine, and sat down.

That's when I saw them.

Eden, Gabby, and Beth were sitting in their usual seats over in the far corner of the canteen, by the window. Watching Eden laughing and joking with them, when two minutes before, she'd been sitting with me while I blurted out that I loved her, made me feel sick, like I'd been winded. I looked back to my hoodie that she'd just been wearing, flung over the back of her chair. As I watched, it slithered off, landing in a crumpled heap on the floor. My stomach curdled.

I stared at her, willing her to look my way so she could see the look on my face. I wanted her to see the tears welling up, the hurt, and the anger. It was so obvious what had happened. Beth and Gabby had arrived in the canteen unexpectedly, and Eden had gone straight over to them, thrusting my hoodie aside like an unwanted rag as fast as she could.

I mean, heaven forbid Gabby or Beth should see her wearing my top.

I kept staring at Eden, but she didn't look my way once. Finally, after what seemed like forever, I picked up my bag and hoodie, leaving behind our coffees and Eden's chocolate bar, and hurried from the canteen.

I didn't look back. I knew, even then, that she wouldn't have seen me leave.

Chapter Forty

I'm sorry.
That was all her text had said. Nothing else.

No apologies for leaving me looking like an idiot in the canteen. No sense of guilt for discarding my hoodie without a thought on the back of her chair, and no remorse for bruising my feelings.

I texted her back, telling her I'd been beyond hurt at coming back to find her gone. I said the fact she'd abandoned me the second Gabby and Beth had come in told me she really didn't care for me as much as I cared for her. Stupidly, perhaps, I told her I understood why she'd done it, but stressed that the way she'd done it had devastated me more than she'd ever know.

She didn't reply.

Instead, I had to endure an evening wondering whether she'd gotten my text and whether to text her again, just in case she hadn't. I was afraid, though. Afraid if I pushed it too much, knowing how fragile Eden felt about the whole me-and-her thing, she'd say she couldn't cope with me being so needy and clingy and call it a day.

It was a risk I couldn't take.

I knew I had to speak to her at school the next day. She was coming to my house that evening, and I wanted to clear the air before she came. If I didn't, I knew we'd spend the evening analysing every little detail of our relationship thus far, and I didn't want that.

Sometimes things happen in life that conspire to make you question everything about yourself, every little detail, and leave you in a messed up bundle on the floor, cast aside, unwanted…like my hoodie.

CHAPTER FORTY-ONE

"Show Eden what was on the noticeboard this morning," Gabby said. She looped her arm round Eden's. "New bar opening up by the King's Road. It's going to be epic there tonight."

"Michelangelo are playing, and it's half-price drinks until nine p.m." Beth delved into her bag and pulled out a flyer. "We'd be crazy to miss it."

We were waiting outside the lab for our lesson.

Me with Greg and Libby, Eden with Gabby and Beth just in front of us.

Always the same scenario.

I was still seething over Eden, both because of my hoodie and the fact she hadn't replied to my text. I mean, what the fuck did she think she was playing at? I wanted her to see I was furious with her. I wanted her to know she couldn't keep treating me the way she had been. I wanted her to know it hurt me so much because I loved her.

If only it were that easy, though.

Eden was right in the midst of her little clique, the cloak of Gabby and Beth surrounding her, making it impossible for me to infiltrate it, let alone even try and catch her attention. Instead, I had to wait, frustrated, as the three of them messed around outside the lab door, Eden looking as if she didn't have a worry in the world.

Unlike me.

"You up for it, Eden?" Gabby teasingly punched Eden on her arm. "Few drinks? Bit of dancing?"

Eden's demeanour changed in a flash.

"I can't." She wavered. At last she looked my way. "I've got to go out tonight. Get something sorted." She bowed her head. "Last-minute thing."

"Again?" Gabby asked. "That's your third last-minute thing in as many weeks."

"It was bad enough when you had to leave Marcus because of an emergency the other week," Beth said. She crossed her arms across her chest.

"Yes. Again." Eden's jaw tightened. "Sorry."

"Why is she apologizing to her?" Libby leant over and whispered in my ear.

"It's what Eden feels compelled to do with those two, I think," I whispered back. "Apologize for having a life that doesn't involve either of them."

"And your plans are more important than coming out and getting wasted on half-price drinks with me and her?" Beth flicked her head towards Gabby and grinned.

"Cancel tonight." Gabby snatched the flyer from Beth's hand and waggled it in Eden's face. "Come with us instead. You'll have way more fun, betcha."

Eden looked to me again, her face a mixture of frustration and anxiety. She swallowed hard. "I can't," she finally said. "It's all planned. Besides, I've got something I really need to get sorted."

"Un-plan it." Beth's raucous voice practically bounced off the corridor walls. "Who are you going out with that's so important anyway? And what do you need to get sorted?"

"No one." Eden stared at the ground. "And nothing."

"A boy?" Gabby flicked a sly look at Beth, then back to Eden.

"Not Marcus, that's for sure," Beth said. "Like he's ever going to bother—"

"Not a boy," Eden snapped, interrupting her. "Why does it always have to be a boy?"

I'd heard enough.

"She's seeing me." I stepped forward. I was angry, frustrated, and infuriated at the way they were pushing Eden. "Problem?" I asked. I stood firm.

"You?" Beth asked.

"Me," I confirmed. "We're spending the evening chilling at mine. Again, problem?"

I looked at Eden. Her eyes were ablaze, but with anger rather than embarrassment.

Gabby slotted her arm through Eden's again and pulled her to her.

"Her?" Gabby's brows pinched. "Since when did you two become best buddies?"

"We chat after philosophy sometimes," Eden replied.

Chat?

"And we hang out sometimes," Eden continued. She still looked angry.

"Hanging out with the gay girl, huh?" Gabby slithered. "Don't you know it's catching? Next thing you know, you'll be cutting your hair short, Eden."

"Like Tabby's." Beth. She had to pipe in too, didn't she? "But being a lesbian is very fashionable these days, apparently."

"I think I'd rather not be a trendsetter on that one, if it's all the same to you." Gabby smirked.

I was incandescent. My breathing became shallow.

"People will talk, you know," Gabby continued. She pulled Eden to her again, and she stumbled slightly. Hadn't she said enough already? Apparently not. "Lezzy Palmer. That's what they'll call you."

"We just hang out sometimes..." Eden's protestations were drowned out by Beth.

"I've seen the way she looks at me." Beth looked me up and down. "You don't want her to do the same to you, do you?"

"It's disgusting." Gabby glared at me, her arm still restricting Eden. "Next thing you know, she'll be dragging you behind the bike sheds." More laughter. Louder this time. People were looking at us.

How freaking insensitive was this pair?

"Do you have any idea how dumb you both sound?" Libby shouldered her way past the others in the queue. She stood face-to-face with Gabby. "And you're sounding positively homophobic again there, Gabby. I'd watch it if I were you."

"Homophobic?" Gabby scoffed. "Me? I don't have a problem with lesbians, Libby. We watched every season of *The L Word*. Didn't we, Beth?"

"We did," Beth looked mischievously back at Gabby. "Didn't you have a total girl-crush on one of them for a while?" I watched, dumbstruck, as Gabby dissolved into a fit of laughter, and felt Greg's hand on my arm, dragging me back away from them all.

"You know what?" Eden's voice splintered through Gabby's laughter.

At last.

"You're right," she continued. "I'd be mad to pass up the chance of seeing Michelangelo tonight. We were only going over some philosophy notes. It can wait."

Gabby stopped laughing. "So you're in?"

"I'm in." Eden turned her back on me and faced the door of the lab. She stepped back as the door suddenly opened, and the previous class began piling out.

"And your hot date with Tabby?" Beth nudged her. She pulled her head back as Eden swung around on her.

"It's not a date." Eden glared. "And if you ever call me a fucking lesbian again, I'll kill you."

❖

I watched, broken, as Eden stormed into the lab, barging her way past students who were still coming out. I'd thought she'd been about to defend me. How wrong had I been?

I made to go after her, only stopping when I felt Greg's arms on mine, pulling me back.

"Don't," he said quietly. "Just leave it."

"Did you hear what she just said?" I turned and faced him, tears brimming in my eyes. "Fucking lesbian? Is that what she thinks?" I threw my bag off my shoulders and hurled it to the ground. "Is that what she thinks of me?"

"She needs time," Libby said. She bent to pick up my bag. "You knew she'd need time."

"To be fair, those two were proper winding her up." Greg steered me away from the rest of the queue, who were now gaping at me. He shepherded me down the corridor a little way. "Enough to make anyone snap."

"She's blown me off just because they were winding her up?" I swivelled round and glared back down the corridor. "How shallow does she have to be?"

"Not shallow, Tabs," Libby said. "Just scared and confused."

"And too chickenshit to tell them the truth," I spat, furious. "Like she's ashamed of who she is. Ashamed of me."

I leant forwards against the wall, palms flat on it in front of me. "She did the same to me yesterday," I said, my insides curling up. "Left me in the lurch in the canteen when those two bitches turned up."

"No way." Libby shot a look at Greg.

"Way," I said bitterly. "How could she do that to me twice in two days? How?"

Libby didn't answer.

"Come with us," Greg said, looking at his watch. "We're going to miss the start of the lesson." He started to walk back into the lab.

"Not a chance." I took my bag from Libby. "She can go fuck herself." My hands were shaking, both from rage and hurt. "In fact, this whole school can do one." I turned to go. "I'm done here."

I stumbled down the corridor. I needed to get away from the school, from the hurt. From Eden.

"When you see her, tell her well done from me," I shouted, my voice echoing back down the corridor to Libby. "Well done for screwing up my life."

Chapter Forty-two

I don't know how long I cried after Eden crushed me like that. As I fled from school, tears blinding me, I was reminded of a nickname Amy used to call me.

Glassheart.

That was it.

All tough and don't give a shit on the outside, but a heart of glass on the inside. That was me, all right. And right at that moment, my already fragile heart of glass was shattering more than it had ever done.

I didn't know what was worse: that Eden had blown me off in favour of Gabby and Beth or that she hadn't stood up to them when they were dissing my sexuality with their repulsive comments.

I went straight home, sitting on the Tube engulfed in my misery. Just another faceless person, but one whose stomach ached from fury and shame and wretchedness. I stared at the floor in front of me as our carriage scudded through the dark tunnels, occasionally looking at a fellow passenger and wondering if they hurt as much as I did right now.

As if to add insult to injury, it seemed as though all around me were adverts for the London Eye. Looming, mocking me. Reminding me of that awesome, perfect day we'd spent together, which I now wished had never happened.

I was relieved to find my parents both still at work and Ed either at university for a change, or still asleep on someone's floor. The house was quiet. Safe. As I entered, the comfort and peacefulness surrounded me like a warm blanket, allowing me precious time to think and to gather my thoughts. I went up to my room and put on some music. I lay on my bed and stared coldly and blindly through the window at the trees shaking in the breeze.

By the time I heard the first key in the door downstairs, around two hours after I'd arrived home, I'd made a decision—one that made my heart of glass smash into a thousand agonizing shards.

❖

My phone vibrated next to me.

Eden.

I rolled over and snatched it up.

How long had I been asleep? Hours? Minutes? I had no idea. All I knew was I'd woken with the worst headache ever and a nauseating sourness in my stomach. Enough already.

"You okay?" Greg's voice sounded at the other end of the phone. "Me and Libby have been waiting for you to text us, let us know you're all right."

"I fell asleep."

Why wasn't it Eden?

I propped myself up on one elbow and peered at my clock, blinking a few times to allow my eyes to focus properly. It was dark, the street light immediately outside my window throwing splashes of orange light around my room.

"Listen," Greg said. "I just wanted you to know we think what Eden did to you today was shitty." He paused. "You so didn't deserve that."

"Thanks," I said. "And, no. No one deserves to be treated like that."

Just because she wanted to save face in front of her friends?

"And what Gabby and Beth were saying as well," Greg continued. "Just narrow-minded, thick, ignorant comments that are best ignored. You should complain to the principal."

"Already forgotten them," I lied. "Comments, I can cope with. Being let down like that, though? That's harder to stomach."

"Come to school tomorrow," Greg urged. "We can talk about it all. Don't let her beat you. You have me and Libby, and we need you...even if Eden doesn't."

"I will," I promised.

My mind was clear. Lucid. I knew what I had to do. If I was going to get past all this, then I'd go to school tomorrow...if only to get the whole mess sorted.

CHAPTER FORTY-THREE

Eden took my hand and pulled me into an empty classroom. I'd come to school, just as I'd promised Greg I would, but I knew that how my day would pan out was entirely dependent on what Eden said to me. I'd either be on top of the world by the end of the day, or in the depths of misery.

"I'm sorry." Genuine.

It didn't make me any less furious, though.

I dropped her hand.

I headed for the door, but she blocked me.

"I'm deeply honoured," I said sarcastically, "that you could spare me five minutes of your precious time, but I'm not interested, Eden."

"Don't be like this." Eden whispered. "Please."

"How do you expect me to be?" I said. "After what you did yesterday? And the day before? All the days before."

Her face fell. "I panicked the other day in the canteen," she said. "Beth and Gabby came back 'cos Beth's rehearsal was postponed and...I dunno." She trembled. "I'm an idiot."

"Panicked?" I repeated. "You panic if you're a cheating husband about to be found out, or if you're a bank robber who's just seen the police. You don't panic when your mates turn up and find you having coffee with someone else. For God's sake, Eden!"

"And yesterday"—Eden stared down at her feet—"I got mad at them 'cos they wouldn't stop having a go."

"For having plans with the gay girl," I said. "Yeah, I was there, remember?"

"You didn't come back to school yesterday," Eden said.

"Oh, you noticed, then?" I stayed cold. Hard.

"Don't."

"You expected me to come back and then face Round Two from you lot?" I said savagely. "Believe it or not, Eden, I've got my pride."

"Please, Tabby," Eden said. "You know how I feel about you." She stepped forward. Reached out to me.

"Don't touch me." I moved away from her. "You know, right now—considering your little show yesterday—I have no idea how you feel about me."

"You know," Eden stressed.

"How could you let them say all that stuff to me?" I asked. The hurt pierced me as I remembered. "Why didn't you say something to stop them?"

"Like what?" Eden said. "What would you have wanted me to say?"

"Really?" I was seething. "Do I have to tell you?"

She didn't reply.

"How about telling them to shut the fuck up?" I said. "Or telling them to stop being so damned bigoted, bearing in mind all the hurtful things they were saying about lesbians, when *hello?* one was standing right behind you. The same one you're supposed to care about. The same one you're supposed to be dating." I glared at her. "And your parting shot—don't call me a fucking lesbian? How do you think that made me feel?" I slumped against the wall, hands in my pockets. Revulsion at the memory seeped through me.

"I was angry," Eden said weakly. "I just said it to make them stop."

"They would have stopped if you'd supported me," I said. "If you had told them the truth."

"They wouldn't." Eden sighed. "You don't know what they're like."

"I know exactly what they're like," I said. "And now I'm beginning to think you're the same." I flashed her a look. "Who are you, Eden? Really?"

The hurt my comment had elicited shone clear in her eyes. Good. I was hurting, too. Time Eden shared the burden.

"I'm not the same," Eden said. "I didn't know what to do." Her face shadowed. "How many more times can I tell you I'm sorry?"

"What do you want?" I asked. "I mean, what do you really want from all this?"

"You," Eden replied. "I just want you."

"But without the hassle of being with me, really being with me," I said. "Am I right?"

"I told you I wanted to take things slowly, didn't I?" Eden protested. A politician's answer. Avoid answering a direct question by throwing a question straight back.

"I know you wanted to take things slowly," I said. "And I think I have. But there's slow, and there's non-existent."

Eden stared at me.

"And there's a whole heap of difference between taking things slowly," I continued, "and just pretending that something isn't happening at all."

"I need time to get used to things," Eden said.

"And I've given you that," I said. "I've been discreet. I've never so much as looked at you when Gabby and Beth are around, let alone spoken to you." I swallowed, not quite able to get the words out. "You want to be with me in secret, without anyone else knowing." I carried on. "I get that. It's not like it's the first time I've had to do it. How do you think Amy and I managed when we were together?"

"I'm not as strong as Amy," Eden said, anger flaring in her eyes. "Amy knew who she was. She knew she was the same as you. I don't."

"Thanks." I clenched my jaw. "Thanks a bunch."

"I didn't mean it like that."

"Then how did you mean it?" I stared, incredulously, at her.

"It's difficult," Eden said. "You don't know what Gabby and Beth are like. How can I explain to them that everything they ever thought about me is untrue?"

"Why do you care what they think?" I snapped. "They're nasty, spiteful bitches. How can you even stand to be around them?"

"I care because I don't want to be given a label." Eden stared down at her feet. "I don't want to be the one that people point at in the corridor, or whisper about behind their hands."

"Seriously?" I looked at her in disbelief. "You'd rather live a lie than have a few people make puerile comments about you?"

"I'm not living a lie." Eden radiated anger. I'd wounded her with the truth.

I fumed, frustrated by this stupid situation we'd managed to get ourselves into. Being with Eden was supposed to be fun. It was supposed to be everything I'd dreamed of. Right now, it was turning into a nightmare, thanks to Gabby and Beth and their influence over Eden.

"You are living a lie if you're pretending to be someone you're not," I said. This time I was more gentle. A change of tack. Maybe anger wasn't the answer any more. "You just don't want to be on the other side of what the three of you have been doling out to others for years, do you?"

That apparently hit a nerve.

"I've never been like that to other people." Eden's face darkened.

"So if you're not like them, then don't act like them," I persisted. "Prove it. Be true to yourself."

"Stop trying to push me into a corner, Tabby."

"I'm not." Impatience reared. "I'm just asking you to stand up for your own principles, even if you're not going to stand up for me."

"I don't know if I can even face that," Eden said. She held my gaze. "I'm scared people will think differently of me."

"You're the same person inside," I said. "So what if they think of you differently? Isn't that their problem? Anyone who matters will know you're the same person. If they can't see that, they're not worth having as a friend."

"But everything will change the second people find out I'm dating a girl, won't it?" she said. Eden was breathing hard. Possibly not as hard as me, though.

"Yes," I said. "I can't tell you things will stay the same, because they won't."

"Maybe I don't want anything to change." Eden scratched at her head, frustrated. "Maybe I like things just the way they are."

Compression on my chest.

"Really?" I said. "You like this? You like making me feel like this? That works for you, does it?"

"No, you know I—" Eden's whole body sagged. She looked overwhelmed, lost and messed up in equal measure. "I don't know. I wish to God I did."

I moved towards the door. Enough of her weakness already. She was choosing to hurt the person she claimed to care for, so as not to rock the boat with people who didn't really care one bit for the real her. I was tired of being railroaded into making a decision I knew Eden wouldn't.

"I thought we loved each other," I said. "If you love someone you aren't ashamed of them. You back them up when they need you."

"I never said I loved you," Eden said quietly. She looked to the floor.

An iron fist punched me. I stood rooted to the spot, trying to regain the breath that felt like it had been hit from me. "Then that makes my decision a damn sight easier," I said, my voice icy cold. "We're through." I shouldered past her and grabbed the door handle.

"Maybe we should have talked more," Eden whispered to me as I opened the door. "Perhaps I should have said more. Explained stuff more."

Eden's words were lost to me.

I'd already cut myself away from her.

CHAPTER FORTY-FOUR

L ife in rewind.
    Leaving her date with Marcus to come and tell me she liked me. The psychoanalysis lecture. The looks in the foyer. The comments on her doorstep. Fencing. Tuesdays. In short, my life for the last four months.

Damn, love could hurt so bad.

It ached.

A real, physical hurting that just got worse every time I thought about Eden and what she'd done to me.

I feigned illness that night when I got home. As if I wanted to explain my tears to my parents? No thanks. My mother would have told me what I'd had with Eden had never been real, so what was the point? Instead, I shut myself in my room, switched off my phone, crawled under my duvet, and tried to convince myself my heart was still beating.

It was a struggle. Nothing made sense. Life was futile again. I'd made the hardest decision ever, but what choice had she left me? How could I have gone on being let down and misused and trampled by her over and over again?

She didn't love me. That's what she'd said.

Even after I'd poured my heart out to her, telling her how much she meant to me, she couldn't do the decent thing and give me the comfort of knowing, despite her misgivings about us, she did actually love me.

She couldn't even give me that.

❖

"Has she contacted you?" Libby asked, early the next morning in school. She'd collared me in the changing rooms next to the gym. I'd neither wanted to return to school nor see Libby, but figured skipping school would have resulted in way too many questions, so I somehow ended up doing both.

She meant well, I knew. But I could have *so* done without it all.

I showed her my phone. Twelve unread texts, six unanswered phone calls.

"Whoa." Libby took my phone from me. "All that since yesterday?"

I shook my head. "Since this morning. I deleted all of yesterday's."

"You didn't want to read them?" Libby asked, handing it back to me.

"I read the first three or four," I said. "They all said the same thing."

"Which was?"

"I'm sorry, please forgive me, please give me another chance." My voice broke. "Please don't give up on me." I cleared my throat. "It's all so fucked up." I wiped my eyes with my sleeve. "She's begging me to forgive her and I'm trying so hard to harden myself to it."

"Even though it's breaking your heart?" Libby asked.

"What else can I do?" I asked. "Give her another chance to stomp on me again? It's clear she's never going to commit." I looked at the messages on my phone. "So I take her back, accept her apologies and try again, then what? I can't cope with her hurting me any more."

"Maybe she really means it?" Libby said. "Perhaps you dumping her has given her a boot up the arse. If she thinks anything of you, then she'll say to hell with her so-called friends and what they think."

"I don't think she cares about me at all," I said.

That thought was horrendous, but it felt good to get it out.

Libby shook her head. "I'm not Eden's greatest fan, but I've seen the looks she's given you when she thinks no one's looking," she said. "And they tell me she cares for you a heck of a lot."

"Yeah, she cares a lot when no one's looking. It's not enough."

"She wants you, Tab. Yeah, she's been stupid, and I'll bet right now she'll be thinking I'm the last person who'd ever back her up. But no one looks at another person the way Eden looks at you without it meaning that they want them unconditionally."

"Unconditionally? How do you figure? She'll cow to the pressure and let me down again, mark my words," I argued. "What part of that is unconditional? Can I put myself through that?"

"Maybe she won't, though," Libby said. "Maybe she's manned up and stopped giving a fuck what Dumb and Dumber think any more."

We both turned our heads as the door opened and Eden walked in, right on cue. I stepped back from Libby, wiping my eyes, still wet with tears, with the insides of my wrists. Eden shut the door behind her and leant back against it. Her face was tired and blotchy from what I assumed were tears. Like me, she kept wiping at them with her sleeves, which were pulled down over her hands.

"I've been looking everywhere for you." Her voice was barely audible.

"Well, you've found me," I said.

"I'll leave you to it." Libby rubbed my arm. "Think about what I've just been saying."

"Hmm." Standard reply in such situations, I'd say.

Eden moved from the door to allow Libby to leave, shooting her a guilty look as she passed.

"Are we alone?" She tossed a look towards the cubicles.

"Still scared of being overheard?" Petty. "Yeah, we're alone."

"Why have you been ignoring me?"

"Really?"

Eden pressed herself against the door again. I guessed so it would stop anyone else coming in. "I've been texting, phoning—"

"I know. What more should I say to you?"

"Even though I was telling you how sorry I am?" Eden asked.

"Sorry is just a word, Eden."

"I've been going out of my mind since yesterday."

"Me, too," I said bluntly. "Wondering what to do for the best."

"What we do for the best"—Eden stepped away from the door and came over to me—"is start again." She rested her hip against the sinks.

"Don't." I took a step away from her and stood next to the hand dryer. "I can't keep being let down by you," I said. "It hurts too much."

"I'm sorry I've hurt you," Eden said. "And I'll keep saying sorry until you believe me."

"Give me one good reason why I should believe you? And believe you until when? What about Gabby? And Beth?" I asked. "You're so worried all the time about what they're going to say. That's never going to change."

"They're my problem," Eden said. "And I'm dealing with it the best way I can."

"By throwing me under the bus every time things get hard? Nuh-uh. I'm done with that game. I deserve better."

She came closer to me slowly, her eyes never leaving mine. I automatically hugged my arms tightly around myself and moved away again.

"I can't be without you, Tab," she said.

"Stop it," I beseeched. "Don't do this. It's unfair."

"Let me prove how much you mean to me," Eden said. Her voice was low and quiet. "Please?"

"I'm so tired of all this, Eden," I said.

"So am I." Eden swallowed. "Tired of how I am. Tired of Gabby and Beth. Tired of fighting."

She stood right in front of me. Her eyes drifted over my face, seeking an answer, or just a hint that I might waver. I was mesmerized, just as I had been the first time I ever saw her. Her gaze pulled me in, sapping any resolve I might have had. I forgot just how much power her eyes had over me as I felt myself drowning in them. In her.

"Do you believe me?" she asked.

I didn't answer. I couldn't. Instead, I let her reach out and take my hand. Without a word, she pulled me with her into a cubicle and shut the door behind her. She locked it. We looked at each other in silence, both breathing quietly, both of us too shy to make the first move.

"Will you let me show you?" Eden asked again. "So you believe me?"

I dropped my eyes.

"Please?" Eden moved towards me and took my face in her hands. She kissed me so slowly and tenderly—a deep pulse travelled the length of my body. I pressed her against the door, my hands reaching up under her top to meet her warm skin, smoothing over the small of her back, over her sides. I sensed her breath quicken when my hands made contact. I impulsively kissed her deeper, lost in her moans and the feel of her body up against mine.

So much for willpower.

"Don't ever leave me again, will you?" Eden spoke through our kisses. "You promise me?"

"I...can't...give you up." I pulled away. "I barely lasted a day without you."

"Things will change, I swear to you." She dusted the hair from my eyes. "I don't want to risk ever losing you again."

"You really mean that?"

Eden nodded. Resolute. Determined.

"Come to my party tomorrow night," she said. "I need you to be there."

"You want me to?" That sure was a bombshell. Enough to send a flicker right through me. "With all your family there? And Beth and Gobby?"

"I do want you to, yes," Eden said. She stroked my cheek and kissed me again. "Tomorrow, everything changes. Please. Say you'll come."

My heart warred with my brain for what seemed like an interminable stretch. Finally, I blew out a sigh. "Last chance, Eden. I mean it."

CHAPTER FORTY-FIVE

Eden's house was lit up by the time I arrived for her party the following night, emboldened by the bolstering presence of Libby and Greg. The brightly coloured balloons and dull thudding of music, combined with excited whooping coming from inside the house, drew us in.

The front door was already open, encouraging everyone to just go on in. A huge cut-out red arrow lay on the hall floor, pointing to the lounge, and we followed. We entered the room uncertainly and looked around at the scattering of people, none of whom we knew.

"Why do I feel so shy all of a sudden?" Libby bent forward and spoke into my ear so she could be heard above the sound of music. "I feel like a five-year-old going to her best friend's birthday party."

"It's 'cos her parents are here," I shouted, all the while seeking a glimpse of Eden. "When was the last time you went to a party where parents were present?"

"I feel like I ought to have a pretty bow in my hair and a present in my hands," Libby said, "rather than this bottle." She waggled a litre bottle of vodka at me.

"You're here!" Eden came across the room towards us, glass in hand. She wrapped her arms around me, spilling some of her drink as she did so. "I've missed you," she breathed into my hair. "Thanks for coming, you two," she said to Libby and Greg, who stood sentry on either side of me.

"Drinks this way." Eden took my hand and led me across the

room and into the kitchen, where an array of bottles of different sizes and colours were lined up on the side. "There are olives in bowls scattered around the lounge." She leant into me and giggled. "My mother is treating this like a Women's Institute soirée rather than her daughter's eighteenth piss-up."

"Are you drunk?" I asked, nodding at her glass.

"No!" Eden laughed. "It's orange juice, honest."

I was dubious.

"Honestly," she said, seeing my unconvinced expression. "I want to have a clear head tonight." She took a sip from her juice. "I'm just happy you're here," she said. "After everything."

"I told you yesterday," I said, reaching over and taking a bottle of beer from the side. "Last chance. I love you, Eden, but I meant it."

"So who's here?" Libby picked up a bottle. She peered at the label, shrugged, then uncapped it. She drank it back, then looked through the kitchen door back into the lounge. "The Wicked Witches coming?"

"They're already here," Eden said. "Gabby's latched on to some random guy she met the second she walked in. No idea where Beth's disappeared to."

"Probably singing at someone," Greg muttered. He reached for a can of cider and opened it noisily, then kissed Libby on the cheek and wandered off into the lounge.

"Who else?" I peered through the kitchen door into the lounge. A sea of unknown faces loomed out at me.

"Mum and Dad, of course," Eden said, taking another drink. "Ben, plus my three cousins. Few neighbours. Oh, and Freya and Liam are here somewhere, too."

"I think everyone's here who should be here now." Eden's mother bustled into the kitchen. She took a knife from the kitchen drawer and turned to Eden. "Your dad would like to say a few words." She rolled her eyes. "Just let him have his moment of being one very proud dad, and then we can cut the cake, okay?"

I downed my beer and glanced at the table, where a large chocolate cake with eighteen candles sat patiently, waiting to be cut. Beth entered the kitchen, two empty glasses in her hands, and I immediately stiffened.

"Gabby's chatting up your cousin Harry in the conservatory, Eden," she said, bumping me as she came past. "She sent me in for more vodka. That okay?"

"I thought she was talking to Ben's friend." Eden frowned.

Beth shrugged. "Got bored."

"Harry's already got a girlfriend," Eden said stiffly. "Does she know that?"

"She does." Beth reached past me, shooting me a look of disdain. She grabbed the bottle of vodka that Libby had brought. "But his girlfriend's not here, is she?" She poured two glasses, filling each liberally.

"So that makes Harry fair game?" Eden's voice was laden with contempt.

"You know Gabby," Beth said. "Never one to pass up an opportunity. Not where a boy is concerned." She grabbed a handful of olives and stuffed them in her mouth. "Just like you, eh?" She mumbled through her olives and winked at Eden. Then, just for good measure, she gave me a look. I presumed it was to wind me up.

Jerk.

In the front room five minutes later, Eden's dad did the most awesome speech about Eden. It was a beautiful and thoughtful tribute to her, both perceptive and funny, and summed her up perfectly. I watched as he was speaking, his eyes full of love as he told the room how proud he was of her and how much he loved her. She stood away from me all the while he was talking, standing over to the side of the room, her mother on one side of her, her brother Ben on the other. Our eyes met across the room all the time her father was talking. She looked beautiful. Radiant. Her face was flushed, both by the warmth of the room and her father's words, giving her a magical glow.

Finally, speech over, a small swell of applause rippled around the room. Eden and I tore our eyes away from one another and focused back on the others around us. Taking a long drink from her glass, and with the sounds of everyone urging her to say a few words, Eden stepped away from her mother and Ben and turned to face the room.

"I just wanted to say..." Eden took another drink. Her hand was shaking slightly. "Thank you to everyone for coming tonight, and thank you for all the gifts, even though it's not my birthday for another five days—"

"Don't think you're getting any more next week as well," a voice called out from the sofa, making everyone laugh.

Eden smiled shyly but didn't reply. "And thank you to Mum and Dad for putting all this on for me tonight." Her voice sounded forced. Unnatural. "And for the awesome speech, Dad." She looked at him. "Although I don't know why you had to tell everyone that story of me feeding the ducks at the park when I was six." Another ebb and flow of laughter.

She traced her finger around the rim of her glass and stared down into it. Her brows, I noticed, were pinched tight. "I wanted to say something else as well," she said, "something that probably needed to be said a while ago."

Eden cleared her throat nervously. "I've managed to make it to being eighteen," she began, "without really knowing what true happiness is." She lifted her head and looked around the room. "But now I do know."

Her mother caught Eden's eye across the room. She smiled.

"Before, I never felt complete," Eden said, looking away from her mother and towards me. "I always knew something was missing from my life, but I could never quite put my finger on what it was." She held my gaze. "But it's not missing any more."

A few murmurs tumbled round the room. An atmosphere was clearly developing, and I began to wish someone would put the music back up again.

"Sometimes, if you're lucky, a person comes into your life," Eden continued, never taking her eyes off me, "who turns everything on its head in the most amazing, beautiful, and unexpected way."

Her father caught the look that passed between me and Eden. "This is very nice, Eden," he said, "but is it going anywhere?" He flashed an anxious look over to Eden's mother.

"Before, I was just going through the motions of life as I was expected to," Eden said, ignoring him. "Just…I don't know… existing, but always sensing there should be something more."

"Is it time to cut the cake?" Eden's mother started to move towards the kitchen, her knife still in her hand.

"Let me finish, please?" Eden turned and faced her mother. "If I don't say this now, I never will."

My grip on the beer bottle tightened.

Her mother's grip on the knife tightened more.

"I was talking to someone not so long ago about love." Eden looked at me. "And that person said what a nice word *love* is, and how people—how she—liked to hear it."

I stared back at her, speechless.

"I should have told her then that I loved her," Eden said, "but like an idiot, I didn't."

"She?" Eden's mother asked. "How much have you had to drink, Eden?"

I zoned in on Eden. The room encased me. The walls began to press up hard against me, crushing the breath from my lungs as I saw the expression on her face.

Suddenly I understood.

Tomorrow, everything changes.

That's what she'd said, wasn't it?

"Eden." Her mother's voice resonated in my head. "Eden, what are you talking about?"

"I'm talking about Tabby," Eden replied, never taking her eyes from mine. "I'm in love with her, Mum. And I don't care if the whole world knows it."

Chapter Forty-six

I don't understand." Eden's mother stared at her. "How can you be in love with another girl? You're being absurd." Confused, her eyes sought out Eden's dad. "Richard, what's she talking about?"

"I am in love with her," Eden said. "And it's not absurd. In fact, it's the most logical thing that's ever happened to me." She smiled. "Because now everything makes sense."

"But I don't understand," her mother repeated. "How can you—"

"I'm gay," Eden said, cutting her mother short. "And I—"

"Don't be ridiculous! Of course you're not gay—look at you. You're beautiful."

Her mother was embarrassed.

She knew it, I knew it.

The whole damn room knew it.

She laughed self-consciously. "This is what happens when you leave an eighteen-year-old in charge of the drinks," she said, as lightly as her wobbling voice would allow. Only one person laughed.

Awkward.

"I am gay," Eden repeated. Her voice was measured and clear. "And I'm in love with Tabby." She turned back to face me. "And you'll never know how sorry I am that I upset you and hurt you—repeatedly—and abandoned you in school last week when you needed me the most," she said. "I really thought I'd lost you. I can't go through that again." She took a step closer to me, ignoring her mother's protests. "I'm scared of running. I'm scared of denying my feelings for you."

Finally, her dad cleared his throat. "Eden, do you really think this is the right time to—"

"When Tabby needed to hear me tell her I loved her," Eden continued, undaunted, "I was too scared of what that would mean. Too scared of the one little word that she really needed to hear. I nearly lost her because I was a coward. Well, I'm not a coward any more." Eden faced her mother.

"What rubbish." Eden's mother dismissed her daughter's statement with a flick of her hand my way. "You've just got yourself all confused because you've been spending too much time with her. She'll have been encouraging you, getting you all mixed up. Making you question things."

"I have a name," I said. My voice was small, but somehow it launched the whole room into action.

Eden's mother spun towards me. "Now I see what your plan was," she said. "Why you were so keen to walk Eden home that night. I thought it strange at the time, but now it all makes perfect sense."

"She wanted to make sure I was safe." Eden slammed her drink back. "For shit's sake, Mum."

"I thought I was being helpful," I stuttered. "I just—"

"Oh my fucking God!"

Who said that? Gobby? Beth? I couldn't be sure. Voices oscillated now.

"Are you telling me you—"

"You listen to me." Another interruption. Eden's mother again. Furious.

Why was the room moving around me?

"I don't know what's been going on between you two," her mother said, "or what twaddle you've been dripping into my daughter's head. I don't want to know. But she is not gay. Do you hear me?"

"I…" I stood, stunned, unable to think or speak.

"What you get up to in your private life is up to you," she continued. "If you want to be gay, then fine. Be gay. Just don't encourage my daughter to experiment with you."

"Megan." Eden's father's voice sounded a warning.

"Why didn't we see this coming?" Eden's mother rounded on him, her face twisted with anger and confusion. "What have we done so wrong to make our own daughter do this to us?"

"What?" Eden's voice rose. "You think my being gay is just me getting at you?"

"Are you seriously telling me that you and she—"

More voices.

Shouting now.

Excitement, the thrill of it all, the scandal.

I spun round. Gabby stood inches from me, glaring.

"Eden, stop saying you're gay." Her mother's voice was measured again. "You've had boyfriends. You can have the pick of any boy in your school."

"I don't want any boy," Eden insisted, trying to contain her frustration. "I want Tabby."

"You poisonous bitch," Gabby hissed in my ear, drowning out Eden and her mother. "What have you done to her? What have you been saying to her to make her like this?"

My heart slammed against my ribcage.

Why wouldn't the room stop spinning?

"I haven't said anything," I faltered. "We've fallen in—"

"Love?" Gabby's voice growled with menace. "Don't give me that shit." She grabbed my arm. "Eden was perfectly normal before you moved down here and started spouting all your lezzy bullshit."

"You turned her," Beth spat. "You couldn't leave her alone, could you?"

"With your revolting lesbian ways," Gabby butted in.

"You see?" Eden's mother flung her hands out. "Listen to your friends. Listen to everyone in here. Every single person in this room will tell you that she"—she pointed towards me—"has turned your head. She"—another jabbing finger—"has put ideas in your head. *She* is the one to blame for all this."

"And *she*"—Libby stepped forward from the shadows of the room where she'd been listening to everything—"is the sweetest, kindest, loveliest person you could ever meet, and Eden is everything to her." She stood behind me and placed a reassuring hand in the small of my back. "So, no," Libby said, "not everyone in this room will tell you that Tabby's turned Eden's head." She looked at Eden's mother. "Your daughter is eighteen. She's not a child. She knows her own mind. Give her some credit at least."

"So why did everything change when Tabby came down here?" Gabby cast her head in my direction. "Eden wasn't like this before she came on the scene."

"Maybe Eden wanted to change!" Libby said, exasperated. "Maybe falling in love changes a person, Gob—"

"Maybe Tabby should go after her own sort," Beth said. "Eden's straight." She swung round to challenge me, her finger aimed towards my face like a dagger. "You got that? She's not like you."

Say something, Eden, please!

I looked at Eden, my eyes pleading with her. All I could hear was my own heart flailing wildly in my ears.

"Stop." Eden finally spoke. Her voice, so soft after all the harshness, was an instant comfort.

Gabby put her hands on her hips. Instant petulant child look achieved.

Loser.

Eden looked evenly at her and Beth. "It's all true," she said. "Every word." She walked over and took my hand. It was cold and clammy with nerves. She gave my fingers an encouraging squeeze. "Don't you dare look at her like she's nothing," she said, "because she's worth a thousand of each of you."

Eden punched her words out, each one said with more conviction and determination than the last. My heart crashed with love for her. I looked at her as she defended me. The expression on her face told me she meant everything she was saying. Slowly, the worries and insecurities of the last few days crumbled to dust.

"How can you say what Tabby and I have is disgusting?" Eden was on a roll.

Was I going to stop her?

Like hell I was.

"You know what's really disgusting?" Eden continued. When neither Gabby or Beth answered, she carried on. "The way you two spoke to Tabby the other day." Her voice faltered for the first time. "You're my oldest friends, but I've never heard you speak as repulsively as you did then."

Beth stepped forward. "I—"

"Shut up." Eden shook her head. "It's sickening," she continued, "the things you've said to her. To anyone. What gives you the right to judge? You should be ashamed of yourselves. I'm ashamed of you. I'm ashamed of myself that it took me this long to say these words."

"You're...really in love with her?" Beth asked.

"I am." Another squeeze of my hand. "So let me ask you this: Do you think I'm vile, too? Because you can either be my friends and support my happiness, or...not."

Gabby turned away. Guess that was her answer, then.

Beth, though, looked meek. Ashamed. "I had no idea you had feelings for Tabby," she said, her tone almost simpering. "Why didn't you say anything?"

"Why do you think?" Eden replied. "Look how the pair of you have acted. How I've acted because of you."

"But I never noticed anything different about you," Beth said. "You're my bestie, and I didn't see any of this coming." She looked disappointed. Upset, even.

"Why would I be different?" Eden asked. "I'm still the same person I was before I met Tabby."

Beth shrugged, at a loss. "I'm sorry." She looked at me properly for the first time.

I waited for Gabby to apologize, too.

Nothing.

"I hate it when you talk about Tabby like she's something to be afraid of or kicked aside," Eden said. "So if I ever hear either of you spouting homophobic filth at her—or me—again, I'll report you, and I'll cut you out of my life forever." She looked from Gabby to Beth and back to Gabby again. "Got that?"

They both nodded like chastised children.

Way to go, Eden.

I felt Eden's grip. Reassuring. Supportive.

I couldn't speak. It was as if I was in a dream, and at any moment my alarm clock would snap me out of it. Faces swam at me: Gabby in a silent, white fury, Beth submissive, Eden's parents, speechless by the kitchen door.

"You're the other half to me, do you know that?" Eden said. She snubbed the room and spoke to me directly, as if there was no one else around. "Without you, I'm hollow. With you, I'm complete. I feel like I can do anything, say anything, go anywhere, as long as I've got you at my side."

"Eden, I—"

"Why deny my feelings when everything inside me is shouting your name?" Eden continued. "Everything reminds me of you. You're with me everywhere I go. I can't shake you from my head."

"That's cute."

"You're cute."

"You're both cute." Ben came up behind us and put his arms round us both. "Now, I don't know about you two, but I'm starving," he said. "And there's a birthday cake in that kitchen with my name on it." He punched his thumb back over his shoulder.

"My name," Eden corrected. "It's my birthday, remember?"

"So, if you two are finished here," he said, "perhaps we could all go eat?"

He peeled his arms from us and walked towards the kitchen, ushering his mother along with him as he did so. Trepidation swept over me as Eden's dad walked over to us. I instantly released her hand. She took it again.

My insides fizzed, not for the first time that evening.

"Not quite the eighteenth speech I was expecting." He looked uncomfortably at our clasped hands.

"I meant every word," Eden said. "And I don't think I'll ever forgive Mum for the things she said to Tabby." Her voice shook.

"You will," I told her.

Her gaze darted to my face, questioning.

"I forgave you." I shrugged, watching her face redden with the memories of all she'd put me through. "You'll forgive her in time, just the same."

Eden's dad held up his hand. "For what it's worth, I think it was very brave, what you just did," he said. "Standing up in a room full of people and saying all that."

"I'm fed up with living a lie," she said. "And past caring about what those two, or anyone else, thinks of me any more." She threw an indifferent look over towards Gabby and Beth, both deep in conversation by the front door.

"Your mum is just shocked, Eden," her father said. "She needs time to get her head around things."

"Just like you needed your own time to get your head around things," I reminded her, hiking one eyebrow to make my point.

"Yes, but she has no need to be shocked." Eden bristled. "I'm not pregnant, or having an affair with a married man. I haven't killed anyone or robbed a bloody bank. I'm. Just. Gay." She emphasized every word.

"And she just needs some time," he said, casting a look towards the kitchen. "That's all I'm saying." Her father took a deep breath. "I better go and see how she is." He looked tired. "I'm sorry," he addressed me, "for the things my wife said to you before. It's a lot for her to get her head round."

"It's okay," I said. "Everyone comes to terms at their own speed. I can understand why she said it."

"I don't agree with what she said, if it's any consolation." Her father made to go. "You appreciate that I have to go and be with my wife, don't you? Talk to her."

I nodded.

"And we'll talk some more later." He touched Eden's arm, then mine, then strode off towards the kitchen.

"You know you didn't have to do all that," I said. I felt humble. Grateful, but humble.

"Yes, I did. I needed you to know I meant every word," Eden said. "And that I'll never reject you or not support you when you need me again."

"And your parents?" I stressed.

"My problem," Eden said. "Like Gabby and Beth are my problems, too."

"Our problem," I corrected.

"Our problem." Eden smiled. "Although I think Beth will be less of a problem than Gobby. Not that I particularly care either way."

"Gobby, huh?"

"Definitely Gobby."

"Always Gobby." Libby appeared beside us. "Some things will never change." She swirled her drink around in her glass. Lifted it up. "To you guys," she said. "And to not giving a shit what people think."

"And happiness." Greg threaded his arm around me and hugged me close. He chinked the bottom of his bottle with mine. "The most important thing of all." He raised his bottle to Eden.

Eden's expression relaxed. The first time that night.

"I do love you, you know," I said. I pulled her into the corner of the room.

Surprisingly, everyone in the room had gone back to doing their own thing again. Drinks were there to be drunk, nibbles to be nibbled. The brief, although embarrassing, floor show was over, and if we weren't exactly forgotten, we were now being…benevolently ignored. Human nature, I guessed. Suited me fine.

"I love you, too," Eden said, tugging gently on my hands so I'd put my arms round her waist. "You do believe me, don't you?"

"After all that?" I asked. I laced my arms around her waist and pitched a look back over to the middle of the room. "I'll never doubt anything you say ever again."

"Shall we go outside? I could use some air."

"Sure."

We headed for the back door, slipped outside.

"Let's hide out here for a bit," she said. She pulled herself up on the small wall that surrounded her parents' conservatory and gestured for me to follow. Her face was illuminated by the light from the moon, giving her a striking, almost ghostly look. Eden held a stone between her finger and thumb. She looked at it like it was the most interesting thing in the world. "I wish they'd all just change the record on the whole *it's a phase* argument."

"But it's not?" I asked. "Just a phase?"

"What—?"

"Not just a hiccup in your normal life?"

"Tab—"

"Are you going to hold your breath one day when you get fed up with the hiccups and hope that makes them—or rather, me—go away again?"

"You said you would believe everything I say from here on out."

"I'm just testing. We've been through a lot, you have to admit."

Eden let the stone fall from her hands. It bounced and rolled away, lost in the darkness of the patio. She took my hand. "I want to take my time to get to know you even better. I want a future with you, Tabs. No hiccups."

We looked at one another, holding each other's eyes for the longest time. Slowly, Eden leaned closer. Still looking into my eyes, she grazed her lips against mine, softly to begin with, then harder as I kissed her back. She looped her arm around my waist, pulling me against her, and kissed me deeper still, the intensity of the moment and her warm lips on mine making my head swirl. Finally, she pulled back, taking my hands in hers. "I love you, Tabs. Very much."

"Three little words." I looked down at our joined hands. "But they mean so much. To me, anyway."

"Then I'll keep saying those three little words until you get tired of hearing them," Eden said.

"I'll never get tired of hearing you say them," I said. "Never."

"Stay with me tonight?" she suddenly said. "Please?"

"Here?" I understood the meaning in her eyes.

"Not here." Eden shook her head. "Take me back to yours? While your parents are out? I really need you tonight, Tabs."

"Are you sure?" I asked.

"Never been more sure of anything in my life," Eden replied.

I took my hand from hers and enveloped her shoulder, drawing her close to me. She rested her head against my neck, occasionally leaning up to kiss my cheek, more often just nestling against me in silence. Then, no more words were needed. We sat like that, enjoying each other's presence, savouring the silence and relishing the cool of the late evening air until the first light raindrops of the night hurried us back inside.

It was perfect. Eden was perfect. She was the girl who changed me, and who brought me closer to my dad, after years of keeping him at arm's length. I'll forever be grateful to her for that.

But most importantly, Eden was the girl who made me grow up and realize that sometimes obstacles appear in your life for a very good reason. And when you stop worrying about them and learn how to jump over them, life can be pretty damn good. Eden taught me that.

Because of her, I finally discovered that sometimes change really can be for the better.

About the Author

KE Payne was born in Bath, the English city, not the tub, and after leaving school she worked for the British government for fifteen years, which probably sounds a lot more exciting than it really was.

Fed up with spending her days moving paperwork around her desk and making models of the Taj Mahal out of paperclips, she packed it all in to go to university in Bristol and graduated as a mature student in 2006 with a degree in linguistics and history.

After graduating, she worked at a university in the Midlands for a while, again moving all that paperwork around, before finally leaving to embark on her dream career as a writer.

She moved to the idyllic English countryside in 2007 where she now lives and works happily surrounded by dogs and guinea pigs.

Soliloquy Titles From Bold Strokes Books

The Unwanted by Jeffrey Ricker. Jamie Thomas is plunged into danger when he discovers his mother is an Amazon who needs his help to save the tribe from a vengeful god. (978-1-62639-048-5)

Because of Her by KE Payne. When Tabby Morton is forced to move to London, she's convinced her life will never be the same again. But the beautiful and intriguing Eden Palmer is about to show her that this time, change is most definitely for the better. (978-1-62639-049-2)

Asher's Fault by Elizabeth Wheeler. Fourteen-year-old Asher Price sees the world in black and white, much like the photos he takes, but when his little brother drowns at the same moment Asher experiences his first same-sex kiss, he can no longer hide behind the lens of his camera and eventually discovers he isn't the only one with a secret. (978-1-60282-982-4)

The Seventh Pleiade by Andrew J. Peters. When Atlantis is besieged by violent storms, tremors, and a barbarian army, it will be up to a young gay prince to find a way for the kingdom's survival. (978-1-60282-960-2)

The Missing Juliet: A Fisher Key Adventure by Sam Cameron. A teenage detective and her friends search for a kidnapped Hollywood star in the Florida Keys. (978-1-60282-959-6)

Meeting Chance by Jennifer Lavoie. When man's best friend turns on Aaron Cassidy, the teen keeps his distance until fate puts Chance in his hands. (978-1-60282-952-7)

Lake Thirteen by Greg Herren. A visit to an old cemetery seems like fun to a group of five teenagers, who soon learn that sometimes it's best to leave old ghosts alone. (978-1-60282-894-0)

The Road to Her by KE Payne. Sparks fly when actress Holly Croft, star of UK soap *Portobello Road*, meets her new on-screen love interest, the enigmatic and sexy Elise Manford. (978-1-60282-887-2)

Swans and Clons by Nora Olsen. In a future world where there are no males, sixteen-year-old Rubric and her girlfriend Salmon Jo must fight to survive when everything they believed in turns out to be a lie. (978-1-60282-874-2)

Kings of Ruin by Sam Cameron. High school student Danny Kelly and loner Kevin Clark must team up to defeat a top-secret alien intelligence that likes to wreak havoc with fiery car, truck, and train accidents. (978-1-60282-864-3)

Wonderland by David-Matthew Barnes. After her mother's sudden death, Destiny Moore is sent to live with her two gay uncles on Avalon Cove, a mysterious island on which she uncovers a secret place called Wonderland, where love and magic prove to be real. (978-1-60282-788-2)

Another 365 Days by KE Payne. Clemmie Atkins is back, and her life is more complicated than ever! Still madly in love with her girlfriend, Clemmie suddenly finds her life turned upside down with distractions, confessions, and the return of a familiar face… (978-1-60282-775-2)

The Secret of Othello by Sam Cameron. Florida teen detectives Steven and Denny risk their lives to search for a sunken NASA satellite—but under the waves, no one can hear you scream… (978-1-60282-742-4)

Andy Squared by Jennifer Lavoie. Andrew never thought anyone could come between him and his twin sister, Andrea...until Ryder rode into town. (978-1-60282-743-1)

Sara by Greg Herren. A mysterious and beautiful new student at Southern Heights High School stirs things up when students start dying. (978-1-60282-674-8)

Boys of Summer, edited by Steve Berman. Stories of young love and adventure, when the sky's ceiling is a bright blue marvel, when another boy's laughter at the beach can distract from dull summer jobs. (978-1-60282-663-2)

Street Dreams by Tama Wise. Tyson Rua has more than his fair share of problems growing up in New Zealand—he's gay, he's falling in love, and he's run afoul of the local hip-hop crew leader just as he's trying to make it as a graffiti artist. (978-1-60282-650-2)

me@you.com by KE Payne. Is it possible to fall in love with someone you've never met? Imogen Summers thinks so because it's happened to her. (978-1-60282-592-5)

Swimming to Chicago by David-Matthew Barnes. As the lives of the adults around them unravel, high school students Alex and Robby form an unbreakable bond, vowing to do anything to stay together—even if it means leaving everything behind. (978-1-60282-572-7)

365 Days by KE Payne. Life sucks when you're seventeen years old and confused about your sexuality, and the girl of your dreams doesn't even know you exist. Then in walks sexy new emo girl, Hannah Harrison. Clemmie Atkins has exactly 365 days to discover herself, and she's going to have a blast doing it! (978-1-60282-540-6)

Timothy by Greg Herren. *Timothy* is a romantic suspense thriller from award-winning mystery writer Greg Herren set in the fabulous Hamptons. (978-1-60282-760-8)